THE DESECRATION OF ALL SAINTS

A STAND-ALONE ACTION MYSTERY

ALAN LEE

SPARKLE PRESS

The Desecration of All Saints

by Alan Lee

First Edition
Printed in USA

Cover by Damonza

Formatting by Vellum

Sparkle Press

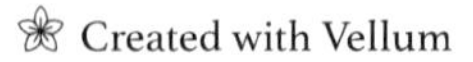

Three Notes From The Author

One - The following story is inspired by true events in Florida.

Two - This story does *not* involve pedophilia, or anything related to recent accusations against the Catholic church.

Three - This is not a canonical book in the Mackenzie August series. This is a stand-alone mystery. Enjoy.

1

Five p.m. and still bright. It was unseasonably warm for spring in Virginia, but humidity hadn't infiltrated the Roanoke Valley yet. The cherry tree in the corner of my lawn was in bloom, like wearing a wedding dress.

Most of the time I met clients at my office or a coffee shop, maybe a restaurant or bar. Food and drink give the hands something to do, a discharge of tension. But the two men I expected had asked to meet at my home. An odd request, yet I remained undaunted—an attorney named Brad Thompson vouched for them, said they wouldn't murder me.

I waited on my front porch drinking a lemonade and rocking back and forth in the chair, issuing an aura of professional competence and wondering what Max Scherzer, ace of the Washington Nationals, was doing right then. Probably drinking lemonade too.

The first man arrived in style. A Toyota FJ40 Land Cruiser. The boxy kind Toyota quit making in the early 1980s, now coveted by robust men everywhere. This guy's was pristine, rebuilt and running better than modern models, sky blue with a white roof. Had a jerry can strapped to the tail next to the spare tire, and I felt the need to swap out my lemonade for something manlier.

The second man arrived with lesser verve and élan; he drove a Porsche. A cherry Boxster with the top down, three hundred horsepower under the hood.

The two men emerged from their disparate vehicles and greeted each other, standing on Windsor Avenue under the shade of budding maple trees. They spoke a moment, ignored by the Grandin neighborhood population returning from work and school, and they came up my walk. They matched their automobiles—polar opposites.

I stood. Never shake a man's hand sitting down.

"Mackenzie August?" asked Porsche. He was a thin guy, like a pencil in pinstriped dark slacks and suspenders. Around his neck, a bowtie; goodness, maybe more verve than I gave him credit for. Wire-framed glasses, black hair, clean shaven, like coming home from Wall Street. He wasn't a stock trader—he was a corporate lawyer. "My name's Hugh Pratt, we spoke on the phone. I didn't realize you were so tall."

"I've tried but I cannot get my impressiveness to convey sonically," I said.

We shook hands. It was fine; I wouldn't remember it.

Then I shook hands with FJ40 Cruiser. I survived. Barely.

This guy growled when he talked. "Robert Wallace. Always liked this neighborhood. Been in Roanoke long as I have. Strong houses built here, before building codes told contractors to do the minimum."

Wallace was a workhorse of a guy, though I'd guess his age at mid-seventies. He had a broad back and beefy forearms like he swung a sledge for a living—he didn't; owned a logging company. He had all his shaggy brown hair, and he wore Levi jeans and a red t-shirt.

I said, "I was admiring your Land Cruiser, the FJ40. It makes me want to be a better man."

Wallace laughed. Hugh Pratt laughed. I reveled.

I asked for drink orders; they requested beer and I brought three cans of PBR and we sat in rocking chairs on my porch.

"I appreciate you meeting with us on short notice," said Hugh Pratt. He drank some beer and heaved a sigh.

I knew the sound. Trouble afoot.

"Emergencies," I said, "are often inopportune."

"Precisely. We find ourselves in unfamiliar territory, in need of a guide."

Wallace made a grumbling sound.

Hugh Pratt continued. "You come highly recommended. I vetted you from three sources. They say you're a former homicide detective in Los Angeles, now on your own and working with local law firms. I'm told you find the truth in dark situations."

I drank some PBR. I tried to do it humbly.

He said, "I won't insult you by asking this conversation to remain confidential."

"I won't point out you just did. Just a couple of guys, not saying stuff."

"We have a situation."

I nodded.

He said, "Rob and I have known each other twenty years. We became friends at church and remain close. We're both on vestry."

"My sixth time serving on vestry," said Robert Wallace.

"What is vestry?" I asked. Humiliated.

"Think of it as a church's board of overseers. I'm the senior warden."

"The CEO of your church?"

Hugh Pratt waffled his hand. "More or less. But the rector is the true leader of a parish."

I winced some. "Rector? Parish?"

"You're not Episcopalian, I see."

"I attend an Episcopal church, in fact. But the jargon eludes me." Infinite mortification. Good thing no single girls were witnessing my ignorance.

"The rector is the head pastor. The parish is the church."

"Got it."

"Our church is the reason we're here," said Hugh.

"Dammit. I fretted you might be."

"Why are you fretting?"

"I prefer it when churches are cities on a hill, rather than gravestones," I said.

"Are you quoting something?"

"Yes. But botching it. Horribly."

"Which Episcopal parish do you attend?" said Hugh Pratt. He pulled a little at his bowtie.

"St. John's."

"Good. No conflict of interest then. The church in question is All Saints."

"Ah. All Saints is the big church."

"Yes. The big church."

"Been there for ninety years," said Wallace. His face wrinkled with pride, like a man discussing his golden son.

"Rob's grandfather helped found All Saints, and he's been a part ever since. Rob's royalty, in my eyes."

"Some things in this world are more important than others," said Robert Wallace. "And church's one of them. I do my part."

"You're here to elicit a large financial donation," I guessed.

Hugh's eyes crinkled. I'm hilarious.

He said, "I wish it was that simple. But All Saints does not hurt for money."

"How nice for God."

"Church is healthy as it's ever been. Keeping something that old running ain't easy," said Wallace.

I indicated his Land Cruiser.

"You like to preserve classics."

"Could say it that way."

"Which is why we're here," said Hugh Pratt. He adjusted his glasses. "Preserving something important. Do you know Louis Lindsey?"

"Know of him. The celebrated, handsome, and gregarious priest. One of Roanoke's most treasured citizens. He's often on television, holding forth."

Wallace nodded with approval, like a big bull would.

"That's him," said Hugh Pratt. "He's our church's rector. Or senior priest, I mean. And someone has come forward with allegations against him."

A Lexus pulled into the drive before I could reply. A model four years old, driven by a man who enjoyed the finer things but refused to purchase new cars. My father climbed out, closed the driver's door, opened the rear door and scooped out an infant. My father's shoes crunched on the gravel.

I stood. "Hugh and Robert, a pause while I greet my family. This is my old man, Timothy August, local elementary school principal. Timothy, these are nameless and faceless prospective clients."

My father, good-looking guy, wise and honest face like a news anchor going grey at the temples, greeted them, "Gentlemen, I know the drill. You were never here."

I collected the infant from his arms. He looked like a bald cherub with bright blue eyes. I guess he wasn't an infant anymore. Time moves fast. But he couldn't walk yet. What did that make him? Whatever he was, he was adorable.

"And this is my boy, Kix," I said.

Both Hugh and Robert wanted to give my son high fives, which Kix suffered with a visible lack of patience. He felt himself above such antics, even if he still had trouble with consonants.

Hugh Pratt and Robert Wallace returned to their rocking chairs and beers to wait while I walked Kix inside. The house felt silent. I set him in his playpen and fetched some juice.

He watched me coolly, like, *Father, I have returned home with lesser fanfare than is our tradition. Usually this is when we have rousing father-son games. Yet today, I cannot help but notice you are distracted.*

"I need to talk with the gentlemen on the porch. Shouldn't be long," I said.

Get rid of them. Immediately.

"Thanks for picking him up."

"Sure," said Timothy August from the kitchen. He poured himself a scotch, took off his tie, and loosened his collar. "I'll make dinner. Your clients staying?"

They are not.

"They are not. I'm about to send them off."

"So quick?" he said.

"Yes. The problem they have is a church problem."

"So you'll refuse the job?"

"Most likely."

"Why?" He added a single cube of ice, sipped his scotch, turned on the stove and hunted for olive oil.

"I don't want to investigate a church."

"You attend a church. Shouldn't its purity matter to you?"

"I'd prefer you not use logic and reason. Not after five in the evening."

"Above all else, son, you are logical and reasonable. This reluctance piques my curiosity, especially since you recently declared your work has not been stimulating."

"This is the wrong stimulation. With churches, seems like it's always the priest diddling some poor kid." I indicated Kix with a tilt of my head. He glared over his juice.

Turn on Sesame Street. This instant.

"You're afraid the case might hit too close to home," said Timothy August.

"Yes."

"If that's the assignment, and if the guy is guilty, clearly he must be stopped. That's what you do. Stop evil people."

"If he's guilty, I might shoot him."

"That happened some in the Old Testament, if I remember Sunday School right. With spears and stones. Righteous zeal and all that."

"That's a sin now. Jesus outlawed it in the New Testament...I think. Focus on cooking, pagan." I went outside into the warm noise while Timothy August pulled chicken out of the refrigerator.

I resumed my seat on the front porch.

"Adorable boy," said Hugh Pratt. "Are you married?"

"I'm not. Long story; the apotheosis of which is, his mother died."

"Oh. Sorry to hear that."

"Must've been tough," said Wallace.

"You were saying that allegations have come forward about the leader of your church, Louis Lindsey," I said.

"Yes."

"Are these allegations of a sexual nature?"

Hugh Pratt nodded, mouth a grim line.

"They are."

"Do the allegations involve unwanted homosexual advances?"

Hugh Pratt set his beer down and held up his hands, as if to slow me down. "It's not like that. Not like the Catholics in the news. He's not accused of molesting children. He's accused of making unwanted advances on a younger clergyman."

"Clergy means priesthood," I said, pleased I knew something at last.

"Yes. A younger man at our church. While far less heinous than molesting children, a priest making unwanted advances on his male clergy is still inappropriate."

"A priest making unwanted advances on anyone is inappropriate. Is Louis married?"

"He is."

Robert Wallace shifted in his chair and cleared his throat. "Listen, August. Louis Lindsey ain't gay. He's been at the church more than a decade. We know him. A great man. Done a lot of good. Then this young guy comes along and accuses him of...you know, hitting on him. No way."

"Still makes a heck of a scandal. Which is why you didn't want anyone seeing you walk into my office. Or talking with me at a restaurant."

"Right." Hugh nodded. Picked up his beer. Set it down again. Rubbed his hands together. "Right. You yourself are somewhat well known for what you do."

"Besides," said Robert Wallace. "Louis's a genius. Hear

me? A genius. Think he'd be stupid enough to get caught? He's the smartest guy you'll ever meet. He ain't gay and he wouldn't get caught if he was. The kid's lying."

"Tell me about the kid and the accusation."

Hugh Pratt said, "The 'kid' is Jeremy Cameron. He's a priest, early thirties. He's been with All Saints a few years. Maybe three. Cameron told me Louis's been making advances on him. But not just him—him and another person. Jeremy refuses to divulge his identity. He says the second person is a younger man with ties to the church."

"When did Jeremy come forward?"

"Last week. I was wrecked, obviously. I spoke with Rob, then we both talked with Jeremy. Now we're here. Looking for answers."

"Does he indicate rape?" I ask.

"No. Nothing forced. No need to involve the police."

"You want to know if Jeremy Cameron is lying."

"Yes. Investigate. Find the truth. We can't believe Father Louis is guilty but...we don't know. You can imagine how messy it's about to get," said Hugh. "Of course Louis will deny it. At least I assume he will, innocent or not. His lawyer will get involved. Our church's lawyer will get involved. The victims might need one too. Jeremy Cameron will talk with the Bishop, our overseer, and who knows how that'll go. Louis is a beloved figure in the news and also in Episcopal circles. It could destroy the church. And here we are, the group charged with leadership of All Saints, clueless what to do. Clueless what to believe. Before shit hits the fan, we need to know the truth."

Wallace frowned at Hugh. "You said shit."

"Ah. Sorry. I'm a Christian but sometimes my mouth has its own power of attorney. That's our request, Mr. August. Find the truth. Can you do that?"

"Sure."

"That easy? Sure?"

"How?" said Robert Wallace. "How can you?"

"This is what I do."

"Yeah, but *how.*" Wallace hadn't moved much. He sat still, like a thick stone.

"Talk to them," I said.

"That's it? Talk to them?"

"Talk to them with brio and panache."

"What's that mean?" asked Wallace.

"Vigorous confidence."

"So you're being funny. I don't like it," he said.

"Even though I'm using big words?"

Hugh Pratt cleared his throat. "I'm still curious what exactly you'll do."

"I'll speak with Jeremy Cameron," I said. "I'll talk to Father Louis. Then talk to the second anonymous guy. Investigate. Poke. Prod. Find the truth. These things are simpler than you think."

"Simple doesn't mean easy," said Hugh Pratt.

"Correct."

"So it's simple but hard?"

"Few can do it."

"And you can," said Wallace, still unhappy.

"Yes."

"Why?"

"Practice. It can be a scary thing and I experience less fear than most, I think. And the truth matters to me."

"And you're a big guy," said Wallace. "Strong hands. You about six feet four? Two fifty?"

"Whatever I am, I'd look ludicrous in the Boxster."

Wallace waved his hand toward the Porsche. "Everyone

does. Even Hugh. Being so big, you have less reason to worry about getting hurt."

"Though it is purity of heart and virtue which protects me. Not muscle."

"You're being funny again." Wallace picked up his untouched can of PBR. Popped it open with a hiss of fizz.

"Can you do this without talking to Father Louis?" said Hugh.

"No."

"Why not?"

"Because," I said. "He holds part of the truth. He'll find out one way or the other."

A car approached—a Camaro. It bypassed the FJ40 and the Porsche and made a u-turn at the intersection beyond. Hugh and Wallace ignored it. I didn't; I typed a quick text message and hit send.

Need a favor. Stay in your car and listen.

Slipped the phone back in my pocket. The Camaro parked and went silent.

The evening air had thickened and street lights would buzz soon. The sky was purple in the east, but pink and orange on the western horizon through the trees.

Hugh Pratt was saying, "Okay. Do what you need to do. Even if it means talking to Father Louis. Good Lord, my stomach's in knots. I have an awful feeling."

"Don't tell him I'm coming," I said.

"You want to spring a trap?"

"Not a trap. But I'd prefer his genuine reaction. Not practiced answers."

"That makes sense. When can you begin?"

"I'll start tomorrow. Nothing on my docket is pressing."

"Perfect." Hugh nodded to himself. "Perfect. Good. What do you need from us?"

"Nothing. I have the names."

"That's all you need?" asked Wallace. He crunched the empty PBR can in his fist. "Names? And you think you can find out who's lying?"

"Like I said. Simple."

"But hard. Like an ax," said Robert Wallace. He nodded to himself, the issue settled in his mind.

Hugh Pratt withdrew a checkbook from his pants and scribbled on it. I remained calm.

"I'll pay for this personally. Keep the church's hands somewhat clean."

"I'm not cheap," I said.

"Good." Wallace grunted approval. "You're the best, you shouldn't be cheap."

Hugh waved away my concern. "I have plenty. And I feel somewhat responsible."

I gave Hugh an amount for my retainer. He doubled the number, signed it, handed it over.

"Okay. Well then..." He stood. Looked like he didn't know what to do with his hands. "Feels like I just signed our church's death warrant."

That was, I thought, hurtful.

2

I went inside. Tossed our cans into the recycling bin.

We lived in a restored 1925 classic brick foursquare. Or so my father told me. It was big. One of those houses with *two* staircases. He bought it when Kix and I moved to town on the condition we live with him. The August boys gotta stick together. The interior was open concept with hints of original craftsman woodwork. I set Kix on the rug in the TV room and I could watch Timothy August over the kitchen countertop as he cooked. Kix played with blocks and I enjoyed the sizzle of chicken and peppers and the roil of pasta.

Timothy August said, "You took the job."

"I had no choice. They begged."

"You had no choice because you couldn't sleep otherwise."

Kix carefully set one block on top of another.

Obviously. Superior genetics. Good men doing nothing? Not in this house. Someone fetch me Cheerios.

The front screen door opened and the final member of our house walked in. Manny Martinez, local U.S. Marshal, and my closest friend. A man so handsome he was almost a woman. Long-limbed, rangy, a passing resemblance to Cristiano Ronaldo, the soccer superstar.

I was easily the least attractive of all the men and babies living under our roof.

Manny walked into the kitchen for a beer. Came back, sat on the leather couch and propped his sneakers on the coffee table.

"I come home, I gotta stay in the car?" he said. "Cause I'm Hispanic?"

"Hispanic? I thought you were sunburnt."

"I should arrest you, *hombré*. But, being a faithful friend and American, I stayed in the car and listened with the windows down." He shifted to pull his badge and gun off his belt. Set both on the couch cushion, away from Kix.

Kix rolled his eyes.

Like I have enough finger strength to pull the trigger. And once I do, I will shoot only pillagers.

"Your two amigos, they are worried. About Louis Lindsey. He's the church guy on television and in the papers."

"That's him."

"They spoke at their cars several minutes while I heaves stopped."

"Eavesdropped."

"*Silencio*, I'm talking. Louis sounds like a fire-breathing monster. Older guy with the weird Jeep, he's worried Louis will quit and find another church. Smaller guy with the bowtie sounds like he wants to find another church before Louis kills him."

"They think he's guilty?"

"Older guy with the Jeep says no way," said Manny. I wanted to correct him—it was a pristine FJ40 Land Cruiser—but he carried on. "Wants to wring the neck of a kid named Jeremy. Not sure what Bowtie believes. They want this kept a secret but they got a good feeling about you," said Manny.

"Obviously."

"How do you bust the city's most powerful and trusted priest?"

"Assuming he's guilty, one must proceed with caution and reverence and perfectly timed aggression."

"How does one do that?"

"One doesn't know," I said.

"What is it with white guys and bowties?"

"Chicks love them."

Manny grinned.

"Then how come you're single?"

"My standards are high. And clearly because I don't own a bowtie," I said.

And he's still hung up on the blonde.

Manny said, "And you're still thinking about the blonde. What's her name?"

"You know it. And that doesn't matter," I said.

Ronnie.

"Ronnie."

"I'm not," I said, "thinking about Ronnie. And if I was, it would be out of platonic concern and civic duty."

He grinned some more. I thought about putting a television remote through his teeth.

"Not cause she's the prettiest señorita in Roanoke?" he said.

"Maybe you should return to the car and wait some more."

"Maybe cutest in the whole damn state."

"Absolutely in the whole state," I said.

"You gonna tangle with this Louis guy?"

"I am."

"Louis's a priest?" said Manny.

"He is."

"Sounds like you need backup."

"Not from someone who flosses after each meal."

"You always been jealous of my smile, amigo."

Kix polished off his juice. Set it down.

Who wouldn't? Look at those teeth. You smile, it's like the sun.

"Dinner's up, boys," said Timothy August, bringing sizzling pans to the table. "Let's celebrate Mackenzie shaking off his slump."

"Slump?" I said.

"You know. Breaking up with the gorgeous blonde. Getting roughed up on one of your last cases. Running low on cash. Maybe it's me who's in a slump because I'm your father and it is indicative of poor parenting."

I patted the check in my pocket. "Low on cash my ass. I'm flushed up."

"Bueno," said Manny. "Because your slump was getting hard to watch, amigo."

"I wasn't in a slump. And also, I make slumping look good."

Kix glared at me.

You said ass.

3

Father Louis Lindsey was born in Maryland, the son of Dr. and Dr. Lindsey. His father a radiologist, his mother an internist. He was an only child. He'd attended Ashdown Forest, a prestigious boarding school in Virginia, and graduated from Dartmouth with honors at the tender age of twenty.

The subsequent twenty-four months of his life were hazy, but I gathered he completed two fellowship programs around Washington D.C. before attending Johns Hopkins for med school.

All this I learned surfing the internet over lunch at Blue 5, a trendy restaurant downtown that boasted live music in the evening and took itself a little seriously. I paused my research while the waitress set a burger with bleu cheese and marinated shiitake mushrooms in front of me. Plus sweet potato waffle fries, because I needed veggies and life was good.

Should I also have a Sam Adams?

Without a doubt I should have a Sam Adams.

Information about Louis Lindsey wasn't scarce online. He had his own webpage, with a blog and links to his articles on religion and philosophy and his lecturing schedule. This past Friday and Saturday he was the keynote speaker at a multi-denominational retreat for married couples. Next weekend he was holding forth at a provincial synod, whatever the hell that was. He had fifty thousand Twitter followers, high for a religious celebrity. His website listed accomplishments such as addressing the National Prayer Breakfast, being an honorable mention for Time's twenty-five most influential evangelicals, guest speaking at a Billy Graham crusade, teaching courses at Duke Divinity, sitting on various leadership councils, etc. Even to potential skeptics, he was an impressive guy and his life had been full and productive and there could be no denying his profound impact.

Oh, and he was a member of Mensa.

Definitely smarter than me. But, I noted with pride, his biceps were less bulky.

All Saints listed him as the rector, but his duties at the church included only teaching and discipleship. He wanted fewer responsibilities, I bet, to free up his schedule. So the more mundane tasks of administration and prayer meetings and counseling and hospital visits and weddings fell to his staff of clergy.

I didn't begrudge him this. Different personalities, different talents, different roles. But my eyes caught on discipleship.

Hmm.

Took a while but I found buried information about his family. A wife and one son. That was it. 'Dr. Lindsey and his wife have one son.' Not an inch more real estate on his website could be spared for the family.

He'd been on a Red Cross medical relief trip to the Congo in his early thirties when he'd felt the call to dedicate his life to God. I was listening to a podcast, wherein he explained his decision to quit medicine and attend Princeton Seminary, when Veronica Summers walked into Blue 5.

The Veronica Summers. Ronnie. Cutest girl in the whole damn state.

We had history. I first met her in this very restaurant, at that very bar, a seminal moment in my life still resonant enough today that I nearly spilled the Sam Adams.

It was close, but I retained my hold on the glass.

Mackenzie August, captain of his own ship.

Ronnie was Aphrodite herself. Taller than most women, maybe 5'10". Still tiny to me. She kept her hair pinned up, a shade brighter than honey. Her high heels had a small white bow over the toe. The bow matched the white belt on her tiny black skirt, and coordinated with her white button-down blouse, collar flicked wide.

I knew my eyes were playing tricks but rooms brightened as she entered them.

Or maybe it wasn't my eyes. Much of the restaurant paused to admire the incoming sun goddess. The bartender waved to her.

Two interesting tidbits about Veronica Summers. Now only reaching her mid-thirties, she already owned her own successful law firm. And she tended bar at Blue 5 on Friday nights.

She strode into the restaurant far enough to let her eyes adjust. Perfect posture. Kept her attaché case pinned to her hip with her elbow.

I remained calm.

Just kidding. My heart, the coward, thundered.

She scanned the restaurant. Her eyes found mine.

We both felt the jolt of electricity and heat. Like eye-contact created a direct current between hearts.

August, calm down. No need for poetry.

She approached my table. She smiled.

I stood. Any man would. One does not remain seated after receiving such a smile.

"Hello Mackenzie." She kissed my cheek.

"Hello Ronnie."

"You were admiring my legs."

"I'm required to," I said. "I could lose my private license if I didn't."

"I hope you noted that my morning yoga classes have produced a slightly firmer muscle tone?"

"I did. And will again."

"And that my recent trip to St. Pete has given me an unusually good tan this early in the year? If you didn't, lie to me for the sake of my insecurities."

"Are you still waging silent war with the girl in your building?"

"The former college cheerleader with excellent calves, yes. She is perfect. At the moment however, in this particular contest, I'm winning."

"There are few moments in which you aren't, Ronnie."

"Thank you, Mackenzie. Who are you meeting for lunch?"

"I am alone."

"May I sit with you?"

"For a moment."

She paused halfway onto her stool. Held me in the blue green of her eyes. Her eyes had always bordered on being too large, like a Disney princess.

"I'm staying longer than a moment, Mackenzie, unless you give me a good reason otherwise."

"Because I remain besotted with you and being in proximity causes exquisite pain."

"How could I possibly leave, then? There's a handsome man at this table who desires me. Every girl's dream," she said. "Are you dating anyone?"

"Objection. That's none of your business."

"Overruled."

"I'm not dating anyone."

"Good. I would wither and die on the spot if you were. My perfect darling baby boy Kix is well, I hope?"

Ronnie had a lot going for her, as if superior intelligence, spirit, and appearance weren't enough: she adored my son; she read bedtime stories to homeless children at the Rescue Mission on Thursday evenings; she was generous with her money; other stuff, probably.

She was still overcoming a profoundly painful past—on a weird level, we connected because both our mothers had died too young. She was a mess. She *knew* she was a mess. But she was trying.

I said, "Kix is still perfect and darling, yes. He misses his ol' pal Ronnie. We both do."

"You, above all people, may not call me *pal*. I haven't seen you in months. I think you've gotten taller and broader."

"That's merely in comparison to the lesser men you spend time with," I said.

"I couldn't agree more. In fact, by contrast, I wouldn't even call them men." We both sat on one side of the raised table, facing each other. She slid out of her heels and crossed her legs, idly kicking her right foot. Her toes made frequent contact with my pant leg. Her toenails were pink.

The bartender brought her a glass of white wine without being asked. The guy adored Ronnie. I did too, but would never stare with gaping mouth as he did, the nincompoop.

"If I had known I'd be on a lunch date with you, Mackenzie, I'd have dressed up."

"This is not a date. And you're not dressed up?"

"What I mean to say is, I might have worn less."

"Ah. I don't mind if you change."

"And yes," she said. "This is a date."

"If we were on a date, I wouldn't be making a slob of myself with a messy hamburger."

She paused to eat one of my waffle fries. I debated chopping her finger with my knife, but I liked that finger. Two waitresses stopped by to say Hello and she introduced me as her date.

They left and she drank more of her white wine. I asked what cases she was working on and she regaled me with stories of rich kids she'd been hired to prove innocent of stupid things they'd definitely done.

"Our jobs aren't so different," I said.

"What mystery are you solving at the moment?"

I told her without using names.

She regarded me over the wine glass's rim. "You aren't happy."

"Why not?"

"Primarily because you miss me. Or at least I hope so. I hope that with all my heart, because I miss you too. But also, you don't want to investigate the church."

"Oh?"

"I know you. You credit the church with saving you from Los Angeles. You're a defender of the church's goodness and necessity. Looking into sexual improprieties within its hallowed walls is like spying on your father, Timothy. Ergo, you aren't happy."

"Only I say things like 'ergo,' Ronnie."

"That's why I said it, Mackenzie."

"Ah."

"Do you miss me?"

"I do. But that doesn't matter."

She swirled her wine. "Isn't it interesting. The only man in Roanoke I want is the only man who won't have me."

"Isn't it heartbreaking, Ronnie. The only girl on earth I want is engaged to another man."

She lowered her wine glass. Wiped her mouth with her manicured thumb and forefinger, a girly motion. Looked down at the table.

I said, "Are you still engaged?"

"I wish you wouldn't bring him up, Mackenzie."

"He's the reason we're not together. You didn't admit you were engaged to a federal prosecutor in Washington until we'd been dating several weeks."

"I remember."

"So now I sit. Alone. Messily devouring a bleu cheese-burger. Not thinking about you."

"Yes you were." She smiled. "If you won't admit it, I will. I think about you. All day."

"Have you visited your fiancé recently?"

"I…have. But truly, he doesn't matter."

"I don't share."

"Why did you come here? To Blue 5?"

"The waffle fries."

"No. You came because it reminds you of me, Mackenzie. And maybe we'd run into each other."

"But mostly it's the fries. How'd you know I was here?"

"I received a deluge of texts. The big gorgeous guy I used to date had arrived."

"Why'd *you* come here today, Ronnie?"

"With hopes that the sight of me might jar you lose from your anger."

"If anything could, it's that skirt."

"Oh?" She smiled again. One of her cheeks held a faint dimple. "That was my strategy. It's hard to covet something you never see."

"It'll come close, but it won't work. I won't date an engaged woman."

She finished her wine. Set it down with a clank. Leaned back in her chair. "Ugh. You and your damned scruples."

"Right?"

"Okay. I'm leaving. I'm late for a hearing as it is. Coming here, I've jeopardized the good will of Judge Chandler."

"Court in that skirt?"

"The judge would open every jail cell in Roanoke for this skirt. But know this, Mackenzie. I'm lonely. Horribly and pathetically lonely. Seeing you has reminded me..." She stood and slid into her heels, a motion I could watch all day. "...how good and perfect of a man you are."

"Well. There's that."

She pressed her hand against my shoulder to prevent me from standing. Bent at the waist to kiss my cheek. Paused, her lips near mine.

I concentrated all willpower on not trembling.

Her fingertips pressed harder against my shoulder.

"I'd forgotten about the muscles too," she said.

"Some girls are worth working out for."

"If you were the type of man to give in too easily, I wouldn't think about you as much."

"Why I'm stubborn."

"Goodbye, Mackenzie. Text me later and tell me if the yoga is paying off, please."

She walked toward the door, her hips moving in an exaggerated swiveling motion, her heels clicking. The restaurant held its breath, witnessing the divine.

Unspoken consensus—the yoga was paying dividends.

4

It wasn't the first encounter with Ronnie that had left me wondering if I should have a cold shower installed at my place of business. She had that effect.

I worked downtown. Roanoke retained an old-world charm despite being a moderately sized city, surrounded by a moderately sized county. Strong hospitals and multiple colleges kept money pouring into the area. My office was on Campbell Avenue, downtown Roanoke, second floor. The building was constructed in the 1920s, like most of the street —classic revival and Beaux-art. The walls were plaster, the floors refinished wood, and the stairs creaked when someone ascended.

Which they did at two that afternoon.

The windows and door were open. I sat at my laptop reading an essay when the wooden slats creaked and snapped in the stairwell, heralding a visitor.

Into my office walked Louis Lindsey, the man himself.

Louis Lindsey bore a remarkable resemblance to Marlon Brando. He was a tall man with broad shoulders, in his early sixties, neatly trimmed hair going gray. He was handsome and fit, from swimming laps at the downtown YMCA. He didn't have jowls but soon might, based on subterranean indications. He'd wear them with class and dignity, the same way he wore his sports jacket and white clerical collar.

He indicated the sign on my door. Said, "Inspector August."

I stood. "Father Louis."

A big voice, built for pulpits. "Inspector August, working on the biggest case of his illustrious career. Trying to prove or disprove that a local priest is gay. How invigorating."

He already knew. Heavens.

Was I surprised? I was.

Did I let it show? I did not. A man's only as good as his stoicism.

"Case of my career? Hardly. Once I rescued a cat from a pine tree. Imagine the sap," I said.

He came farther into the room. Pulled back his sports jacket so he could rest his hands on his belt. He stared through my window with a disapproving shake of his head, a father lecturing his son.

"It grieves me, you given this assignment. That the church considers *this* its most pressing issue. Do we worry about the homeless? Are we concerned with Roanoke's widows and orphans? No, we're anxious about the gossip. Run along, Inspector. Get your magnifying glass. Free us from this scourge, this intolerable rumor."

"I hear sarcasm is the lowest form of communication."

"No. Gossip is. Trust me, son. Here I am, a happily married man, still with the bride of my youth, dodging sniper fire from my own congregation. The hardest part of my job isn't the grueling schedule. It's not the hurting people or the sick. Nor the teaching or the preparation. No, the hardest part is enduring the backstabbing. It's suffering through unsigned emails laden with criticism." He moved away from the window to stand in front of my shelves, hands still on his hips, scrutinizing my panoply of worldly possessions. I sat, to better absorb the haranguing. He carried forth. "That is the hardest part. It's the *inspectors* bought to pry into my private life. Some southwest Virginia boy with bourbon on his shelf thinking he understands the mysteries of the universe. Who holds himself in the position of judge, who can preach to *me*, the ordained priest of thirty years."

"You got all that from my office shelves?"

"Gossip—the lowest form of communication. I despise it. Other than that, Inspector, do you know which vice I consider the worst? For human beings to indulge in?"

"Let me guess. Sounds fun, like ontological Jeopardy."

I saw him pause. Shoulders bunch a little and he pivoted at the waist to regard me.

"Ontological," he repeated.

"Ontological, a fancy word us idiot southwest Virginia boys use. My first guess about the worst vice is acedia."

He turned the rest of his body to face me. Placed his hand on my client chair.

"I'm impressed, Inspector. But no, it's not spiritual sloth."

"My second guess. Onanistic sins."

He smiled. A bit chagrined.

"You are putting me in my place," he said.

"Unless you know what onanism means, I win."

He pulled my chair an inch. Came around and lowered into it. I got the impression he was staring at my mouth.

"The politest way to say it is coitus interruptus. I sized you up too rashly, Inspector. I apologize."

I steepled my fingers. Regarded him shrewdly. Remained silent and mystical.

"I am unaccustomed," he said, "to enormous and powerful men like you being well-read. And here I am, the hypocrite. It is judgment itself which I despise most of all."

There was something about Father Louis Lindsey that even enormous and powerful and erudite men like me found arresting. He was handsome, sure. Moved with the self-awareness and prepossessed grace of someone accustomed to cameras and sermons. But more than that, he carried an *otherness.*

On the outside, a celebrated priest.

Under the skin, something more. Something alien.

Maybe it was his eyes. They were pale, and they changed temperature.

He said, "Have you ever pondered why God placed the tree of the forbidden knowledge in the middle of Eden?"

"I rarely think of anything else."

He smiled. It wasn't fake but, I thought, it was for my benefit.

I said, "It's an unusual placement and an unusual prohibition."

"Quite. Eating of the forbidden fruit, eating of the knowledge of good and evil, one becomes *aware* of goodness and of evilness. Adam and Eve, once innocent, lost their innocence. They suddenly realized, 'Oh no, I'm naked.' Before then, they didn't mind. After? They experienced shame. They decided, being naked isn't good. They judged their nakedness. They became judges. Before then, only God was judge. And thus it should have remained. Because once they started judging one another, they could no longer remain in paradise. The very act of judgment places you above others. And that is poison, and poison must be respected. We must respect the corrosive power of judgment. God put the tree in the middle for them to see and respect, not on the outskirts where one might sneak in secret. Your sin is only as big as your secret."

"Insightful, Father Louis."

"Isn't it."

"My initial reaction is to ponder the difference between judgment and discernment."

"Oh yes. Despite their similarities, the first is a poison. The other, a godly skill. So you understand..." He paused. Scanned my desk. His eyes hovered on my belt—like he could see the pistol I wore, though from his point of view he couldn't. "You understand why the hardest part of my job is enduring the judgment of my own congregation. Especially when it's aimed at me."

"Sure."

"Especially when they hire a private detective who is blindly convinced the mere rumor of homosexuality is worth wrecking lives over."

"I am?"

"Aren't you?"

"Did I give indications I believed thusly?"

He tapped his pursed lips. "Perhaps not. Have I sized you up incorrectly a second time?"

"Maybe you are projecting your own misgivings onto me," I said.

With a finger, I swiveled my laptop around so he could see the monitor. On it was an article he'd written several years ago, titled, *The Looming Threat Above Our Adolescents: Society's Blind Eye to the Evils of Homosexuality.*

His eyes heated four degrees. Anger and...something else. Something excited.

"I regret that article," he said. "Even if it did earn me a rich lecturing tour. I did more harm than good, however."

"I have found no public retraction."

"Nor will you. Christian leaders expressing sympathy for homosexuality are essentially excommunicated."

"The truth isn't worth the price?" I said.

His fingertips were white, gripping the chair rails. He was experiencing a lot of emotion but I couldn't tell what kind.

"Is that judgment? Or discernment, Inspector?"

"You wouldn't be excommunicated from the Episcopalian church. They're somewhat sympathetic to the LGBT crowd."

"My influence far exceeds my local church. And my denomination."

"Wow. You're quite a guy. With all your influence."

"I wonder, son. Where does this obstinance come from? What are you afraid of?"

"A life of quiet desperation."

"You crack a joke. But the truth rings beneath it. Few men operate out of terror as much as you do. That was obvious within a minute of our meeting."

I didn't think he was correct. I did my best to operate out of core principles and convictions. And yet...the man was anything but unintelligent. Did I operate out of terror?

Shucks. The list of things that would keep me awake tonight was lengthening.

He took my pause as assent.

He said, "Did you lose someone? Where does this pain and anger come from?"

I stayed quiet.

"I see it under your myriad of defense mechanisms. We're all afraid, Inspector. Aren't we. So it's best we don't scurry around this planet during our short lives and waste it hurling rocks at one another."

"And your fear?"

"That's easy—purposelessness. Lack of achievement. And if you perpetuate the gossip, Inspector, you'll participate in the evil. I am not gay. Inform those who hired you and consider your job complete."

"I will," I said.

"Thank you."

"As soon as the investigation is, in fact, complete."

He stood. Face a little red against the white collar, but his eyes were still pale. Walked away and came back. Placed his hands on the back of my client chair. He lost the lofty pulpit voice, now mean and low.

"You play games," he said. I still retained the impression he watched my mouth. "You play games with me? You tell me *no*. Like it's a...like you and I are playing a game?"

"I told you *no* because that's the answer."

"You think a private license gives you the right to play God."

"No. It gives me the right to find truth."

"Truth is subjective, boy. You flatter yourself. You're a glorified cop who likes writing tickets."

"Are you speeding? Have you something to confess?" I said. But I regretted it. Instantly. A clumsy metaphor. Come on, Mackenzie, you're better than that.

"I see a young boy in a framed photograph on your shelf. Your son?" He said it without looking.

I didn't respond.

"But I see no indication of his mother. Let me guess why, Inspector. You're no innocent man either."

"By no means."

"You wallow in sexual transgressions the same as the rest of this broken planet. Your hands are red. Guilty as sin. And yet you want to ruin others, ruin me, for the same sin.

Alleged sin. I'm leaving, Inspector. You will not uncover any of my private life."

I didn't want him gone yet. I had the man babbling with emotion. Ready to undo himself. Could be the shortest investigation of my career. He needed only a nudge.

"You misunderstand the point of my investigation, Father."

"Oh?" Said it with a sneer. And it was a good one. I almost ducked.

"I wasn't hired to discover if you're gay."

That stopped him. He raised up. The hands squeezing the fabric of my client chair slackened. His brows furrowed. He searched my lips for answers.

"Then...?"

"I was hired to look into accusations against you."

"Accusations that I'm gay," he said.

"No. Accusations that you're making unwanted sexual advances."

"Unwanted?" he said.

"Yes."

"Someone is accusing me of *unwanted* advances."

I nodded helpfully.

"Unwanted," he repeated. It was the undesired nature of the advances that he was stuck on.

"Sexual advances often are."

"Someone...complained," he said.

"Several someones."

"Several. That's not true." He tried to say something else but couldn't. The Adam's apple in his throat bobbed. He squeezed the chair back until his nails dug small holes in the fabric. Made a growling noise. "That *cannot* be true."

"Which part?"

He threw my chair to the floor.

"Who?" Low seething voice. For a dangerous moment, he looked as though he considered trashing my shelves. "Tell me *who.*"

"No."

"Give me a name!"

"Nooo."

"I've done *nothing* wrong."

"Except," I said. "My favorite chair is sideways."

"You're making a mistake. A *big* mistake." He turned and stormed from the office. Thankfully the staircase survived his wrath. The door leading to the street slammed.

"Heavens," I said again.

5

With haste and investigatorial wiles, I looked up the phone number for All Saints on my laptop and dialed it.

"I need to speak with Jeremy Cameron, please."

The nice woman on the other end said, "One moment please." I listened to an instrumental version of "I Can Only Imagine" for a minute, and she came back on. "I'm sorry, sir, but Jeremy is gone for the day. Can I send you to his voicemail?"

"Jeremy asked me to get ahold of him today, but I don't have his cell," I said. It was deceit. Lying to a church receptionist. Mackenzie August, maybe going to hell. "This is Elvis Cole at St. John's. Could you either have him call me or pass me his cell number?"

"Elvis Cole, you say?"

"At St. John's, yes."

"Well I don't see the harm, then. I'll give you his cellphone number," she said, and she did.

I hung up and dialed Jeremy Cameron. He answered on the third ring.

"Mr. Cameron, my name is Mackenzie August. We haven't met yet, but I wanted to give you a heads-up."

The voice on the end uttered a chuckle. I could tell he was driving. "Okay, sure. A heads-up about what?"

"I was hired to investigate Father Louis' sexual improprieties."

Brief pause. "Oh. Alright, I'm listening."

"I only just started but Father Louis himself surprised me at my office. Somehow he knew I'd been hired."

"Oh no. That's not good. Wow, that's...that'll sure stir the drink, I guess. How'd he know?"

"I haven't had time to guess yet. Either someone at the church told him, which would severely reduce the number of suspects, or someone eavesdropped on a conversation. Or some other avenue I haven't thought of yet. However, I get the impression he doesn't know *who* made the accusation."

"Hang on a sec. I'm pulling over so I can think," said the voice. The drone of the motor reduced. Then more noise, like static or distortion, and I visualized him rubbing his face in a panic. "Okay. So...he knows about the accusation, but he doesn't know who."

"That's my guess. But again, this happened fast."

A blast of noise, like he sharply exhaled against the receiver. "All of a sudden this is happening fast. But the past year has felt like an eternity for me."

I normally didn't make calls like this. I hadn't been hired to protect anyone. I wasn't a bodyguard. Jeremy Cameron could be lying for all I knew. For reasons I hadn't yet processed, I was worried for Jeremy.

I said, "I have no educated opinion yet on the authenticity of your claim. That's not what this phone call is about. But if you are telling the truth, that puts you on his list. He wanted to know who made the accusations, and he'll narrow his search to those he has assaulted or seduced, if in fact he has."

"That makes sense. I appreciate the heads-up. A lot."

I put my feet on the desk. I had butterflies in my stomach, anxiety on his behalf. "Let's meet tomorrow and talk about this."

"Yes, absolutely."

"Maybe you can lay low until then to avoid a confrontation with Father Louis. He could be on a warpath. Go home. Turn off your phone. Avail yourself of peace and quiet."

"Jeez. This is...that might be a good idea. Father Louis is intense. A force of nature that I'd prefer to duck. Situations like this aren't taught at seminary," said Jeremy Cameron.

"Very little of life is."

"Tomorrow morning work for you? I'm feeling alone in all this. The men on vestry don't believe me, I could tell."

"Tomorrow morning works. If you're telling the truth, you've got friends."

"That's, ahh..." His voice tightened with emotion. In my head, he closed his eyes and lowered his head. Thirty seconds passed before he tried again. "That's not easy to believe. But it'd be nice."

"Believe it, kid."

6

"You said 'Believe it, kid'?"

"I'm not proud of it."

"Were you drunk?" asked Manny.

"Drunk on altruism and testosterone."

We had just finished a three-mile jog, me pushing Kix in his stroller. Despite the early morning breeze, I sweated and sucked wind.

Manny, on the other hand, did not. He was more of a natural athlete than me. He grew up running and fighting on the streets of Puerto Rico and Argentina, though that stage of his life was a fog hard to penetrate. He bounced and dashed like a professional soccer striker did, legs moving like springs. A pristine man in the prime of his life, so naturally arresting that several women stumbled as we passed. I wasn't bad to look at, I'd been told, but I also wasn't Adonis himself.

"Altruism," he said. "That's like estrogen?"

"Often, yes. Unfortunately."

Kix snorted.

He got me.

We were on the Greenway headed home, passing the upscale River House apartments, a former industrial building now housing urban elite millennials and a taproom.

Ronnie Summers lived in the River House. *The* Ronnie Summers.

I wondered if she'd wear a skirt again today; temperatures were supposed to be lower.

Kix shouted at me. I'd run the left wheels of his stroller off the path and into the grass. I corrected my trajectory but he pivoted in the chair to glare.

You know, if you'd bought the BOB jogging stroller with the nicer shocks, instead of this used model, the grass wouldn't be an issue.

"What're you going to do," said Manny, "if Padre Louis is gay?"

"I don't care if Louis Lindsey is gay. That's tertiary."

"Then I am confused about why you were hired."

"Do *you* care if Louis Lindsey is gay?" I said.

"No."

"Why should I?"

"Because you go to church. And you believe in the Bible and you pray and all that."

"So do you," I said.

"I believe in God because of heritage. You believe in God because you care, hombre."

We reached the playground I referred to as the Alligator Playground, and the sun moved above the dappled trees.

For several minutes I didn't speak. I remained within myself.

"Let me rephrase," he said. "You and I, we are amigos for years. I know you don't care if someone's gay. And I was just a *pendejo* for in sue and eating you do care."

"You mean insinuating."

"Sí. I was a jerk for *insinuating* you care if someone's gay. And even worse, I *insinuated* you would take a job trying to 'out' someone. It was a jackass thing for me to say."

"Who says we aren't jackasses?"

"What I meant to ask was...does going to church mean you should care? No, that's not what...but, isn't that a big deal for them? The church? Is it a sin? Don't they... *Aye caramba*, this is hard to discuss and stay correct politically."

"How about this. Let's admit the media and other outside forces are making you and me walk on eggshells about this issue. But that's dumb because, as you say, we've been amigos forever. Let's speak plainly and between us forgo the political correctness. We'll do our best and forgive each other missteps."

"*Ay dios mio, gracias*. Because I am but a confused and humble Hispanic."

Kix gasped from his stroller. *There she is. See her? The brunette in pigtails wearing the purple neoprene shirt? She's going down the slide. See her? The little barefoot girl. She knows I like that purple shirt. Everyone be cool. Is she looking at me? Cough once for yes.*

I said, "You know why the church has traditionally been extra judgmental against homosexuality? Because very few of them are homosexuals. It's painless to point the finger. On the other hand, you know why the church goes easy on gluttony? Even though the Bible warns against it?"

"Got a guess. Cause a lot of them are fatties?"

"That's my opinion."

"They should give up carbs," said Manny.

"Clearly. Same goes for laziness. Harder to wave signs admonishing sloth if you are lazy. That'd be pointing out a speck in another's eye when you have a plank in your own."

"Weird ass thing to say, amigo."

"Wasn't me who came up with it. So, no I don't care if Louis Lindsey is gay. Not my business and I wouldn't take a job 'outting' him. But things change if Louis Lindsey is sexually harassing others. Male or female."

"Because assault is different than sexual preference."

"Correct. Sexual indiscretion disqualifies Father Louis Lindsey from church leadership. Especially if it's unconfessed and unrepentant indiscretion. The church leaders need to know the truth."

"And that's what you do. You find truth."

"Yes," I said.

"Harder than what I do. I just run the bad guys down."

Father, pull over. I'll give you five cookies to pass a message to the mother of that brunette vixen over there. Tell her...I'm interested. But only if she is. Tell her I've got a lot of options. Go on.

I said, "Bad can be subjective. Being unfit for leadership doesn't necessarily make one bad."

"Are you splitting hairs, as you white people say?"

"I am. But I think they are important hairs."

"You think Father Louis is guilty of sexual harassment?"

"Way too early to tell," I said.

"But...?"

"Man's guilty as sin. In my humble and confused opinion."

7

I dropped Kix off at his sitter's—a neighbor named Roxanne, mother to a little girl Kix's age—and I drove to the McDonalds off Interstate 81, exit 145. Far enough away from Roanoke City and All Saints that we could talk without prying eyes or eavesdropping ears.

A lesser detective would've been dismayed to see that Father Louis Lindsey smiled on our rendezvous from a wide billboard inviting passersby to attend a service at his church. But not me; I was merely unsettled.

Jeremy Cameron looked young. Technically not far from my age but I felt like I could be his grandfather in terms of world experience. Stylish tortoiseshell glasses, tight jeans, leather boots, and a knit cardigan. He had freckles and blonde hair that would be floppy if he didn't cut it soon.

I got coffee. McDonalds had upped their java game but primarily through the use of corn syrup. Or so Manny told me. I didn't used to care about corn syrup but now I understood that it was pernicious and to be avoided at all costs. Or so Manny told me. So I got the coffee black and I suffered.

Jeremy Cameron got a breakfast platter but didn't touch it.

"You sleep?" I asked.

"A little, thanks to a couple drams of bourbon. Sorry to drag you all the way up here."

"No problem."

"I didn't want to risk an encounter with Father Louis until you and I spoke and I had some idea what to do."

"Are you afraid of him?" I asked.

"A little. I've seen him angry and he doesn't control his rage well."

"I saw that too. When I wouldn't reveal his accuser."

Jeremy Cameron paled. "Yeah."

We were sitting in the corner booth, removed from other patrons.

"You're single," I said.

"Correct. I'm not anti-marriage. It just hasn't happened yet."

"You went to Vanderbilt Divinity. Graduated when you were twenty-eight? And immediately started working at All Saints."

"Right."

"Tell me about him, including the harassment," I said.

"I'll start with the positive. He does a lot of good. He's generous with his money. He's a very engaging speaker and teacher. He's well-liked and respected. A tireless worker. Doesn't drink, smoke, curse, gossip, none of that. Of course, he's brilliant. Far more intelligent than I am."

"Do you know the definition of onanism or acedia?" I asked.

"No. Should I?"

"No," I replied, with no sign of the inward smugness that

I felt. Just me and Father Louis knew those words. Maybe I was brilliant too. "Only curious. Carry on."

"I've been with All Saints for three years. I caught signs of his anger issues during the first year, but hey, nobody's perfect. Plus he's my church supervisor and spiritual mentor, so I wasn't about to correct him. Then last year he started calling me into his office for closed sessions. Counseling, you could say. He wanted to know more about my past, my future plans, those kind of things. Then he started to probe deeper. My fears. My sins. My dreams. Sexual experiences growing up. Really intimate stuff."

"You told him everything?"

"I did. Confessed it all. In my late twenties, being mentored by this larger-than-life and celebrated figure, of course I did. I felt honored. Soon afterwards he asked me to accompany him on trips. Again, I was thrilled.

"The first trip, we went to celebrate the sacraments at a church south of Richmond, stayed overnight, came home. Nothing happened.

"The second trip was to an overnight conference in northern Virginia. We get to the hotel. I park the car. Father Louis checks in at reception. I get the luggage. In the elevator he says, 'You'll never believe it, Jeremy. The hotel botched our reservations. We have to share a room. But at least there are two queen beds.' And I don't think twice about it."

"The third trip was to the same hotel in northern Virginia," I guessed. "And they'd mismanaged the reservation again?"

"Yes," said Jeremy.

"But there was only one bed this time."

"That's right. He offered to take the floor, but I refused.

That was crazy. No reason two grown men can't share a bed."

"You still didn't suspect anything."

"Not until later that night. Going to bed, he said we should pray. Sure, I thought. I mean, that's what we do. Father Louis wanted to hold hands. So we do, we hold hands. When we finish praying, he says, 'Amen,' and he kisses my fingers. Which I was *not* okay with. Suddenly the moment goes from being holy to alien. And he must've known it was too much too soon because he immediately said 'Good night' and got into bed and fell asleep. But I was...I was weirded out."

"You were being groomed," I said.

"Yes. There are different definitions for that word, not all of them evil, but in retrospect I see he was trying to soften me. Making inroads and inquiries about a potential sexual relationship; I didn't fully realize it at the time. He arrived at my home weeks later. In the late evening. He asked to come in and I let him. Big mistake. I had more or less dismissed the kissing by then, because he'd returned to normal. But that night, he said he and his wife hadn't been intimate for years. He looked awful. He asked if he could sleep over. Asked if I was lonely. Asked to hold hands and pray."

"Inappropriate behavior for one's supervisor."

Jeremy's eyebrows went up. "Very. I kept asking Father Louis to leave. He wouldn't. He told me I was lonely too. We were both lonely. I sensed disaster. So I stood up and went into the kitchen. Maybe he thought I was getting a drink, but I grabbed my keys and left. Went to the church and spent the night on the floor. The next day he emailed me a note, saying he appreciated my support and my counsel and that he was feeling much better now."

"How long ago was that?"

"Three months. Since then he's been normal. Every now and then he jokes about it, when we're alone. Like he thinks he's teasing me."

"That night, at your house, you realized he was gay."

"I decided..." He looked up at the ceiling. His fists were clenched. This was difficult. "I decided he was bisexual. Or, I mean to say, he was willing to experiment with being a bisexual. Or...I don't know. Let's not give it a name. How about, that night I realized he was trying to seduce me."

"Yes. Well said. Why wait three months to speak with the vestry?"

"Because I'm a coward. Because I was shaken to the core and scared. I was mad at him. At God."

"And at yourself," I said.

"Yes. Isn't that stupid?"

"Not at all. He didn't get what he wanted, but you were still violated on some level. And with that comes a lot of baggage. And much of the baggage isn't rational or reasonable, including blaming yourself."

"Yeah." He nodded. His eyes pooled and he pushed up his glasses to rub them. "Yeah. I know. I've told others that in the past. But internalizing is easier said than done."

I gave him a minute. Finished my God-awful coffee. Stood and went for more. Decided to add in some cream and sugar because I'd rather die early than do that again. Somehow black coffee was better at home.

I came back. "Why'd you decide to speak with vestry?"

"Because I realized he was grooming others." A sudden fire to his voice. He leaned toward me. "He's running through the *same* routine he did with me but with others. I know of one man, at least. I checked his schedule and talked with him. It's not just me. And I...I can't just watch."

"But that man won't come forward."

"When I talked with him, he admitted it. Kind of. But he doesn't want to go public."

"The public is not always kind to...whistle-blowers, for lack of a better word."

"Exactly," said Jeremy Cameron. "I don't know why that is. But it's true. We think worse of the victim sometimes than of the accused. I have an awful feeling Father Louis might be getting more of what he wants from the other man than he got from me."

"And you won't tell me who he is," I said.

"No. Not yet."

"Then it's only your word versus Father Louis's."

"I know. And no one will believe me, I'm aware. But..." He raised his hands, palms up, like, *What am I supposed to do?* His eyes teared again. "I fully expect to be fired. And to never be hired by another church."

"A heavy burden you're carrying."

"I hate him. I despise Father Louis now. He makes me sick. I'd rather fight this and be fired, over letting him continue. Did you know most presbyters or priests don't like being called Father? It's a term we don't use much anymore. But he demands it. Use it enough and you start to think of him as a father, like he's trustworthy. It churns my stomach now."

"Did you alert the other man that Louis might be on the warpath?"

He nodded and said, "I did. Were you hired by vestry? Hugh Pratt?"

"Him and Robert Wallace."

He said, "Robert Wallace doesn't believe me, I know."

"Rob Wallace is interested in preserving the church. Right now he's worried about collateral damage. Which is not an entirely ignoble position to take. Though," I said, "it's mostly ignoble."

"And Hugh Pratt?"

"He doesn't know what to believe. Which is why I was hired. He wants the truth."

Jeremy leaned forward. Strained with the words. "*Believe* me, Mr. August. I'm telling the truth."

"It would help, Jeremy, if I could talk to the other man."

"No," he said.

"What if I find out who he is? Through methods other than you?"

"How would you do that?"

I shrugged. "Chicanery and a plucky amount of derring-do."

"Do all private detectives talk like this?"

"Only the greats. Does Louis ever email you?"

"Sure, all the time. But it's never incriminating. He's too smart to leave evidence lying around," said Jeremy.

"What about texts?"

"Same thing. Professional or friendly notes only."

"Be nice to look at Louis's phone and the history of texts. And yours too. Does the church provide staff with cellphone plans?" I said.

"No but we get an allowance to help pay our own. Why?"

"If the phones were owned by the church, it'd be easy to procure the devices and records."

"You're welcome to look at mine anytime. I know our emails are technically owned by the church. But I'm telling you, Father Louis is brilliant. He wouldn't produce hard evidence that incriminates himself."

"You're probably right. But even lucid men can let sexual obsessions suborn them into criminal stupidity," I said.

He watched me a moment and smiled. It reminded me

that Jeremy was a good-looking guy. "You're just showing off now, with the vocabulary," he said.

"I was on a roll. I apologize."

"What should I do, in the meantime? Excuse the expression, but it appears shit is hitting the fan."

"I got a feeling Louis might play this cool. If he's guilty, he's been in disguise for a long time. He can be patient. So you play it cool too. Any encounter with him, record it. Either audibly or with a camera. If you ever feel threatened, call me," I said.

"What would you do?"

"What do you mean?"

"If I'm being threatened, how would you help?"

"I would stop him. Or them," I said. "Obviously."

"*Them?*"

"Maybe. Probably not. But I would stop them."

"You can do that? How?"

"Because I'm wearing a spring jacket, you cannot tell that I am ferocious and tough. Trust me. I could stop them."

"Do you carry a gun?"

"Yes. Though I don't need one. Again, it's the jacket throwing you off." I stood.

"What will you do now?"

"Research. Investigate," I said. Added defensively, "And maybe do some one-handed pushups."

8

I parked in the bank lot across from All Saints, watching, detecting, and vigilantly listening to baseball podcasts. It was only April yet I already felt forlorn about the Nationals fading in September.

Might be time to switch to self-improvement podcasts instead. One about parenting young boys; Kix deserved a father who wasn't depressed about baseball games not yet played.

While I waited, I scoured the internet for Jeremy Cameron. He was intermittently active on Reddit—discussing movies and books—and he had a public Photobucket folder, plus obligatory Facebook and Instagram accounts. No Twitter or Snapchat that I could find. His Masters of Divinity dissertation was published to an online library—one hundred and eleven pages on modern day transubstantiation trends and instruction among Anglican, Episcopal, and Catholic seminaries. Yuck. I went backwards through social media photos and comments far enough to determine who his closest friends were in undergrad and grad school. Bonus—I found an old girlfriend named Miriam.

Further research yielded phone numbers for her and an undergrad buddy. I left a message with Miriam, but Tommy Houston answered; I explained Jeremy Cameron was up for a grant to pay off his student loans and Tommy Houston was one of six references listed; did he know of any reason why Jeremy shouldn't receive the grant? I grilled Tommy thoroughly—no no, Jeremy Cameron was the best, great guy, the voice of reason in the shared house of seniors at UVA, was always the designated driver, played guitar at his wedding, really terrific, tell him I said Hello.

Miriam called back an hour later—Jeremy was the sweetest, cried when they broke up, wouldn't hurt a fly, prayed with her when her grandfather died, Jeremy made the best priest she was sure, he absolutely deserved the grant, tell him I said Hello.

Jeremy sounded like a hoot in college. As long as you were into late night studying at the library.

Louis Lindsey appeared from the church's heavy wooden doors at 3:15.

Ah hah. Bingo. He would lead me to all the clues.

He slid into a white Audi convertible. The canvas top rolled back and disappeared into the car's trunk. I glared accusingly at my Honda; it didn't even have a moon roof.

Louis Lindsey pulled out onto Church Street, rolled through a stop sign, made an illegal right turn, and sped into the South Roanoke neighborhoods. I gave him a little distance and followed two cars back. He took the Franklin bridge near Virginia Tech's medical college, passed River's Edge fields, and parked in the drive of an impressive colonial on tony Avenham Avenue; the house was a hundred years old, preserved and updated and perfectly manicured. Hot *dang* those were splendid red maples.

I parked on 26th and watched him enter the house. I pulled up the title of the house online—the colonial belonged to Louis Lindsey.

I'd followed him home. *Not* to all the clues.

I observed and reconnoitered and monitored until dinnertime. By then I had convinced myself I'd seen his face watching me through windows on the top floor, but that was mere imagination and boredom. I drove to Kix's sitter's house feeling glum and useless. On the bright side, I found a parenting podcast that convinced me I wasn't an irredeemable wreck of a father. But I should probably read more books to him, which I was willing to do.

Unless he asked for James Patterson.

I had standards.

9

That night Kix and I watched Dora the Explorer and played with trains on the coffee table. Kix was not, I thought, an effective nor a safe engineer; the locomotives crashed with frequency and violence.

Listening to the sounds from the kitchen, I judged dinner almost ready. I stood to help move food. Manny brought grilled chicken thighs from the back porch. I set a Caesar salad on the table.

"Manny. You beautiful nitwit," I said. "You set the table for too many."

"We got a guest coming."

My father arrived in the kitchen; he'd changed out of his button-down shirt and into a cotton pullover.

He asked, "You have a date, Manny?"

"No, señor. I don't bring girls home. They bring me home."

"Then who?"

Outside a car parked in our gravel driveway. The engine switched off and we heard the alluring sound of heels on the sidewalk.

Kix's ears perked. We both knew that particular cadence. He started bouncing; I nearly did too.

Ronnie Summers opened the screen door and stepped into our home. A bottle of chilled champagne gripped in her left fist.

None of us budged. Just sort of admired. Afraid sudden movements or surrendering to instincts might spook the angel away.

She had that effect on guys.

She had that effect on everyone.

She wore khakis today, the kind that hugged her hips and flared at the strappy black leather heels. A white blouse that wasn't translucent but it hinted that it could be in the right light. Business casual, though it looked like formal evening wear on her.

She closed her eyes. Took a deep breath. Let it out slow. "I've missed everything about this house," she said. "The absolute cleanliness. The order. The peace. The dark and gleaming woodwork. The men. The beautiful sexy men. And especially the scents." She opened her eyes. My heart, the coward, skipped. "This house smells like leather couches and books and good bourbon and cologne and soap, and this is the happiest I've been in months."

"Hello Ronnie."

"Hello Mackenzie. And hello *gorgeous*." She slipped out of her heels, set down the bottle, and scooped Kix, who'd been hyperventilating for attention. I knew the feeling. "Oh goodness, he's gotten more perfect. I just can't." She bounced him and wiped her eyes. "Dammit, Kix. Seeing you always wrecks me. Reminds me of how emotionally unstable I am."

He patted her face.

I forgive you for the profanity. Always.

"Manny," I said. Quietly. "You beautiful nitwit. You invite her?"

"She texted me. Asked to come over. Only a dumbass say No to Ronnie Summers."

"I agree, Manuel," said my father. "Only a dumbass."

We finished setting the table. We were not floating but almost.

Ronnie slid Kix into his highchair. She lowered into the chair across from me; she smiled and the chandelier's lambency intensified.

"Mackenzie, can you say grace? I've missed that too."

"I will. Although you do not believe the God to whom I pray exists."

"The closest I get is listening to you talk with him."

I said grace. The room seemed to take on a supernal hum, as though more was going on than we could see.

Ronnie cut up Kix's chicken and we took turns plying her with questions about her practice. Timothy August and Manny enjoyed Ronnie almost as much as I did; they plied me with rampant scorn and bitterness when I ended my relationship with her. She told us she was busy with work sent by her father, a man I'd never met.

She asked Manny after his career, and they laughed over two pending hearings, men whom Manny arrested and now Ronnie represented. The malfeasants had money; destitute criminals couldn't afford Ronnie Summers.

She asked after Timothy August's elementary school, and he regaled us with woes about the failings of modern day parenting.

Her bare toe slid under my pant leg now. When I glanced in her direction, she was absorbed in conversations down the table.

We finished dinner. The men cleaned. Ronnie read a

book to Kix on Dad's reading chair in the far corner and put him to bed.

She came downstairs, helped me dry dishes, poured herself a flute of champagne, and took my hand. Whispered in my ear.

"Sit with me on the porch. I promise not to molest you."

I followed with mixed feelings about her promise.

We sat in rocking chairs. The spring evening held a loose chill, the sky a dark and dotted blue blanket.

She set down her flute. Took a shaky breath.

"Coming here might not be worth the pain," she said. "I miss this so much."

I couldn't think of a great response. Nothing came to mind. So I went with that.

She said, "Did Manny tell you I was coming?"

"He did not."

"Then why are you wearing that shirt? You know I like how you look in that shirt."

"You are confused. I look this good in all shirts."

"You do. I'd almost forgotten. I'm used to other men. Their hands aren't big like yours. They don't have forearms like you or the shoulders. Goodness, the shoulders. And the hair and cheekbones and your perfect lips...whew, I'm getting worked up. There are no men like you, Mackenzie."

"I might quote you on my business cards."

"And your house! The corners are swept, the remote controllers are lined up, the marble counters are polished. Even the bathroom is spotless. The men in this house never cease to amaze. If I had more money, I would produce a reality television show about this home and pitch it to TLC and every woman in America would watch."

I was feeling exposed and confused and hurt, trying to play nice, act like this was normal. Being with her was like sunbathing—intense and hot, I'd been burned before and I was feeling raw.

"You and I can't be friends, Ronnie."

"Because you want more."

"I'm predisposed by nature to."

"But you won't," she said.

"But I won't."

"I don't want to be away from you, Mackenzie. And I don't want to just be friends. Our months apart made that crystal clear. Coming here tonight is like a hammer of clarity. I want you to be happy, and I want to be the girl who makes you so."

"And yet."

"I *can't* end my engagement," she said. "I know...I know that doesn't make sense. I know my logic is flawed. But that's how I feel about you."

"So here we are again."

"Maybe..." She picked up the flute of champagne and finished it. "Maybe there are levels of togetherness on the spectrum between Completely Separated and Married. We could try? We could shift around to find our spot on the spectrum that works best?"

She was trying not to cry.

"I bounced around the lower end of that spectrum in Los Angeles," I said. "Hurting others. Ruining myself. Pretending it was normal as I withered. I'm at a healthy place now. But my hold on sanity is gossamer thin. It's peace but its tenuous. And you're a wrecking ball. Unless you plan on building something permanent here, I can't let you demolish me. I'm not sure I can rebuild again."

"I'm alone and you are too. I know you miss me. We can help each other. Keep the hurt away."

"The way heroin keeps the hurt away."

"I'm tempted to take that as a compliment." She withdrew a cellphone from her pocket. Ran her finger across the screen a few times and the phone in my pocket buzzed. "That's from me. May I borrow your cell?"

I withdrew it—she'd sent me some kind of message—and handed it over. She pushed buttons on my screen and returned it.

A map was displayed. My location was blue, and it indicated I was at my house on Windsor. Next to my blue dot, there was a little icon of her. A photo of her smiling, and we overlapped.

"What's this?"

"I shared my location with you," she said. "And vice versa."

"So I always know where your phone is?"

"Yes. And by extension, where I am."

"Why?"

She seemed pleased with herself. A little more vigor and charm. "Because it's hard to covet something you never see. I'm hoping you'll be tempted to check my location occasionally. Maybe daily. The more you look, the more you'll think of me. And the more you think of me, the more you'll think of me."

"Profound."

"Isn't it? I thought of this clever little plan myself. A plan to win you over," she said.

"It won't work. I am an oak."

But I wasn't so sure. Her plan was sneakily grounded in fact and the frail and fallen nature of our human condition. It struck me as effective.

She said, "It might. Maybe at night, maybe a dark and desolate evening, you'll feel alone. I'll come to mind. You will open the map to locate me. See that I'm at home. Alone. And you'll be tempted."

"This location sharing, is that the primary reason you came over tonight?"

"I want you to be happy, and I want to be in your life. So..."

"Ronnie."

"Yes Mackenzie."

"This plan of yours?"

"Yes Mackenzie."

"It is egregiously sinister."

"I'll play dirty to get you, if I must. But now I'm tired. It's been a long day." She stood and stretched, a move designed to get attention. As she raised her arms over her head, her blouse tugged free at her left hip. "Does Manny still sleep on your floor?"

"He does."

"Have you deduced why?" she said.

"Not with certainty. But, as with us, it has to do with hurt and solitude and a broken history."

"He gets to sleep in your room. Why can't I?"

"There is plenty of floor space for you."

A curve of pearlescent white in the darkness—her smile. "You're saying you'd rather me bunk with Manny than with you?"

"Never mind. You may not bunk with Manny. Your children would be too beautiful and the fabric of our reality would unravel." I stood. Took her hand and walked her to her car. "You're barefoot."

"I know. I'm leaving my high heels by the front door intentionally."

"So I will think about you."

"Yes. It's a multifaceted assault on your ethics."

I kissed her forehead. She smelled like perfume and expensive shampoo and my overloaded sensorium turned the world shades of red and pink. She trembled under my lips and in a flash of lucidity I saw us from the outside, saw that she was just a girl and I was just a boy and that sometimes grown-ups ache like we did as kids. I saw myself, saw her, saw the broken pieces, saw that maturity doesn't always bring understanding and wholeness but sometimes the longings intensify without relief and we crash into people who can't complete us but we try anyway desperately.

Two needy humans. Trying. And mostly failing.

Dust in the wind.

I came back to myself to hear her whisper, "Sometimes, Mackenzie, at night, I wish I'd never met you."

I stepped away. "I understand."

"But, since I did, I can't stop."

"I understand that too."

"You're distancing yourself from me quickly, Mackenzie." She kind of chuckled. "Am I so awful?"

"Good night, Ronnie."

"Good night, Mackenzie."

I didn't trust myself to look at her again. She'd almost broken through with her whispers, with her scent, her big eyes catching the stars, her vulnerability. I went inside and closed the door.

Manny was on the couch.

"I didn't listen, amigo. But I watched. You have the willpower of...of an amazing person. Bruce Lee or Chuck Norris or the Pope."

I sat in the leather chair. Tingling. "An outré selection of people on your list."

"That is an estúpido word. I thought I might be banished to my own bedroom tonight."

"Came close. But I am an oak. An oak who needs another cold shower."

He returned to his low carb beer and the baseball game.

I withdrew my phone. Opened the map.

Watched Ronnie the whole way home. A mere three miles away.

10

Here's the thing about proving someone guilty.

It's troublesome.

So far the case of Father Louis didn't involve the justice system, so I didn't have to prove him guilty beyond reasonable doubt to a jury or judge; I just had to convince the vestry. However, I wasn't familiar with the inner workings of Episcopalian by-laws; presuming Father Louis had a high-priced attorney on retainer, things would go better if I *could* prove him culpable beyond reasonable doubt. Assuming he was.

A few ways to do that. I could...

One—Get him to confess.

Two—Accumulate overwhelming evidence.

Three—Take the first-person testimony of multiple victims or eyewitnesses.

Though a brilliant and stalwart and intrepid investigator, neither flagging nor failing in the face of danger, dressed with class and a touch of irreverence, and currently the obsession of Roanoke's most desirable blonde attorney, I preferred to not do more work than necessary. Ergo, getting testimony from alleged victims would be my first choice.

But. The only alleged victim I knew about, other than Jeremy Cameron, didn't want to speak with me. Which I took in professional stride. Maybe if he knew I was currently the obsession of Roanoke's most desirable blonde attorney he would feel differently.

I sat at my office, sorting through spreadsheets of All Saints's expenses. For reasons of transparency, they published a budget online. Specific individual salaries weren't detailed, but they were included in the personnel section. I didn't know what I was searching for. Merely hoping something jumped out, like a Louis Illicit Sex fund hidden in the back.

Stupendously banal work. I therefore withdrew my sacred bottle of Johnnie Walker Blue from the drawer and poured a finger of scotch. I preferred to cut strong liquors with ice, but I could manage neat in an emergency.

I was contemplating a taste while examining the church's missionary expenditures when my phone rang. Jeremy Cameron on the line.

"Mr. August, sorry to bother you again. I know this isn't part of your job. I need advice and I'm not sure where else I can turn," he said.

"Happy to help. Is not the church's vestry a resource available to you?"

"I called Hugh Pratt, but he said we should speak in front of an attorney to be safe. And I don't have that much time."

"Ugh. Attorneys. They ruin everything. Even the most desirable blonde ones," I said, staring with deep reverence into my scotch.

"I suppose you're right. But I think he has the best

interest of the parish…err, church at heart. He still doesn't know whether to trust me or not."

"I get it. Calling me's a good idea."

Technically I didn't know yet whether to trust him or not. But I did. More than I trusted Louis. Call it veteran intuition. And he'd been nicer to me than Louis had been.

Through the phone he said, "Father Louis just announced an unscheduled staff meeting later today. I should go. Right?"

"He's your supervisor. So probably."

"What if he questions us about the accusations? I don't like lying. But…should I?"

"Use your best judgment. Lying can serve a purpose. But so can the white hot truth. It rattles people. Either way, record it."

"This is nuts," he said. "This is not why I went to seminary. I never fully realized the absolute power he wields."

"Explain."

"He's the rector. He has full control. The staff of receptionists and grounds keepers and accountants and childcare workers and administrators and deacons…they are in awe of him. His word is law," said Jeremy. His voice was hushed and throaty, probably in his office and he didn't want his words leaking through the walls.

"What about the bishop? How's it work? He's Louis's supervisor?"

"Bishop Glenn. Louis is far more influential and beloved than him. Sometimes I get the impression Bishop Glenn takes his direction from Louis. I asked for a meeting and he put me off. He didn't return my recent call either. I don't suspect collusion; I just don't rate high enough. Soon I'll lay on his doorstep until he deals with me."

While he spoke, I sipped some scotch. It justified the wait, and life was worth living once more.

I said, "What about other clergy in the church?"

"There's only three clergy here. Father Louis and us."

"Us?" My Clue Detector beeped. "Who is us?"

A pause. "Sorry. I forgot you don't attend All Saints. Us, me and the other clergyman: the worship leader," he said. Even as he spoke, I was surfing to the church's webpage. Opened up the clergy section and examined the pictures. Nicholas McBride. Good-looking guy, young, fresh out of seminary. He said, "Nicholas and I, we're clergy but we don't count in terms of power structure."

"Why?"

"Because we're young. We're kids to Father Louis and the deacons and the vestry. I'm the eldest and I'm only thirty. Technically I'm the curate, or associate rector, but no one thinks of me that way."

"All Saints is a big church," I said. "Is it abnormal to have such a young group of clergy?"

"I suppose you could say that."

I opened up Facebook, the investigatorial tool of champions, and found the page for Nicholas McBride. I celebrated with another dram of Johnnie Walker. It cost a billion dollars per bottle, approximately, so it was vital to milk the experience.

"So at this staff meeting, Father Louis is the king," I said.

"Correct."

"Did he invite the vestry?"

"No, he would never. Not that they would oppose him, not to his face. Remember, they hired you in secret. Besides he doesn't...sorry I gotta go," he said in a rush and he hung up.

The sudden silence in my ear felt loud.

11

I stood and dashed down the final swirl of scotch. Locked the office and drove to All Saints. On the way, I sent Jeremy Cameron a text message.

I'll be in the parking lot of your church. Need me, I'm here.

I doubted Jeremy was in physical danger.

Heck, I didn't even know if he was telling the truth or not. But the kid felt so young, and Father Louis had intimidated even me a little.

Well. A very little. I had a gun, after all. And I did some pushups last night.

I had a mental image of a scared kid being afraid of his tyrannical and violent father. I didn't know if that was an accurate picture of what was going on, but I assumed it would help Jeremy Cameron if he knew I was close.

I parked in the paved lot and lowered my windows. Roanoke's downtown was breezily industrious, a self-contained and satisfied world that moved a couple miles per hour slower than bigger cities.

Louis Lindsey's voice flooded my car. An All Saints

commercial on the radio, enlightening listeners that life had meaning and he would be honored to help them navigate it at either the early or late service on Sunday. I turned the volume down and wished things were that easy in real life.

I'm so profound. Kix would be amazed.

He would also demand I work more efficiently, because I was checking Ronnie's location on my phone. Relax kid, it's harmless to look. (She was at her office) But then I got busy searching the photos on Nicholas McBride's Facebook page.

Nicholas McBride, Roanoke, Virginia, clergy, worship leader and children's director at All Saints. He was married and had a baby. The wife and baby made him look older than Jeremy Cameron. In his photos Nicholas was playing the guitar, giving his baby a bath, holding hands with his wife at the beach. Like Jeremy, Nicholas was attractive. White, trim, athletic, looked like a long-distance runner. Dressed in tight jeans and trendy tight shirts. I found a photo of him smiling with his mother.

Something inside me was disquiet. My inner eye spotting clues the rest of me was too dense to see. Or maybe I was hungry.

I walked down the street to Bread Craft and got two doughnuts and an iced latte and prayed Manny wouldn't see me with all the carbs. Came back and resumed my digital investigation.

I found Nicholas McBride's Instagram account and stared at the collection. Then I jumped to Jeremy Cameron's collection, and back. I stared for thirty minutes until I identified the nagging disquiet.

"Ah hah," I told myself. Because we all need encouragement.

I went through all of Jeremy Cameron's Facebook timeline and searched his photo collection again. Further confirmation.

Neither guy had a photograph with his father. Multiple shots with Mom, and none with Dad. Did that matter? Maybe. Maybe not.

Mackenzie August, master of deduction.

What else did they have in common? Young guys. Fit. Fancy hair on the longer side, always in place. Handsome. But their faces each held the same type of handsome. In fact, handsome might not be the right word. These weren't overly masculine guys. They were...pretty wasn't the right word either. Nothing effeminate about them. Nor androgynous. But they were organized. Their outfits matched, more than most men their age. They wore good shoes and belts. Not slobs, not messy. Nice bright eyes, good lashes, big smiles. They posed well for the camera...

I snapped my fingers.

That was it. They looked like guys raised by their mother. No father around telling the mom to quit fussing with his hair, it's good for the kid to get dirty, don't baby the boy, he's supposed to get banged up and scraped.

I looked at myself in the mirror. My hair was short and in place...mostly. I had a little powdered sugar from the doughnut on my chin. I could use a shave. I looked down—my shirt wasn't tucked in. My sneakers needed to be washed. Or replaced.

My mother had died years ago, eliminating her gentrifying influence. My father never offered to help me pick out clothes and he never demanded I pose for pictures. Therefore I was a bit of a mess.

Fascinating.

Manny had been raised without his father. And that guy looked perfect. How'd he do that?

I was contemplating my own short-comings when Father Louis appeared out of the church. I was close enough to see his face was red, veins bulging in his neck. He hurled a computer bag into the back of his white Audi convertible, got inside, and roared off.

I thought maybe our eyes locked for an instant. But that was my imagination.

I texted Jeremy Cameron.

If you're still alive, I'm still outside.

He appeared a few minutes later. Scanned the parking lot and saw me. I beckoned. He came on shaky legs, opened the door, and kinda fell in.

"Good grief," he said. "That was like being in the principal's office. And the police station. And purgatory."

"Father Louis lambast his staff?"

"He paced back and forth like an angry lion. He told us about someone trying to tear the church apart. Unfounded accusations meant to assassinate his character. That he and God would deal swiftly and with justice against the wicked. That we shouldn't believe the rumors, and we should report directly to him if we hear anything. At the end, he was irate to the extent of incoherence."

I gave him a minute to decompress. We stared out our respective windows and thought things without speaking.

A curious system, this church hierarchy. The head of the church, or rector, seemed to have an inordinate amount of power. He wasn't hired or fired by the congregation, but by a distant Bishop. And if the rector was gregarious enough and filling the coffers, who stood in the way of absolute control?

God, I supposed. But did he involve himself in the management of such things?

I said, "How did Nicholas handle it?"

"Fine. Other than Father Louis, no one in the room spoke much."

"Would you care to reveal the identity of the other man Father Louis has allegedly molested?"

"I promised I wouldn't," said Jeremy. "So I can't."

"You promised you wouldn't tell the vestry who he is. And by extension, you promised you wouldn't tell *me* who he is."

"Correct."

"I'll find out without your help. And I will keep his secret as thoroughly as you are."

He nodded. "I believe you. The less people who know, the better."

"Fewer."

"What?"

"The *fewer* people who know, the better. I know it's weird because 'people' seems like an uncountable entity, but...you know, let's move on. Did Father Louis hire you personally?"

"He did. In the Episcopalian church, hiring is the purview of the rector," said Jeremy.

"Did he interview you?"

"Yes."

"Did he ask about your father?"

He blinked. Blinked again. "Maybe. Does that matter? It was three years ago."

"Try to remember. Certainly he asked about your family and your history. He'd be an irresponsible maniac not to."

"I have no relationship with my father."

"That's the point."

"How is that the point?"

"I'm gathering evidence. You want the vestry and me to believe this married and well-known religious leader is secretly a homosexual and a predator. Predators are careful.

Predators don't pick their victims at random. Predators often select young men who have no relationship with their father. They are malleable. Vulnerable to predation."

The color in his face graduated down from a healthy pink to sickly pale. He stared through my dash into the distant history, recalling a job interview three years ago.

"You're saying...that's the reason I was chosen? He hired me with this in mind?"

"Maybe."

"Somehow that makes it even worse. Yes. At the interview, he asked several questions about my father."

"If he's guilty, then it's no coincidence," I said, "that Nicholas doesn't have a healthy relationship with his father either."

"Good Lord."

"The church staff appears curated with tempting targets for a sexual predator."

Jeremy covered his eyes with his hands. Took a deep breath. "How do you know Nicholas doesn't have a relationship with his father?"

"Elementary, my dear Jeremy Cameron. To be specific, it's seventy-five percent the result of a quick and rigorous investigation, and twenty-five percent a guess. I'm right, aren't I?"

He didn't answer. Instead, in something of a monotone voice, "People say the two of us look alike."

"You do, a little."

"The receptionists at All Saints tease us. Say we dress like we're gay."

"Although I'd take that as a compliment, the receptionists are misguided. You two dress like you care. Like you were taught how and you listened. Don't have to be gay to care how you look. Does Nicholas have an unhealthy or nonexistent relationship with his father?"

"I think so. He's more reserved concerning these things than me."

"I'm making an educated guess that Nicholas is the other victim. He is younger and still in awe of Louis and doesn't want to lose his job," I said. Again, twenty-five percent a guess.

I had the best guesses.

"I cannot answer that," he said.

"I know."

"Also, I don't like being called a victim."

"You're right. Poor word choice," I said.

"I know what you meant. And I know you don't intend any harm. But it helps if I don't allow myself to feel victimized. You know?"

"I don't think of you as a victim, so I shouldn't use the word."

"Thank you," he said.

"For the sake of this conversation, let's proceed on a plank of hypothetical presumption. A presumption that Nicholas is the other man Louis attempted to molest. Or successfully molested. Why does he refuse to speak with the vestry?"

"Probably for the same reason I delayed for months. I knew I wouldn't be believed. I never felt so alone as when confiding in Hugh Pratt and Robert Wallace. There's a strong chance my reputation will be ruined and I won't find another job in a church. Even if I'm proven correct, I'll still bear a stigma."

"America hates snitches," I said. "Might as well have that in our pledge of allegiance."

"Even the Christian community hates them. That's

something I'm learning. Parishioners pledge allegiance to their pastor or priest; he becomes their idol and suddenly your church is fractured. Most of All Saints will think I'm being unfaithful to Father Louis."

"That's a universal problem mature churches should be immune from. But. Trouble with churches is, they're constituted by people. Fallen and broken people feel personally implicated and betrayed by snitches, which is absurd," I said.

He was crying. Looking away from me.

I said, "But you can't think of it that way. You can't look through that broken lens. Paul Revere wasn't a snitch. Neither was Martin Luther King, Jr. They were men telling the truth about a danger."

"Doesn't matter how I look at it. I still carry the burden."

I popped open my glove compartment near his knees and withdrew a box of travel tissues. Dropped them in his lap.

"It's a heavy burden, too," I said. "Not able to be carried by many men. Which is why Nicholas doesn't want to come forward. Yet. Hypothetically."

He wiped his eyes. Blew his nose. Gave a sad smile.

"These things never work out well for the testifying victim, do they. No, I don't want to say victim. I mean...I don't know what I mean."

"It can't be made fair. Not really. But you're still going through with it," I said.

"I am."

"Why?"

"Because I remain a believer. I still believe in the holiness of God. The goodness of the church. I refuse to let one man ruin it for me. We live in a fallen world, as you said. We're meant to walk with our creator but we wallow in squalor and lesser realities, distanced from God. The church is his primary tool on this planet to get us out of our mire. It's a broken and leaky ship but it's the only one headed in the right direction. You know, most of the time. If a wicked man is at the wheel, he has to be removed. Even if it costs me everything."

"Holy smokes, Jeremy."

He chuckled. "I've given this a lot of thought, you can see. And my convictions are only getting stronger."

"If I was an inch more emotional, I'd be choked up."

"You need the tissues?" he asked.

"No. But I might come listen to you preach one day soon."

"You should hear Nicholas. He's a gifted orator."

"What happened to your father?" I said.

"He was a drunk. Still is, I assume. He abused Mom. She left him when I was ten. He came around some, and I had to call the police on him when I was twelve."

"That leaves a mark."

"It does," he said. But he sounded less sad now. "Do you believe me now? About Father Louis?"

"Getting that way."

"Even if you correctly identified the other man Father Louis is assaulting, hypothetically, he still won't testify to vestry or in court. So how will you prove Louis's guilty?"

"Jeremy," I said. "I'm not sure. Yet."

12

Temperatures that evening dipped into the forties and our heat clicked on at eleven. The radiators gurgled and hummed, the only sound in our quiet house.

I laid under my covers reading a Frederick Forsyth book and wondered *how* he knew all that stuff.

Manny reclined on a fancy Therm-a-Rest air mattress on the floor at the foot of my bed, reading a Hemingway novel and occasionally correcting the guy's Spanish.

Just a couple librocubicularists in our element. A dramatic and intentional correction from our previous lifestyle.

Manny and I had worked together in Los Angeles. I was homicide, he was vice, and we became friends after crossing paths on a couple cases. We worked eighty-hour weeks and spent our minimal free time drinking and fighting. I'd been unusually good at the job but the work had been hard, and I self-destructed after only a decade. I came home to Roanoke, Virginia in search of sanity. Leaving behind the corpses and the hate. A year later Manny appeared on my porch unannounced, a haunted man. He moved into the spare bedroom but chose to sleep on my floor. Every night.

Something horrific had happened. I didn't ask what. He didn't offer. We were both grateful for the friendship. Building a new life with new routines wasn't likely. But I could do it because of Kix. And he could do it, maybe, with enough August support.

He was, without a doubt, the most dangerous man I knew. Plus the most patriotic. Shockingly well equipped to be a federal marshal.

And so we dipped our toes into dangerous waters during the day and, pacified, watched baseball and read novels at night. It worked for us. So far.

I was learning about the hell that was Vietnam and the brave men who went into the tunnels beneath it when Manny sat up from his air mattress. Cocked his head.

Very quiet. "Amigo."

"Sí?" I inquired.

"Someone is outside. They just tried the door."

"Which door?"

"Rattle sounded like the rear doorknob."

I set my book down. "You made enemies recently?"

"*Por supuesto.*" Of course. "But they are smart enough not to come here."

He stood, his big .357 revolver withdrawn from under his pillow and ready in his fist.

I reached into my nightstand and withdrew the Kimber 1911. Better safe than shot. We moved into the hallway; he turned right, and I went left. Took opposing staircases down.

No reason to wake Dad. He hated shooting people anyway.

Who'd try to enter our house this late? Random interloper? Doubtful. Not in this neighborhood. One of

Manny's recent captures, out on bail? Maybe, but most of them understood that Marshal Martinez was not a man to anger.

The main level was dark. Doors still closed and locked. So were the windows. I never noticed how many windows this house had until now that I felt exposed by them. Tactical nightmare. A car drove down Windsor, the headlights and reflections limning the furniture and rushing around the far walls.

No intruder had penetrated our house. I was certain. But maybe he was still trying.

The neighbor's black Labrador began barking. Mr. Welch lived alone in the house behind ours and he let his dog, Fargo, out late each evening. Fargo was not often noisy but at the moment he was yowling.

Whoever the intruder was, he would be on the run now. Or she.

I moved to the front door. Unlocked it and went out. Cleared the porch and moved toward the driveway, sliding sideways and backing up, facing the house and facing the unseen Fargo beyond. And facing whatever caused Fargo to lose his mind

The bright night felt crisp and cold. No clouds. A couple degrees fewer and I would see my breath.

I continued backing up, enlarging my field of view. No one getting past me. I knew without witnessing it that Manny had gone through the back door, cleared the rear deck, and was chasing down the disturbance.

I kept moving sideways to the street. A mere shadow. Kimber pointed at the earth. From my point of view at the corner of our lot, I had a long look down all four streets of the intersection.

Cars passed on Grandin over the hill.

Deeper inside the neighborhood, maybe two blocks in, a car door slammed. An engine droned and faded.

Manny whistled and I moved down the line of crape myrtles, looking under and around the cars, slipping along the west side of our house, until finding his silhouette at the neighbor's fence. Mr. Welch had taken Fargo indoors.

"Señor Welch says his dog started barking and someone ran that way. He didn't get a good look." Manny pointed away from the position I'd taken. "Footprints in the grass."

"Maybe a local neighborhood kid?"

"Not a kid, not a woman. A man, and not a small one. But I never saw the hombre. Heard a car drive off in the distance. Long gone now."

"What kind of engine?"

"Quiet kind."

"You let him get away," I said.

"Not on purpose."

"Means you're getting old."

"Old? I was sleepy. But I'll kick your ass right now."

"Doesn't seem helpful." We returned to the house. I locked the front door.

"I kick enough asses, amigo, I get a bonus from Uncle Sam."

"Any guess who it was?"

"Nada. Someone kinda sneaky."

I went around the house's interior. Checked every door and every window, even in the dusty basement. I laid back down in bed.

On a whim, I opened Ronnie's location. Manny said the footprints didn't look like a woman's, but...

Ronnie's dot blinked onto my screen. She was at Blue 5, probably tending bar, her bizarre after-hours hobby.

Of course it hadn't been her outside. She had too much

dignity and class to be a prowler. Girls like Ronnie didn't stalk. They got stalked.

I wondered when Ronnie's shift ended. Wondered if she worried about stalkers late at night outside the restaurant as she hurried to her car. She'd probably feel safer if I was there. I'd recently done pushups, after all. Maybe I should offer. I'd be a fool not to. Maybe we'd go back to her apartment for a while.

Manny shifted on his air mattress. Book down, probably asleep.

Five minutes later I still stared at her dot on my map. Debated driving to the restaurant. To Ronnie.

What I had in Roanoke was good. Stable. A safe and healthy environment for my son. I had a family. And a Manny. A job I enjoyed that paid the bills. Enough stimuli to sate the urges. Though sometimes at night I missed the noise and the fights and the girls and the drugs.

And other nights I missed them a lot.

Ronnie Summers would scratch a lot of itches. Sate a lot of urges.

But those were urges I willfully decided not to satisfy. Itches I volitionally didn't scratch because of the chaos down that path. Chaos that knew me well. Those were scars waiting to rip open. By a woman engaged to another man.

"Good grief," I told the ceiling.

Mackenzie August. Still trying to grow up.

I set the phone down. Closed my eyes. Forced them to stay closed. Not tonight, Ronnie. Not tonight, chaos.

Our prowler was already forgotten. Because although I didn't get out of bed, I couldn't get Ronnie out of my mind.

I'll be darned.

Her plan was working.

13

I dropped Kix off early at Roxanne's, rented a white Chevy Malibu, and parked two blocks from Louis Lindsey's stately colonial house on Avenham. If he'd seen me driving my Honda, he wouldn't be expecting the Malibu. I donned a baseball cap in the rented car and waited for him, replete in my foolproof disguise.

So good at this I scare myself. I queued up more of the parenting podcasts and drank coffee.

He surprised me, returning from an early morning jog. He came up Avenham and walked his front lawn a few times, hands on his hips and sucking cool air. His shirt clung to him. He checked his pulse and went inside.

Thirty minutes later he emerged showered and fresh, tossed a leather satchel into his Audi and headed out. I couldn't break into his home because although I'd never seen her I assumed his wife was inside. So I tailed him instead. To the church.

I parked and pondered just how much of my life I was willing to waste following him to and from his home and office. I walked to Bread Craft to replenish the coffee, a selfish and unprofessional move that nearly cost me—Louis Lindsey was back in his car and leaving the lot on my return. I ducked behind the Malibu as manfully as possible to avoid detection, and then drove after him.

He wove through traffic to Roanoke Country Club. I stopped at the deserted end of the parking lot and used binoculars to observe him withdraw a bag of golf clubs from his trunk and join a group heading for the clubhouse. From this distance, the men looked identical—white, handsome the way retired quarterbacks are, wealthy, and pleased with all the above.

A round of golf meant Louis was engaged for five hours. And for that time, I was free.

I drove to the YMCA, changed clothes, struggled through fifty burpees, lifted weights and overturned tires, punched the heavy bag, jumped rope, ran two miles, stripped and soaked in the hot tub, took a cold shower, changed back, and left to meet Manny for lunch. We ate at Billy's because of a deal he had with one of the managers; Manny had caught the manager's kid with cocaine and he let the boy off with a warning in exchange for eating free for twelve months.

It wasn't bribery. It was bartering, the way deals used to be struck in a simpler time. Or that's how he explained it. He ordered two sandwiches with no bun, and I got a burger. We each had a beer and debated the validity of Jason Bourne beating John Wick in a fight.

No, we decided. A resounding negative.

Still two hours to spare. I swung by Roxanne's to get Kix. We drove to the playground off Brandon near the pond, and we tried all the slides, and ran after squirrels, and fell off the monkey bars, and cried, and climbed, and slid some more until he explained it was time for his nap. I deposited the exhausted two-year-old with Roxanne and returned to Roanoke Country Club, invigorated by the supernal break in the boredom.

Louis Lindsey emerged forty-five minutes later, early afternoon. He shook hands with his friends, the masters of the universe, and left.

He did not drive home. He did not drive to the office.

Progress.

He parked at a house in western Roanoke County, near the Salem border. A red-brick ranch, Ford pickup inside the carport. Box shrubs. Brick walkway. Chain-link fence with a swing set in the back. Nice enough place. I eased to a stop two blocks away on the opposite side, peering around a cable service truck. Louis straightened his shirt, glanced around the neighborhood, and went inside. After waiting five minutes, I got off the brake and motored past the home. Noted the address and returned to my hiding spot. Pulled up the house's title online.

Belonged to George and Dianne Saunders. They purchased the house two years ago.

I called Jeremy Cameron.

"You know a George or Dianne Saunders?" I said.

"Name rings a bell. Should I?"

"I'm not sure. Just chasing leads."

I heard clicking. A keyboard.

"Oh, I know this guy. Found him on our church's directory. They used to attend All Saints. They still might, I suppose, but I haven't seen them in months. Maybe a year. He's a morning manager at Home Depot, I think. Why?"

"I'll let you know. Thanks."

I watched the innocuous house and wondered what was happening inside. Had Louis Lindsey visited the ranch at night, I would've snuck to a window and snooped. But in the daylight I'd be seen, a very visible and minacious simpleton.

If I was a consummate and thorough professional, I would be tailing Jeremy Cameron every other day, not just Louis Lindsey. After all, Jeremy could be lying. And much was learned about a person through snooping. I'd been investigating idiots and criminals and malfeasants for a decade, however, and veteran instincts told me to ignore Jeremy and focus on Louis, at least until Louis proved to be squeaky clean.

Which he wasn't.

And also, consummate and thorough professionals were boring.

Half an hour later a Chrysler minivan arrived. The van squealed hard to a stop behind the pickup truck and a woman got out. Left the door open and she stormed through the front door. Even two blocks removed, I heard shouting. The woman came back out and removed a baby from the van. Using binoculars I saw her face was red, her jaw set. Louis Lindsey emerged from the house, said a few quiet things to the woman—looked like potential apologies or explanations—and he departed in the Audi. The woman slammed the front door. More shouting was audible as I drove by.

I tailed Lindsey to his home, left him there, and returned the Malibu.

Fascinating.

The hell just happened?

14

Someone knocked on my front door at 9 p.m.

I closed my laptop—I'd been playing and losing a game of chess against the computer—and answered the knock. A woman stood there, talking on her phone. She was fifty, she looked forty, a good forty, brown hair glinting with silver. Excellent physique made even more commendable through plastic surgery, or so the rumors and the physical evidence indicated. I'd seen her face earlier today on the cover of a magazine published in Roanoke.

We'd helped each other on cases before. A collegial arrangement. She was probably my prettiest colleague. And probably the prettiest sheriff on the East Coast.

She held up a finger. Said, "I'll call you back," and hung up. Texted something and put away her phone. "Hey babe. Sorry this is late. Got a minute?"

"Sheriff Stackhouse." I stepped aside to let her in. "You have me on the cusp of alarm."

"There aren't many good reasons for the sheriff to knock on your door after dark, are there."

"I can think of more with you than with the typical sheriff."

"Thanks. But don't be alarmed. I'm here to compare notes."

I led her to the kitchen. Held up a beer and a bottle of Woodford bourbon. She nodded at the bourbon and slid onto a stool. Her khaki uniform was snug and she hadn't buttoned it all the way to her neck and the collar gapped, but I did *not* look.

"Compare notes," I said. Dropped two ice cubes into a highball glass and poured bourbon. Slid it to her. And did *not* look. "On Margaret Atwood's most recent novel?"

She finished the bourbon in one pronounced gulp. Held it out for more.

"I don't know who that is, babe." I thought she sounded husky, like Demi Moore. "A kid's gone missing. And your name came up."

I poured another shot.

Said, "I'm not on any missing children."

"This is a weird one. Two years ago, maybe around the time you moved here, a teenager disappeared. Jon Young. Good kid, lived with his grandmother, plenty of friends. Sixteen, I think, made solid grades, and then he was gone. No clues. A month later his body surfaced in the Roanoke River, down near North Carolina at the John Kerr reservoir. Waters were high. M.E. saw no significant signs of mistreatment, but he'd been shot two days before floating onto the shore. Shook Roanoke up good.

"This morning, a mom reports her teenage son missing. Happens a lot. Usually it's a non-issue; the kid's a prick or the parents are assholes, he's staying at a friend's or girl-friend's, boyfriend's, whatever, and comes home soon. These things resolve themselves. This one caught my eye, though."

"Why's that?"

"His name's Alec Ward. I kinda know who his parents are. Both Alec and the boy who died two years ago regularly attended All Saints," she said.

"Ah." The hairs on my arm raised.

"Yes. Ah. So that sparks my interest—two missing kids from All Saints? God, I don't want to go through that again. I go over there today and I'm chatting with Jeremy Cameron in his office about Alec Ward and Jeremy's phone rings. He answers it, talks a minute, and hangs up. He looks a little spooked and I ask, anything wrong? No, he said. That was just a friend, Mackenzie August."

"I'm so friendly."

She sipped her bourbon. She watched me over the rim with green eyes. I don't think she was doing it to seduce me, but it had an effect just the same.

She said, "No you're not. I didn't mention to Jeremy Cameron that you being involved is often trouble. Looks like he's got enough on his plate. But I thought I'd come talk to you as soon as I could."

"My tax dollars hard at work."

"Speaking of hard at work, Manny around?"

"He," I said, "is not. Sometimes he's gone for a couple days without explanation."

"You wouldn't believe the ruckus he causes walking through my office. No one can focus the next ten minutes."

"I sleep in the same room with him every night. Doesn't bother me. I am an oak."

"You two share a room?" she said.

"Not really. But also yes."

"That's the juiciest damned gossip I've ever heard, sweetie. The girls will lose their minds, I tell them about this. And speaking of a girl losing her mind, where's your father?"

"I'm here," said Timothy August coming down the rear staircase. He was rolling up the sleeves of the shirt he'd just thrown on. "I thought I detected the most lovely bachelorette in Roanoke."

"In Roanoke?" she said.

"In the state, I mean, of course."

She held out her hand. He took it and squeezed.

She hadn't held out her hand to me. Weird.

Timothy kissed her cheek. "You're here on business."

"Yes. Unfortunately."

"Drinks after?" he said.

"I wish." She pulled out her phone to check the time. Scanned the waiting text messages. "Got a missing kid, a 7-11 clerk shot in northwest, a transport broken down in Danville with prisoners inside, and a deputy in custody for beating the shit out of an inmate. What about tomorrow evening?"

"I am yours," said Timothy August. "Dinner? Drinks? Dancing?"

"Just drinks. I'm having dinner at the cancer research fundraiser. But I'll be dying to get out of that room."

"Hey. I'm still here," I said with a sense of vertigo. My father was single and somewhat active in Roanoke's Wealthy And Hot Over Forty-Five scene, a lurid world where rules seemed looser. I'd seen him and Stackhouse orbit one another before, enough that I anticipated them crashing together at some point. But I prefer not to witness it.

They ignored me.

My father said, "Tomorrow it is. Drinks at Stellina?"

She pursed her lips in contemplation. "Let's make it the Pine Room."

"The Hotel Roanoke's bar."

"You know, just in case."

She smiled. It was a good one.

He smiled back.

I covered my face with my hand. "Holy hell."

"Yes. Just in case," he said.

"Actually, Timothy, I don't have a date for the fundraiser. I'd like to bring the handsomest widower in Roanoke, if you could manage..."

"I'll be there, Sheriff," he said.

"You didn't even let me promise a reward."

"I will implode," I said. "Any second. From atavistic outrage. And familial mortification. And—"

"Okay, son. I'm going. Calm yourself."

"I'm the one who needs to calm himself?"

"Goodnight, Sheriff," he said.

"Goodnight, Timothy. See you soon."

Dad winked and went back upstairs.

I poured myself a glass of bourbon.

Stackhouse watched the empty staircase a moment and said, "He doesn't have your breadth of shoulders, but that is one sexy man."

"Keep it up and next election I'm voting for someone else."

"You're jealous because I have a date tomorrow night and you don't," said the Sheriff.

"That's...unnecessarily deleterious. Let's get back to the endangered children."

"You aren't friends with pastor Jeremy Cameron. You don't have normal friends. You're working for him?"

"For the church," I said.

"How long?"

"A few days."

"And now a kid's missing. Coincidence?"

"Better be," I said.

"Tell me about the job."

"Top secret."

"Tell me anyway."

"Louis Lindsey is accused of being a sexual predator. His targets are male."

She said, "Ah," and sipped her drink.

"You do not appear poleaxed."

"I'm not poleaxed, whatever the hell that means."

"You knew he was gay?"

"Babe, I'm fifty and single. I spent a fortune to look this good. I spend all day with seedy attorneys and all night at parties with bored rich people. I see things. I hear things."

"Such as?"

"He's often at soirees without his wife. He's flirtatious and aggressive. Father Louis has a sexiness about him that's hard to deny. His followers are rabid, they eat him up. Plus there are whispers and rumors that when he, ah, strays from home, it's with members of his own gender."

I put both hands on the counter and leaned on them. Stared at my glass of bourbon. Sucked at my lip.

She said, "Sorry. That bum you out?"

"It bums me out that the leader of a church is widely rumored to be promiscuous and prominent citizens accept that as normal."

"The church at large doesn't have a great reputation the last couple years."

"No," I said. "We don't. Thus I am lugubrious."

"Talk normal, Mack. Jesus. So what does your investigation have to do with Alec Ward disappearing?"

"Nothing."

"That's a big coincidence."

"Too big."

"Let's play Worst Case Scenario. Assume the two disappearances are related. Assume the same guy got them both, and will treat them similarly. That means Alec Ward is alive but potentially abducted and the clock is ticking; he'll soon be shot and dumped into a river, and we'll never know why."

"A lot of assumptions."

"Humor me."

"The first kid disappeared two years ago. Hard to involve me or my current investigation. But still, I don't like it."

"I agree, and I'll take all the help I can get. Bringing Jon Young out of the river and burying him was godawful."

"Sure."

"Who accused Father Louis?"

"I'll tell you when I'm able to. At the moment, these incidents do not correlate."

"Understood." She drained the final drop from her glass. Stood. "Okay, babe. I'll go. Update me and I'll return the favor."

"Just us law keepers sharing ammunition."

She paused at the door. "Speaking of fathers who are predatory..."

"No. Shut up. Don't."

"Tell your old man I'm looking forward to tomorrow."

15

Hugh Pratt called early and asked to rendezvous at his office after breakfast. I took an elevator up the Wells Fargo tower to floor ten and followed his directions through the hallowed corporate hallways. I stopped at a southern facing window and then at a western. This high, Roanoke City opened like a map, blurry and gray through the lashing rain.

Hugh welcomed me and closed the door.

"I didn't realize how small my office is until now you're standing in it," he said.

"It is my Batman-like prognathous altering your perception of reality."

"Should I know what prognat-whatever means?"

"It helps my sense of superiority," I said, "that you don't."

He went behind his desk. Outrageously he sat oriented away from his view of Roanoke. I remained calm about his absurd furniture placement. Barely. His desk held one keyboard, two monitors, neat stacks of papers, a phone, and an orderly container of pens and pencils. Today he wore suspenders and no bowtie.

He punched up Robert Wallace's cell and put him on speaker. By the sound of it, Wallace was drinking coffee and not feeling talkative; I respected that.

Hugh Pratt said, "Thanks for coming, Mr. August. I hope this isn't inappropriate, but I wanted to hear how you're progressing."

"Sure. What occasions your request?"

He made a wincing face. Looked away. Appeared as though he hoped I wouldn't ask. Released a long breath through his nose.

"Father Louis called me the day after we met, indignant and furious. I don't know how he found out. I assured him we were working to disprove his accuser, and I refused to reveal Jeremy's name. He called me again last night. He demands we curtail your services or he'll pray about leaving the church."

"Ergo, you need an update."

"Please."

"Louis Lindsey appears to be more unsavory than you, the vestry, or the congregation realizes. Or at least it doesn't appear that you realize it," I said.

"Can you be more specific?"

"I can. But understand I can prove nothing yet. Inside a courtroom or out, inside a vestry meeting or out, this is hearsay so far. But hearsay I trust."

"I understand," said Hugh. His speakerphone rattled with a grumble from Robert Wallace.

"I spoke with Lindsey. Spoke with Jeremy Cameron. Of the two, I trust Jeremy. I have personally witnessed strange behavior from Lindsey. Also there are rumors about town that he runs around on his wife and could potentially be in the closet."

"Rumors."

"Unsubstantiated."

He nodded. Like a man relieved to hear no hard evidence had been found because it delayed the hard decisions he'd have to make.

"You trust Jeremy and you trust the rumors?" he said, emphasizing the final word.

"I do. A gut feeling thus far. But if I were you, I wouldn't act on my gut. I need a few more days."

"Rob Wallace wants Jeremy Cameron fired. Today."

"Yesterday would be better," said Wallace through the phone. "Damage to the church is irresponsible and unnecessary."

Hugh said, "Clergy decisions are technically the privilege of Father Louis and the Bishop, baring drastic circumstances. I think Rob and I are willing to wait a few more days to get hard evidence before taking action."

"What do you know about Alec Ward?"

He paused. Held my eyes a moment. Frowned.

"Who?"

"The Ward family and their son Alec. They attend All Saints," I said.

"I don't know them," he said. Pulled a little at his collar. "Rob?"

"I know them. Late-service people," said Wallace. "Hugh and me, we attend the early."

"Alec is missing," I said.

Hugh Pratt swallowed. "Missing?"

"Gone a couple days."

"I'm sorry to hear that. Is that germane to your investigation?"

"Don't see how it could be. Especially in light of Jon Young."

"Who?" Hugh asked.

"Jon Young attended your church until two years ago. Went missing and showed up dead in the Roanoke River."

"Oh! Yes of course. That was awful. Sorry, I should remember his name. I often have a narrow scope of focus."

"Did you ever have suspicions or guesses why Jon Young was murdered?" I said. "Or hear unsubstantiated rumors?"

"No. Should I? Should we?"

"Not necessarily. But it's unwise to ignore coincidence," I said.

"In your profession, I can understand that. Okay, well… that's all I needed. Rob, anything else?"

"No," said the phone.

Hugh stood. Our meeting was over. "Please let me know if you discover hard evidence against Father Louis or Jeremy Cameron. In the meantime, we'll be praying he's innocent. Father Louis, I mean."

"And Alec Ward?"

"The missing kid? What about him?"

"I am concerned," I said. Still seated.

"If you don't mind, let's allow the police to do what they do and you focus on Father Louis."

"You're the one writing checks."

"Thank you."

"Though seems to me, Alec Ward is probably worth caring about."

He stiffened. "I didn't say I don't care. That's an unprofessional thing to insinuate, Mr. August."

"I'll let you know," I said and stood, "when I have evidence one way or another."

"That's what you're being paid to do."

"Lovely view." I nodded at his window. "Only an ass would ignore it."

A chuckle from the phone.

I DROVE TO ALL SAINTS, feeling smug that I'd be early, when my phone rang. It was, what do you know, All Saints.

"Yes, hello, Mr. August," said a warm and pleasant voice. "You have an appointment this morning with Nicholas McBride, our worship minister and children's coordinator?"

"That's right I do. And I'll be, get this, a few minutes early."

"I'm very sorry, Mr. August, Nicholas has to cancel. Something popped up and he can't make it," she said.

"I'll wait in your reception area. I'm in no hurry."

"I'm afraid he says he's unavailable all day."

"No problem. How about tomorrow, same time?"

"Nicholas said he'll call you when he's free. He has your number," she said, a new note of strength in her syllables.

"How about I show up right now and knock on his office door, whether he likes it or not?"

She paused. I fretted my stock was plummeting.

"Mr. August, that will *not* be—"

"Twas a joke. Can't you infer I'm hilarious? Tell Nicholas McBride to call me immediately. Only a coward hides from his problems. Tell him I said so."

16

Yesterday's bizarre confrontation at the home of George Saunders had me intrigued. Louis had clearly been an unwelcome visitor in the eyes of Dianne Saunders. She'd been furious. But why, I pondered, would that be.

I wanted to talk with George, the morning manager at Home Depot, and then hopefully his wife Dianne. I swung by George's place of work and asked for him, but was told he was busy in the back, would I mind waiting? I'd try again later, I said.

I'd try at his house, approximately the same time Louis had visited yesterday, though I withheld this from the grumpy guy at Home Depot's customer service counter.

At my office I spent ninety minutes on research, including scouring a dozen websites, placing five polite phone calls, and sending three querying emails. I formulated a resultant list comprised of four names and four personal telephone numbers—former colleagues or associates of Louis Lindsey that struck me as worth contacting. One colleague from a hospital, one from a church, one from a mission trip, and one more who had attended Louis's boarding school and was now the dean.

Would I learn anything significant from contacting these four? Possibly not. But I was stalwart and industrious and as handsome as Tom Hardy.

Was being handsome pertinent to the phone calls? Possibly not. But some things in life should be noted occasionally.

The better part of valor won out as I debated who to call first—ergo, I checked Ronnie's location using my phone. In case her car was broken down on the interstate or she was trapped under something heavy.

Heavens.

She was a mere one block away. Potentially having an early lunch at the market. Who was she missing more, I wondered. Me or her fiancé?

Just kidding. It was me.

She might require company to stay the loneliness. Only a heartless monster denies succor in times of need.

Before I could rise and go visit the woman engaged to another man, the wooden stairs leading up to my second-floor office creaked and snapped. Someone outside my office.

A woman entered. With caution. She looked maybe sixty, wore the blue jeans and white sneakers favored by women who were in fact sixty, and a turtleneck with gold necklace outside the shirt. Her hair was short and brown, no gray showing.

"Hello, Mr. August?"

"Yes." I stood. "Did you think I might be Tom Hardy, the actor?"

"Oh. I'm...I don't know who that is."

"Please come in and have a seat."

"Thank you." She ventured in like the floor might shake. Smiled at my bookshelves. "You have a Bible. That's nice."

"A Bible does not a saint make, I'm learning. How can I help?"

She sat in my client chair. I sat in my private investigator chair. She closed her eyes and when she opened them again she was crying.

"This is difficult."

"No rush. Tissues on the corner of my desk."

"You're a very large man."

"I try."

"My name is Bonnie Young. Earlier today Sheriff Stackhouse came to speak with me," she said.

I nodded.

"Before she left, the sheriff suggested I tell you what I told her. So here I am."

"Bonnie Young," I said. "Any relation to Jon Young?"

"Yes." She smiled like a doting grandmother should. "I raised Jon. He is the son of my only daughter. Was the son."

"I learned of your grandson's death just yesterday. I know that was hard."

"It was. He was shot and thrown into a river and I still don't know why. I keep his room exactly as it was. His mother had Jon before she was ready, and she lives in California. I was essentially his mother."

"A mother should never have to bury her son. Or grandson."

"Precisely." She took a tissue and dabbed. "And obviously I'm still not over the experience."

"Sheriff Stackhouse told you Alec Ward was missing."

"She did. And now I'm having flashbacks."

"The two disappearances are probably unrelated. But she's being careful," I said.

She looked down at the crumpled tissue in her hand.

"As she should, in my opinion. Anything to avoid what I went through."

"What exactly did you tell Stackhouse that she thought I should know?"

"We discussed a lot. She asked questions, and many answers I couldn't remember. I tried to forget, you understand. But she got stuck on two details."

"Okay."

"I told the police at the time, but maybe it's more important now? The first is, before he vanished, Jon had recently come out of the closet to me. He was gay. I didn't mind and I'd already had my suspicions. I wanted him to be happy. But he wasn't. He didn't want to be gay. And the second thing, I suggested he talk with someone about being gay and his desire to be straight. We attended All Saints, so he began counseling sessions with Father Louis."

"Oh," I said, feeling the room tilt a little.

"That's the same face the sheriff made. Except she said, 'Shit.'" Bonnie blushed a little at the word.

"I probably should have. The police knew this at the time?"

"Of course."

"What did Jon say about the counseling sessions?"

"Not much. They only had three or four before he disappeared. He was enjoying them, I think. Mr. August, why is that detail suddenly so interesting?"

"If Alec Ward comes home today, it's not. But if Alec has vanished the way Jon did, it's a potential clue the police can use," I said.

"But there's more, isn't there. That you can't tell me."

"There's more."

"Why did the sheriff want you to know? You in particular, I mean."

"The more eyes on this, the better. I'm in the profession of finding things. Finding people and finding the truth," I said.

"I hope I helped, even though it hurts. And I hope you find Alec."

"If I do, you'll be one of the girls I call to celebrate."

She smiled, a relief of pressure. "If he's truly missing, I bet you find him. You're good at this, I can tell."

"I am," I said. "Shockingly so."

17

George Saunders returned from Home Depot at 3:15. I waited in my Honda across the street. He parked behind the minivan and stepped out of his truck. I got out of my car.

He reached back inside for a backpack and closed the door.

"George Saunders," I said, approaching through the cold drizzle. "I'm Mackenzie August. Hoping we can talk."

He looked at me. Didn't like it.

"Yeah? Okay, why's that?"

George was handsome. Unusually good looking, a Roanoke ten. Tall and strong, wide back, nice jaw, hard hands, but an open face, predisposed to kindness. I'd kill for those lashes. He shrugged his black Home Depot shirt against the misting rain.

I wasn't sure how to get there. Too much I didn't know. Was he friends with Louis? His wife wasn't. Could the two men be more than friends? Would he be loyal to the priest? Maybe he was like Jeremy Cameron and sick of the man? Or perhaps my reading of yesterday was all wrong.

No compass on this. So I went straight at him.

"I need information on Louis Lindsey."

George Saunders looked as though I'd pulled a gun on him.

"Father Louis? I don't know'im."

"Sure you do. He was here yesterday."

He backed into his truck door.

"How'd you know that?"

"The whole neighborhood knows that. He parked and walked in. Then your wife vivaciously ran him out."

"Listen, guy, this isn't, I'm not gonna, maybe you ought to take off."

"People are coming forward with accusations against Louis, George. Serious and sexual in nature. That he's making unwanted advances, and maybe worse."

George had the backpack in front of him like a shield. A timid position for a man so impressive in architecture. If rattled, maybe something useful would fall out of him.

"He is? They are? Who said that?"

"This is weird. I understand you don't know me. I don't know who you are either. And this is sudden," I said.

"Are you the police? How does this involve the police?"

"I'm not the police."

"Who is accusing him?

"Does that matter?" I said.

"What? No, I don't know. Why're you telling me this?"

"I'm gathering evidence. Louis is in hot water, George. The more evidence the better."

"So why're you here?"

"You know something," I said, an educated guess. Rattle rattle rattle the cage.

"Me? I don't, I don't know..."

"Does it bother you that he's preying on other people?"

"Sure, I guess, I don't know. Like who?"

"Who what?" I said.

"Who told you about Father Louis? What's his name?"

"How'd you know it was a guy?"

"I..." His mouth moved without sound. He started edging around the truck for safety. "Get on out of here. I'm going inside now. I'd appreciate you leaving me alone. I can't help."

The rain picked up a little. No longer just a drizzle.

The front door opened. A woman came out in a storm of agitation.

"Hey. *Hey!* George, who's this?" she said.

"It's nobody. He's leaving."

"Oh. Great. Another *nobody.*" She came down the steps stomping and pushing back her sleeves.

"I told him he had to get."

"Who're you?" She marched into my personal space. "A fag? You another fag?"

"Damn it, Dianne, you can't say that."

"He's right; it's rude," I said.

"What is it with you fags, think you can take things don't belong to you? George isn't gay!"

"Dianne! That ain't...he ain't either. Lower your voice."

"He isn't gay? Yeah, neither was the last guy," she said and she rolled her eyes, crossed her arms.

I said, "My name's Mackenzie, and—"

She kinda snorted. "Gay name."

"That's what some friends told me in middle school. My father pointed out that's not really an insult. So neeners."

"George is *married.* To me. He is my *husband.* Doesn't that matter to you? What you *want* or think you *need* is irrelevant."

I winced. For an instant, Ronnie's face was superimposed into my vision. My head swam. Dianne's words floated through my ears again, *Ronnie is engaged. She is his fiancée. Doesn't that matter to you? What you want or think you need is irrelevant.*

Ronnie was taken. It *should* matter to me. *I* should be irrelevant. And yet I...I kept wandering onto private property. Just like Louis.

Being lumped into the same category as Louis Lindsey stung.

Assuming he was guilty.

"Hello?" said Dianne Saunders. "You hear me?"

My world snapped back into focus. Ronnie vanished.

"Come on, Dianne. Come on inside," said her husband.

"My name is Mackenzie August. I'm gathering evidence to determine if Louis Lindsey is guilty of sexual indiscretions. If you know anything, I'd like to hear it."

"You're what? Say that again?"

"Get on out of here, Mack," said George. "Last time I tell you."

I withdrew my card. Laid it on the truck. "Louis Lindsey is being accused of assault. Preying on impressionable men. I'm gathering evidence. The more the better, to determine if he's guilty or innocent."

Dianne watched me with wide eyes. At a loss for words, finally.

George snatched my card off the truck. Grabbed her by the arm and pulled her toward the house.

"Mackenzie August," I said. "You can find me online. Mackenzie August, private investigator."

"You're trying to catch Father Louis?" she said.

"I'm trying to catch the truth."

And then she was inside and the door closed hard.

18

You said that? That you were trying to catch the truth?

Kix and I trotted along the Greenway. The April drizzle had abated, yielding to thin fog. Like jogging through a mystery.

"I am humiliated."

Yeah that's a mortifying thing to say. Catch the truth.

"I'm getting dramatic in my old age."

You're what, thirty-five? That is so old. I'll never be that old. Is it scary, close to death?

Dusk descended early because of the fog. We were alone and I took the turn near the middle playground and increased pace. Kix bounced around, enjoying himself.

You seem angry, Father.

"I'm angry, Kix."

I don't much care for omphalopsychites or their self-involved musings. But I'm willing to suffer yours.

"I'm angry that Ronnie is engaged and won't break it off, either with me or with the other guy, the prick." I was breathing hard and working to keep the stroller on the path.

In this situation the blame is mostly hers. But not entirely.

"It's my fault for letting her back in. For not having self-control. But now she's back, I can't stop thinking about...I like her."

You like her? Quite the poet you are.

"On a pro and con list, she's almost entirely pros. But that one conflict..."

Yes, she's engaged. That's a doozie. Also, be a darling and keep your eyes on the path. You're veering into the grass and I'm afraid I've spilt my juice.

"That's why I'm mad."

We overtook another patron of the Greenway, went by so fast I barely noted it was a woman wearing the hell out of her spandex running outfit.

"And something else..." I said, sucking a lot of air now.

More? You're a conflicted guy. Do you see that fallen tree branch? Please do not push the stroller overtop. Do you see? Watch out...Well there's juice just everywhere now.

"I'm angry because a kid is missing. Alec Ward. I'm angry because this has happened before and it ended in disaster for Jon Young and his family. And I'm mad because it overlaps with my investigation, and I don't enjoy coincidences."

Kix remained quiet.

"I don't *want* a kid to be missing. I don't *want* the leader of a church to be promiscuous. I don't want the church to have such a bad reputation that pastors' affairs are barely worth mentioning."

We reached the parking lot. I slowed to a walk and paced behind our car to cool off. Without the street lights, it would soon be dark. My sneakers crunched on gravel and the nearby Roanoke River gurgled beyond the grass bank.

So what happens now?

"I need hard evidence that Louis is pressuring his way

into sex with persons not his wife. Although that's gross too. Maybe it's not rape because he doesn't use physical force, but if I can prove he's coercing others who were unwilling, that's enough for the vestry."

How do you do that?

"I need to keep pressuring Louis. Make him mad. Talk with Nicholas, the other clergy on staff. Locate more of Louis's sexual partners and get them to confess. Videos would be ideal."

Sex tapes? Gross. You adults.

"I want to find more than enough evidence for his vestry and Bishop to fire him. I want to nail his ass to a jail wall. Assuming he's guilty."

It's almost like you're taking this personally. Is it time to go? I need a change.

"I'm taking this personally. I'm not sure why—still working that out. I'm unreasonably furious with him."

Maybe because you're worried you're culpable for the missing kid on some level.

"I've already decided Louis is involved with that missing kid somehow. He's guilty until proven otherwise. Which is prejudiced and wrong, but that's my frame of mind."

Oh my.

"I'm feeling a little more orderly and codified, saying all this out loud."

Hey, here comes the girl wearing the tight black pants.

My breathing had slowed. I unbuckled Kix and hoisted him out of the stroller.

She's walking by. Right there. She's pretty. She's looking your way. Do you not even care?

"You're wet, Kix. You spilled your juice," I said, setting him into his car seat.

For an investigator, you're unusually dense. Good thing I love you.

THAT NIGHT, as hypnagogia settled like a blanket, my phone beeped. A text message. From Ronnie Summers. *The* Ronnie Summers.

She'd sent a selfie, displaying her from the navel up. She was wearing…it wasn't quite lingerie and it wasn't quite a tank top. Some kind of red, diaphanous, silky, lacy, tight… wonderful garment that shouldn't be sent to a lonely bachelor. Also it had tiny shoulder straps.

>> **Come have a drink?**

I issued a masculine grunt. *Not* a groan.

Manny said, "Amigo. You having a bad dream? Or maybe a good dream."

"I'm fine. Everything's fine. Everything super fine and I'm not miserable. Going to sleep now. Probably."

"Bueno. Glad to hear it. Keep it down up there. Some of us on the floor are trying to sleep."

19

For days Alec Ward waited in the dark.

Intermittent light came into the black from the far corner; not enough to illuminate his world, but enough to convince him days were passing. Days or lifetimes.

Try as he might, he remembered nothing about this nightmare. He didn't know where he was. Didn't know how he got there. He recalled school and walking home...and that was it.

He couldn't cry anymore. His throat was raw from screaming. When he shouted now it came out hoarse. He couldn't stand because some kind of harness was locked around his waist, and the restraint coupled to a chain that bolted into the floor. His hands were bound too. He tugged until his wrists were slick with blood. He pulled at the chain long enough to know it would never budge.

Soon after waking he'd blindly explored and found a plate of peanut butter sandwiches, two water bottles, and an empty bucket. He resisted as long as he could, fearing poison, but boredom and fear and thirst had won. Now, days later, he starved and ached for water.

Alec hadn't been hurt. Yet that was part of the problem; there was nothing and nobody. His existence was a void. Underground, he thought. A small room, based on acoustics. Smelled like musty earth.

He understood death came soon. He'd seen enough movies. This wasn't a basement people got out of. But on screen, it always happened to idiots or people who deserved it. Not to...

Not to him.

The void was complete. He didn't know when his eyelids were open or closed.

Until at last the light erupted. He hadn't heard footsteps but suddenly the sun filled his enclosure. The sun or a flashlight. Instantly blind, he writhed backwards and whispered, "No! *Please!* Whoever...please, I need—"

"You need water," said the voice. A man's voice.

He did need water. His tongue was swollen and thick.

"Please, sir, my name is Alec Ward, and my parents will—"

"Won't be much longer." A gloved hand patted his head and Alec shuddered. He couldn't back up anymore without the restraints pulling. "Depends on how things go."

Alec tried opening his eyes. Near him, inside the agonizing light, two big bottles of Smart Water and more sandwiches.

He started crying. "Please let me go home."

"Maybe. That's not up to me."

Who *was* this, Alec wondered. Did he recognize the voice? It belonged to a man.

"Drink the water. I'll come back."

"No, please, don't go."

"Be over soon. I hope."

"*Please!*"

Footsteps. A heavy door closed. Soundproof.

Alec's cries couldn't escape the black.

20

A warm April gust rattled my office windows. Dying spring petals from dogwood trees whisked by like pinkish snow. Some constellated against the glass and marred my view of the Orvis across the street.

I called the receptionist at Louis Lindsey's former church, a smaller Episcopal parish in Virginia Beach. He worked there half a decade before his celebrity grew and he transferred to a larger congregation with deeper pockets—All Saints. I didn't disparage that decision; pastors and priests moved around and some fit better than others, and churches needed money to survive.

The nice woman on the other end answered a handful of Lindsey questions before asking, "Why do you need to know all this?"

"Writing a piece on him for the paper," I said. "I need background on the famous man, you know? He's becoming quite influential."

"Isn't he a doll?"

"Such a doll."

"I just love him. Cried my eyes out when he left."

"Who wouldn't."

"Not us! We were a wreck, I can tell you."

"Why did he leave?" I said.

"It was time. These things happen. Just this year alone we lost our children's minister and two deacons. What paper are you with?"

"Roanoke Post," I said. No such paper.

"How exciting. You'll tell him I said hello?"

"Of course. Were you friends with his wife?"

"Oh no. His wife stayed to herself. Such a pretty woman but I never really knew her. No one did, I suspect. But *such* a good dresser."

My phone beeped—incoming call. It was Dr. Scott Osborne, former colleague of Louis Lindsey. I hung up with the nice receptionist and answered Dr. Osborne.

"It's not often I get calls from private detectives," he said.

Zounds. He must've looked me up by the phone number, because I hadn't revealed that in the voice mail. There went my Roanoke Post cover story.

"You're among the few and proud," I said. "I'm looking into Louis Lindsey. In search of background information."

"Dr. Lindsey? Haven't heard that name in a while. He settled in Roanoke?"

"He did."

"The man's in trouble or something like that?"

"He's an Episcopal priest now," I said.

"No kidding! I hadn't heard. What a strange guy. No wonder he dropped off the grid. I quit seeing him at the functions and conferences, you know."

"I did a little research. You two worked closely for several years. Friends, I assume."

"We were..." He paused. I smelled blood. "...we were colleagues. Both internists at MedStar Georgetown. Those were fun days, back when things didn't matter. But Louis moved to a different floor...no, that wasn't it. Forgive my memory, it's been twenty years, I think. He left the department and we lost touch. Damn, an Episcopalian priest? I never would've guessed."

"Not the priestly type?"

"You could say that." He chuckled. "He earned his Medical Doctorate and a Masters of Divinity, I assume? Hell, if anyone could handle that it'd be Lindsey. Can't fault his brain power, either side."

"You weren't sad to see him leave the department?"

"I didn't complain, no. This town ain't big enough, you get it?"

"Why'd he leave?" I said.

"I'm remembering a little more now, and it was a private matter and I better not say anything else about that. Maybe talk to our HR department? I don't recall if they got involved or not."

"Did it have anything to do with rumors of sexual indiscretion?"

Another pause. I pictured him staring at the ceiling. "I won't answer that directly, Mr. August, but I'll tell you this. That man didn't like being told 'No.' On any matter. He didn't want to hear it from his patients, his consults, his colleagues, or his supervisors. The temper on that guy, well, it was infamous enough that I don't mind admitting it to you, because it was public knowledge."

"The legendary physician's God complex."

"And some of us are more legendary than others. At least in our own eyes," he said.

"If I were inclined to look, would I find his name in police records? Missing person reports or assault?"

"Not that I know of. Shit, nothing like that. What exactly is the man being accused of?"

"Unofficial accusations thus far, nothing involving the police. But I thought I'd ask."

"I bet you'll have a hard time. Guaran-damn-tee it. The guy's fan base was rabid and devoted. Dr. Lindsey could slap you in the face and you'd still love him. He never got sued, to my knowledge, which is rare in our profession. His bedside manner was remarkably polished. An excellent actor."

"I heard once about the statistics..."

"Yeah, if a physician spends ten minutes or more with a patient, talking, chatting, the chances of him or her being sued are miniscule. Because he'll be liked and the patient will give him the benefit of the doubt. That statistic? It's true."

I ended the call quick. "Fascinating. Thanks for the help."

I pressed End on my cellphone.

Because Louis Lindsey was standing in my doorway.

21

Louis Lindsey radiated power. I'd forgotten that about him.

He was brooding and conflict thundered in his face. The resemblance to Brando was startling. He smiled at me but there was fury beneath the pale eyes. Fury and passion and hurt. Or maybe I was being dramatic. I felt like his eyes lingered on my mouth, anticipating what I would say next.

I stood up but I didn't feel taller.

"Big strong handsome Mackenzie August," he said. "Pursuer of holy justice. Finder of facts. How's work, Inspector?"

"Some days are effortless. Certain nincompoops make it easy on me. Come in, Louis."

He did.

He made a show of withdrawing his cellphone and setting it on my desk. It was a common gesture I'd seen the mafioso guys do. A ritualistic way to symbolize there would be no recording.

Wonder where he learned it.

I set mine beside his.

Today his outfit was jeans and a tailored oxford. He sat

in my client chair. Crossed his legs and laced his fingers. Watched as I did the same.

“Are you enjoying my life, Inspector?”

“I am not.”

“Oh?”

“Early indications are, you’re relentlessly predatory.”

“The way to ascend any ladder, Inspector, is not passivity.”

“Your ladders do not interest me. I’m concerned with the lives you’re ruining.”

“How noble and heroic of you. Did you dream of this lifestyle as a boy? Fearlessly prying into the sexuality of others?”

“Only,” I said, “if that sexuality was Princess Leia’s.”

He permitted a slight smile. Eyes on my mouth.

“Of course, you’re a child of the 80s. Early 90s? The princess in the golden bikini, who needed a good rescue. What was it, exactly? Her blonde hair, the blue green eyes, the skimpy royal outfits? The prominent position she held?”

“Blonde hair and blue green eyes? The hell kinda Leia are you thinking about?”

“I’m hazy on the details. She wasn’t exactly my type. So update me, Inspector. What has your investigation unearthed? Perhaps I can fill in missing links.”

“You aren’t as careful as you think, Louis. Evidence abounds like fruit ripe for the plucking.”

He remained in total stillness. If he was startled, he gave no sign.

“Oh dear,” he said. “My my. Plucked away, have you? Yet somehow I think, if pressed, you could not present two pieces of concrete evidence. How frustrating for you.”

“Maybe we can strike a deal.”

“A *deal*.”

"You come clean on the parts I don't know, you avoid jail," I said.

"That's adorable, Inspector. The whole thing, your career. Adorable. Do you have a plastic gold badge to go with your costume?"

"I'd rather you go to prison anyway. I'll visit, you know. To see you in orange."

"Do I detect a hint of animosity?" he said.

"The animosity comes free of charge."

"Taking this personally. I'm flattered. A holy warrior full of righteous zeal. Doing God's work. Making the little boy in the photo proud, chasing away the pretend ghosts and rumors."

"Testimonies aren't rumors, Louis."

"You have no testimonies, Inspector. And if you did, what then? Oh no, goodness gracious, Father Lindsey is human after all. Gasp. Oh well, let's all move on. Someone make sure the pretend police officer gets a check on the way out."

"Hurtful. I'm private, not pretend."

"Is this fun game you're playing worth the career of poor little Jeremy Cameron?"

I remained in absolute stillness. Or tried. Because he'd startled me. Did he know it was Jeremy who'd come forward? Or was he guessing.

"Jeremy Cameron, the clergy at your church. I imagine he'd say Yes," I said.

"Oh but what can we expect from children? All heart and no brawn, no muscles intended for the marathon. Little Jeremy needs guidance, not heavy responsibility. No one believes the word of a child."

"There hasn't been an adult in this room for years."

"Yes, adulthood. Still not there, Inspector? A slippery and diaphanous thing, maturity. Do you know why people use their phones to film firework shows? Concerts and birthday parties are recorded, instead of enjoyed. The attendees watch through a lens, why is that? Because life promises us meaningful moments and the moments do not deliver. Because of the gaping holes in our lives that we desperately need to fill, and when the moment of truth arrives, it arrives flat. There is no healing power. So what do we do? We film the moment, we film the birthday party. We layer in potential future meaning to stave off the immanent desperation. Maybe one day in the future this moment will have meaning, we hope, and we try to preserve it for redemption with an *iPhone*. But it doesn't work. Does it, Inspector? Your desperation reeks. The gaping holes are obvious. What wounds are you trying to heal? This job, you pretending to care, pretending to help, to find truth, what hurt are you trying to redeem? It won't work. Vanity, vanity, all is vanity. A griffin is more real than any redemption you'll find on this inane odyssey."

"A griffin?"

"Come now, Mackenzie. Head of an eagle, body of a lion. It's pretend. That's my point."

"I know what a griffin is. But following the ravings of a sexual degenerate is not simple," I said. He made no big movements but his eyes seemed to darken with shadow and his nostrils flared. "I do this job for reasons of self-preservation, you mean. Not nobility?"

He made a tsk'ing noise. "Of course. You chase after the wind because God put eternity in your heart, and it's too much for the poor inspector to bear."

"Or perhaps my chief end is to fear God and to enjoy the labor."

He issued a small gasp and sat up straighter. "So you *have* read your Bible. Or at least Ecclesiastes. My my."

"I admit, part of the work is selfish. But a selfish investigation can sublimate into something better," I said.

"Such as redemption?"

"Such as an exposure of objective innocence. Or guilt. Your guilt."

"Objective," he said. "That's a joke, I assume. We all like sheep have gone astray. Are you a sexually innocent man?"

"By no means."

"Of course not. A strong virile man like yourself, oceans of testosterone and urges. Of course there's some hot little blonde running through your mind all day and through your bed at night."

"Wouldn't that be nice."

"You have nothing, Inspector. You'll get nothing. My personal life remains out of your reach. You wish to disrupt my career but you can't. Is your life so pathetic that you need this? Are you so broke? I thought you a man of import."

"I would investigate you for free, Louis, propelled solely by thoughts of giving evidence at your trial."

"Let us communicate as though you were civilized. I can give you things to do. You need to be occupied? I fraternize with the wealthiest and most prominent citizens in the state and beyond. You think they don't need services you provide? Of course they do; they're wretched disasters. Let this wild goose chase go, Inspector. Move on to something lucrative, something worth your time. With my contacts, you'll be rich."

"How rich?"

"Who knows. If you're industrious, perhaps retirement ten years early."

"Pass," I said.

"Why?"

"I'm obdurate. One of my loveliest traits."

His fists clenched and he stood. The chair banged backwards, tipped on its rear legs, counterbalanced a second, and landed forward again.

That was close.

He leaned toward me a little.

"One of my loveliest traits? *Power*. I have followers. Devoted disciples," he said, and pale madness flashed as he did. "I'm holding them back from destroying you, Inspector. But how long will hounds obey their master if they're rabid and angry?"

"Gasp. A threat. I am overcome with your power."

"You're interfering with my church. A church in crisis. One of our young men is missing. Perhaps you heard? I am the shepherd and my sheep need me. And yet here I sit, wasting time with you, asking you to stop harassing us," he said.

"Did you know Alec?"

"I know him, present tense. He's not dead."

"You're sure?" I said, tingling up the back of my neck.

"Ye of little faith. He's alive, and in God's hands. I know if we pray and work hard enough, he'll return. He's a good boy. He was in counseling with me, and so his disappearance is especially painful. But you—"

"Alec came to you for counseling?"

"Many do," he said.

"Like Jon Young?"

"Your childish investigation is inflicting harm. Let's be crystal clear, Inspector; the suffering is because of you."

I stood too. Wanted some height advantage.

"Be more clear."

"If you continue, the pain intensifies," he said.

"You're threatening me."

"I'm making a demand. Stop."

"No," I said.

His eyes bounced from my lips to my belt, to my gun.

"My church and the people within suffer. Because of you."

"Do you have Alec Ward?" I said.

"Don't be insulting, Inspector. Of course I don't have Alec Ward."

"Of course not, Father."

"I'm leaving. Time for you to stop being obdurate. Before others get hurt."

22

We glared over the desk. An impasse. Louis had asked me to stop and then threatened repercussions if I didn't. I said no and refused to budge.

He winked at me, the way a gunslinger would at high noon. Turned to go.

I grabbed him and threw him across the room and his head cracked the wall and his skull split open and he died and I loved it.

But…

Nope.

That didn't happen. I wanted it to.

What I actually did was, I glared more as he left. He wasn't the first to threaten me. Wouldn't be the last, maybe not even this week. I suspected he had abducted a kid, however, and that gave his warning extra teeth. And if I threw him, he could involve the police and effectively end my inspection.

Not yet, Louis. I'm not finished.

The door downstairs slammed. He was gone. I dedicated sixty seconds to fuming and cursing, and then got proactive.

I dialed Jeremy Cameron as I walked to my car.

"How you doing," I said.

"Alec Ward is still missing, so I'm trying to reach his friends to offer support and prayer. Tough conversations."

"Louis Lindsey just left my office. Threatened to hurt people if I didn't stop the investigation. He mentioned you by name."

A long sigh from Jeremy. "He knows. Someone on the vestry must've spilled the beans. Our deacons quit returning my calls. People stop talking when I enter a room. Any sort of authority or leadership I had vanished. This...this just sucks."

"It does. Where do you live?"

"Does that matter?" he said.

"I'm not worried about your safety. But I'm also not *not* worried either. He mentioned rabid devotees."

"He has those in spades. I live in a townhouse downtown, off Williamson, near the market. It's a busy place. I'm safe."

"Call Nicholas and warn him too. Don't go anywhere strange. Don't go anywhere alone. Don't accept unusual requests for meetings. I'm sure you're fine. I'm sure you're not in danger. But also, call me if you get suspicious. About anything."

"Thank God for you, Mack."

"Maybe. Not yet, though." I hung up, got in my car, and drove to the Sheriff's Office.

I knew the bailiff at the checkpoint and he waved for me to bypass security. Up the stairs, into the offices, through the deputy bullpen, and beyond the two assistant desks. One of the women tried to stop me but I went straight into the inner sanctum.

"This office," I told Stackhouse, who was sitting beyond a double-wide desk loaded with folders and a computer monitor, "is hideous."

She looked like a movie star on a trashy set. Her hair was up and she wore hoop earrings. Some sheriffs got their way through bullying and force of will; Stackhouse got her way because the public fell over themselves obeying her.

"It's okay, Trish," Stackhouse told the woman pulling on my arm. "He's an ass and he won't leave no matter what we do, anyway."

Trish reluctantly released, but I thought she gave my bicep an extra squeeze.

Stackhouse's walls were decorated with pictures of her smiling with diplomats, including a previous VP and the current president.

"What's up, babe," she said.

"Louis has Alec Ward."

"How do you know?"

"I don't. And I haven't a shred of evidence to back up the claim," I said.

"Then...?"

"Don't make sexy eyes at me. They won't work."

"These are my regular eyes. Your judgment of Father Louis is clouded because you're angry and because of your current case," she said, going back to her paperwork.

"He was counseling Jon Young. He was counseling Alec Ward. And he told me Alec is still alive and Alec will return if I discontinue my investigation."

"He didn't say that."

"He came close."

She looked back up. "Father Louis was counseling Alec? His parents didn't mention it."

"Lindsey just told me he was."

"Alec wasn't gay. *Isn't* gay, I mean. He had a girlfriend. *Has* a girlfriend. Jesus. The hell is wrong with me," she said.

"Being gay doesn't necessitate counseling. And there are many reasons to seek counsel."

She shrugged.

"Okay. I'll call the parents. We're striking out anyway."

"And find out where Louis was the afternoon Alec vanished."

"Babe..."

"If you don't, I will. And it will involve hitting Louis until he tells me," I said.

"Fine, I'll ask the police chief to send a detective to verify. I'll call you with the answers soon as I get them. By the way, I like it when you're mad. It's a good look on you."

"Didn't you recently go on a date with my father?"

"I did. Want the details?"

"You're a vile harlot," I said.

She smiled, one of those that landed her on magazine covers.

"You shouldn't talk that way to your mother." She stood quickly, held out her hands. "Whoa, whoa, okay, relax, babe. I was kidding, I'm sorry. Let go of my desk, these papers won't sort themselves. Release. Please release."

I let go of the lip of her desk. It took effort.

"Find out where Louis was. And ask about the counseling," I said.

"You got it. I think you get taller when you're angry."

I turned to leave.

"Hey. Several girls in my office won't say No if you ask them out. Trust me. Want their names?"

I left, going back through the maze of desks.

"Mackenzie?" she called. "Are you sure? Some of them have no scruples, I know for a fact!"

No one had scruples anymore.

Apparently I was the only one holding onto mine.

Barely.

23

April produced another warm day, the kind with no clouds and a crisp blue sky. Manny met me downtown for lunch and we walked along the row of market vendors hawking wares grown in Floyd and Franklin County and Botetourt. The fruit wasn't ripe yet, so I bought a loaf of yeast bread, homemade honey peanut butter, and strawberry preserves. We were contemplating vegetables and cold cuts when Manny spotted a clue.

"Ah hah," he said.

"You don't say Ah hah. Only I say Ah hah."

"I spotted a señorita in distress." He pointed across Market Street to a small table outside Jack Brown's burger joint. Ronnie Summers sat there with two men, waiting for lunch.

"Ah hah," I said.

"That's what I thought. We gonna...what'cha call it?"

"Instigate mischief. Yes."

"Because of jealous rage?" he asked.

"You betcha."

I purchased a pint carton of cherry tomatoes and we

lined up across from her table, thirty yards distant. I threw a tomato, which arced over the street. My distance was perfect but the aim was lacking, and the tomato bounced harmlessly against the wall.

Manny went next. His parabola was notably less noble than mine, and I told him so, and he connected solidly with Jack Brown's display window.

The tomato's impact got Ronnie's attention. Her two male suitors were too involved with her many perfections and their own excitations to notice.

I threw again, missing, but Ronnie saw us.

The market vendors observed our fatuous onslaught with dismay, but no one was brave enough to reproach Manny. He had that effect. And a badge.

Ronnie covered her mouth with one hand. With the other she picked up her cell.

My phone buzzed.

>> **You two are children.**

>> **Don't go anywhere! I'll order you both a hamburger and join you for lunch. Purchase a bottle of wine, please, at the store behind you. Something chilled.**

>> **These guys are ass hats anyway.**

Manny threw once more and connected with the shoulder of Ronnie's friend. The guy sat straighter and turned but Manny and I were already hiding behind a delivery truck.

"What are we doing, señor?" he said.

"Acting puerile and precocious."

"Stupid words. I am not an hombre who hides."

"I do it all the time. Called snooping."

"We snooping right now?" he said.

"More like, getting free hamburgers from Jack Brown's

burger joint. Let's go before the tiny lawyers threaten us with scary litigation."

RONNIE ARRIVED twenty minutes later bearing two greasy translucent bags. Her scent combined with the hamburgers' and I had never been so happy.

"Who were you eating with, señorita?" said Manny.

"Sycophants. Idiots after a date and a settlement to a personal injury case."

She distributed the hamburgers and fries, and I poured white wine into plastic cups. Ronnie wore khakis and she kicked off her heels, and we sat on my rug crisscross. She daintily sipped her wine; Manny removed the bun from his burger and carved off chunks of beef and bacon with a knife and fork; I ate like a savage.

"Will you?" I said.

"Go on a date with the ass hats? Absolutely not. Settle the case? Not until they add a zero."

"They're offering a hundred grand but you want a million?" said Manny.

"Something like that."

"Aggressive," I noted.

She smiled at me. Such a preternaturally arresting sight that Manny and I paused eating to admire it.

"Yes. I am. My track record with judges and juries is sterling, so I can demand a lot."

"We should feel grateful that a demanding, fearsome, and sterling attorney bought us lunch, eh amigo?"

"You should, yes," she said. "But it was my pleasure. I'm demanding, aggressive, fearsome, but also rich."

"You're rich?"

She shrugged. It was a good motion; she knew it was a good motion; so did we.

"Relatively. I am the proprietor of my own law firm, and you boys chose professions that limit your significant earning potential. I bet my salary laps your combined income. But then I spend it all on shoes, so who knows."

"I spend mine on diapers," I said.

"And me? Expensive tequila and more expensive watches," said Manny.

Ronnie raised her plastic cup.

"A toast. To you two, Roanoke's most desirable and destitute fighters of injustice and sin. And to me; all the eligible women within fifty miles would kill to sit where I am."

We banged plastic cups together and drank.

"What injury has your client sustained?" I asked.

"He broke his scapula on a malfunctioning escalator."

"And you're asking a million."

"I am."

"For a broken scapula?"

"No, silly." She finished a french fry and carefully wiped her fingers and her lips with a napkin. "Not for a broken scapula. That's not how our justice system works. I can ask that much because my client is a gorgeous twenty-two-year-old Grecian boy in med school who cries easily. He will tell the opposing counsel, and the judge, and the jury if necessary, that his hopes of being a surgeon are ruined, even though that's not provable. It's not his scapula that will get a million; it's his dreamy appearance, his dashed dreams, and my aforementioned track record."

"I have concerns," I said, "about the robust goodness of our courts."

"You should. Speaking of goodness and cases, how is yours?"

I told her, not omitting names any longer. About the accusations and the religious megastar. About Jeremy Cameron and the missing kid. About the secrets and the suppressed pain. I didn't realize how angry I was until it began flowing. I was on my feet and pacing by the end.

"I know Father Louis," she said. "We were at a cocktail thing last week. He's as sexy as sixty gets."

"He hit on you?" said Manny.

"He did not."

"Ay dios mio. He *is* gay."

"Why're you so angry, Mackenzie?" she said.

"Lots of reasons."

"Because the priest is gay?"

"It's not the gender of his victims that bothers me."

"Most Christians consider homosexuality a sin, right?"

"Tendentious but true," I said.

"Do you not take sin seriously?"

"I take it seriously enough to know I shouldn't be the judge. I leave that to God. I assume he's better at it, after all. You're talking to a guy who spent ten years in Los Angeles, working homicide. Pulling bullets out of bodies and trying to find the guy who fired them. Consoling grieving families and orphaned kids. My opinion, God takes sin even more seriously than I do. But of greater concern to him than the gender is the assault itself."

"So tell me why you're angrier than usual," she said.

"Because I'm a little stuck. There are people I need answers from but I don't want to push hard, because they're already under duress. Because our culture crushes whistle-blowers for doing the right thing. Because I like the church and it's under attack. Because a kid is missing and I'm worried I helped cause it. This thing went from a simple 'employment' case—trying to prove a man is unfaithful to his wife and ergo his profession—to a larger and more important investigation and I'm on an unforgiving clock, especially if Alec is being held somewhere."

"There's another reason he's angry," said Manny.

"Which is?" Ronnie asked.

"You're the third person to *insinuate* Mack would care more about the homosexuality than the assault."

"I meant no offense. In fact that's not what I meant at all. I know Mackenzie; he's not that sensitive," she said.

"He didn't take offense, that's not it. It's that the questions are...indicative, that right? The questions are indicative of society. It's that, he doesn't want the gay man to have kidnapped the kid. Right?"

I nodded. "I think Louis took him. But I don't want it to be true."

"Because he's gay?" she asked.

"Yes."

She pursed and tapped her lips. Scrutinized me a moment.

"I think I get it. You're worried that if Father Louis took Alec Ward, it will reinforce the false stereotypes."

"Yes."

"The false stereotype that all Christians have got it in for the LGBT crowd. Or that homosexuals are pedophiles, you don't want to perpetuate that. Yet the results of your investigation might incidentally give credence to the stereotypes, potentially creating a greater rift between the local church and the gay community," she said.

"I hadn't adumbrated it quite so clearly in my mind. But yes."

"You can't save everyone, Mackenzie.

"I'm not trying."

"Yes you are," she said.

"How so."

"You want to save Alec Ward. You want to save Jeremy What's His Name, the clergy kid. You want to rescue the church from their mess. And you want to preserve homosexuals from bad press."

"And me, you let me sleep on your floor," said Manny.

"Lastly," she said, "on some level, you're trying to save me."

"Nerds," I said. "You two are nerds."

"You are, though. You think I shouldn't marry Darren and you want to rescue me from it."

"First of all, Darren is a stupid name. And second, I'm not interested in saving you," I said.

"I hope that's not true. Because believing it helps me fall asleep at night."

"In this instance, unless it's far worse than I know, you can save yourself. Even though it's hard. And if I interfere, I'll be sending the signal that you can't. That I don't believe you could, which isn't true."

"Oh." She stared at her empty cup. "Would that be so bad?"

"I think so. It would put us on uneven footing. And if we have any future together, a fun but doubtful dream, I wouldn't want to begin it with an unfair or false moral advantage."

She grew somber. Her cheeks colored and she inspected her toes. "You've thought a lot about this."

"Some girls are worth it."

"At every turn, Mackenzie, I am reminded of your depth. It is always a pleasant and humbling surprise."

"And I say," said Manny and he finished his wine, "white people think about stuff too much."

24

We were cleaning up—Ronnie staying close but unable to make eye contact; turbulent emotions desperate for equipoise—when a light knock sounded on my door frame.

I knew the woman standing there. Dianne Saunders, wife of George the Home Depot manager. In her right fist, my business card. Her husband George was an unusually attractive man; now that she wasn't fuming and screaming at me, I could see she wasn't bad either. She had a wide mouth, the kind necessary to model, and large green eyes, dark hair, absurdly high cheekbones. Freckles too.

Ronnie sucked a little air. Under her breath, she told Manny, "Oh shit. A beautiful woman is here for him. I'm insanely jealous."

"Mrs. Saunders, come in, please," I said. Of all the people on earth, she might have been my first choice to come knocking. "Our lunch is concluded."

She took another long look at Manny and Ronnie.

"Was it a lunch for Roanoke's most beautiful people? Something like that?" she said.

Manny nodded.

"Sí, mamita. And you belong."

Polite smile. "Not sure my husband would approve."

"Approval is overrated."

Ronnie kissed my cheek. Stepped into her shoes and grabbed Manny by the arm.

"Come on, Marshal. We were just leaving," she said.

"We were?"

"Yes. We were."

"Ah. Bueno. Mack, tell the lovely señorita good things about me," he said.

Dianne Saunders blushed a little. Pressed her lips together.

"He sleeps on the floor of my bedroom," I said.

"Ay! Dios mio, not that."

Then he was gone, forcefully tugged by Ronnie.

I closed the door. Dianne moved to my chair. I grabbed another and set it near her, not wishing to grill her over a desk.

"I know I should have called," she said.

"Not a problem."

"Your friends are beautiful."

"I am surrounded by a surplus of it," I said. "Dianne, I regret ambushing your husband at home. I needed information and sometimes the best way to get it is through surprise. I see now I was poking an open wound."

She met my eyes. A muscle in her jaw flexed.

"I hate Father Louis," she said.

"I might also."

"Somehow he seems to know when I'll be gone. And that's when he visits my husband."

"What for?"

Her head dropped. She rubbed at her eyes with her

thumb and forefinger. She spoke toward her knees. "This can't leave the room."

"I understand."

"You promise?"

"Cross my heart," I said.

"When I first met George, he was...call it bisexual. He doesn't like that term. He was into heroin and cocaine, and he...was promiscuous with anyone he could find when he was high. We met when he was twenty-five, at rehab. He was trying to quit drugs, and I was an alcoholic. Still am, I guess, but dry. You know? We fell in love, which they told us *not* to do. A good marriage needs to have one stable partner, they said. They were right. It's been hard."

"From what I've seen, marriage is hard even without the addictions."

"Yes. That's exactly right. And more so when you both... well... Listen, I apologize about the language I used on the street. I don't hate gay people. I shouldn't use the vulgar slang. I was furious and protective."

I said, "How does Louis Lindsey fit into this?"

I already had a hunch.

"I'll answer that. But it cannot leave the room. Father Louis is the one who got George into rehab. George refused to go until Louis made him, essentially. They were close. They partied together and...they were more than good friends. You understand?"

I nodded.

I *knew* it.

But I didn't tell her so; might kill the mood.

She continued, "Isn't that gross? The age difference? The man's sixty. Anyway. George goes to rehab, starts to get clean. Meets me, also getting clean. I think Louis's reasons for making George go to rehab were good, at least partly. But it backfired. George decided the promiscuity was unhealthy and he wanted to only be with women. Me, in particular. Louis didn't handle it well, you can imagine."

"I can."

"It's been three years. *Three.* And George still has former *friends* looking him up for a good time."

"Some addictions are hard to break," I said.

"They are. For both of us. And George is trying. He really is. But these temptations keep ringing our doorbell and he..." She stopped. Ran her fingers through her dark hair and gathered her fists at the base of her neck. "Well. I won't go into details. George and me, we're both from the country. Both grew up on farms, part of what attracted me to him. We're getting out of Roanoke soon as we can."

"Until then, you're dealing with Louis."

"Father Louis comes by the house every month or so. Usually when I'm not there, pretending to offer counseling. It's bullshit, Mr. August."

"His counseling services are also being plied elsewhere for nefarious purposes."

"Nefarious?" she said.

"Wicked."

"You told me you're trying to catch him, right?"

"Someone in a position of prominence leveled accusations against him. Alleged unwanted sexual advances. Very similar to your situation with George. If I can prove it, he'll be fired and most likely forced to leave Roanoke. If I can prove abuse, he could spend time in prison."

"George and me, we'll never testify. But I want to show you something." She pulled a cell phone from her pocket. Queued a video and handed it to me. "Recorded this last night. See what you think. Maybe it'll help."

I accepted the phone and hit play.

The video was blurry as the camera took a few seconds to focus. The speaker buzzed and the screen jumped. The person recording—Dianne, I assumed—was shooting through a window, between curtains. Through the window, two men were distorted but visible. Louis and George.

Dianne's voice came through the speaker loud, because her mouth had been close to the mic.

"*That's Father Louis. We told him not to come back, but here he is again. In our backyard.*"

The screen jumped again.

"*Hang on...I'm opening...the window.*"

The camera settled and the voices of the men became audible, but barely. I maxed out the volume. Louis was, without a doubt, drunk.

"*Bastard little kid, thinks he'll ruin me,*" Louis was saying. Sounded like, 'Basard lil kid, thinks hill rune me.' "*I gave him every...everything. Gave him the job. Found him a place to live. Even...even the got'damn car he drives, that's from me. Jeremy Cameron. Jeremy got'damn Cameron and his dumbass inspector... Mackenzie. Can you...can you* believe..."

He stumbled through my name just as he stumbled through their backyard. He banged his shin on a wrought iron chair.

"*Father Louis, you shouldn't be here. Not like this. You know how to use Uber?*" said George.

"*Be sure your sin will find you out, Jeremy Cameron. Be sure of it. How could he do...to me? To me! I am Louis Lindsey. Father Louis. The Father Louis. Do this to me? I can...I can crush him.*"

"*Go take a walk, Father Louis. I'll call you a cab.*"

"*You shut up, George. You shut the hell up! You used to be my... And you left...left me. A true friend sticks closer than a brother. As iron sharpens iron, George. But not you. You left. Son of a bitch, you just...left me.*"

"It goes on like that for a while. See the wine glass Louis's holding? He brought it with him. Full," said Dianne.

I watched to the end as Louis was staggering away and the video cut off. Louis was unquestionably drunk and irate and abusive. He threatened both George and Jeremy. And if one knew what to look for, there were sexual inferences to be drawn.

"Not ideal behavior from a pastor," I said.

"Take the video. Show it to the people at his church. Will it be enough?"

"Maybe. I was hired to determine if Louis was abusing Jeremy Cameron. He doesn't admit it in this video. But…it's still damaging. His vestry might fire him over it. Does your husband know?"

She nodded.

"George knows. He said you could have it. He hates Louis too. Can I text the video to your phone?"

"Please do."

"And you'll show it to the church people? You can force Father Louis to leave us alone?" she said.

"I'm going to try."

25

I had hope.

I had mixed feelings too.

Also some heartburn from the beef, cheddar, bacon, and fries. But that seemed less relevant than hope.

I watched the video half a dozen times. It was rough. The leader of a church, drunk and swearing and bragging and making threats. According to the video's whispered voiceover, this wasn't Louis's first unwelcome visit, so add trespassing to the list of sins.

But...what had I been hired to do? What specifically? Drag Louis's name through mud? Make damn well sure his church knew he was human? Humiliate and embarrass a pastor? That'd be easier.

I'd been hired to determine if Jeremy Cameron's accusations were true. And this neither proved nor disproved it. I was glad no one followed *me* around with a camera, capturing my worst moments and presenting them to the public. Yet that's what I held in my hand.

So.

What to do? What to do.

Mackenzie August. Going nowhere fast.

I watched it again. Used my thumb to rewind a little and listened.

"How could he do...to me? To me? I am Louis Lindsey. Father Louis. The Father Louis. Do this to me? I can...I can crush him."

Crush him. Crush Jeremy.

That settled it, gave me the permission I needed. The man was making threats against Jeremy Cameron. Technically Jeremy wasn't my client; the vestry was. But I'd extended that umbrella to include him.

I forwarded the video to Jeremy Cameron with the note, **We're getting closer.**

I also forwarded it to Hugh Pratt and Robert Wallace, the vestry guys, and texted, **Let's talk.**

Ten minutes later, Hugh called.

"Mr. August, thanks for the message. That's a hard video to watch," he said.

"Even harder to endure in person, I bet."

"Can you meet with the vestry after church this Sunday? Father Louis's out of town. I'll call Rob and set it up."

"I'll be there."

"Great. We'll figure this thing out in person. See you then."

We hung up.

Jeremy Cameron texted soon after.

>> **So that's why you asked about George Saunders.**

>> **That poor family.**

I remained motionless in my chair a while longer. Something nagged at my conscience and code. Didn't take long to identify the source.

I shouldn't have texted the video to Jeremy, Hugh Pratt, and Robert Wallace. I should have shown them, but not given out copies. What was I thinking? Blindly spreading evidence around was unprofessional and foolish.

A feeling of uneasiness settled over me. And I hated it.

THAT EVENING Kix and I rocked in the chair next to his crib. The nightlight glowed and his blinds held a faint ambiance from the streetlights, but otherwise the room was dim. An air freshener filled the space with a clean linen scent. We rocked and sang in our cocoon of serenity until my eyelids drooped and he was breathing heavily.

The phone in my pocket buzzed. I blinked myself awake and checked—unknown caller, the number blocked. I answered.

A low throaty voice said, "Good evening, Inspector."

It was the voice of Louis Lindsey.

"Am I interrupting anything important?"

"You are," I said.

"I'm curious. How often do you have urges and not act on them?"

"All day, every day. For example, I debated throwing my chair at you but didn't."

Kix stirred in my lap.

"I mean sexual, Inspector. Surely a powerful young ram such as yourself is practically throttled by sexual urges."

"That's what separates us from the animals, Louis. Denial of self, delayed gratification. You should try it."

"Should I?" He chuckled, and I could tell he sipped a drink. "An odd accusation. Especially since you can prove exactly and precisely nothing. You possess no evidence that I ever...consummated an illicit thought."

"I'm swimming in evidence, Louis."

He didn't listen. "We agree the denial of self imputes a kind of heightened virtue. To have an urge and to not act, that is something one can be proud of."

"Such as homosexual urges and tendencies beyond the vows you made to your wife?"

"One could see how acting on them would be improper for a man in my position."

"For a married man in a position of power over others, improper as hell, Louis."

"Too bad, Inspector. Too bad you can't prove it."

"Is that so."

"Cute video you have. Of me and George," he said. "Believe me, I have better."

I didn't drop the phone. But I came close.

Damn it. This was my fault. I shouldn't have shared the video Dianne gave me. Who knew how many people had seen it now. Mackenzie August, the amateur ass.

"I wouldn't call it cute," I said.

"It's embarrassing, I admit. Not my finest moment. You have successfully caused me shame. Are you proud?"

I stayed quiet.

"You didn't heed my advice, Inspector. I warned that you would cause suffering. And now you have. The fallout is on your shoulders."

"Alec Ward? Where is he, Louis?" I said.

The line disconnected.

26

The next day was a rainy Saturday.

Kix and I stayed indoors other than a foray to the children's museum downtown. Afterwards we watched intolerable shows on PBS Kids and practiced our army crawl and made tacos for dinner.

All day long I worried...*no*, not worried, because stalwart inspectors do not worry...I wondered about Louis's augured fallout. That evening I fell asleep thinking about Alec Ward.

The next day, Timothy August kept Kix while I attended the late service at All Saints. The cathedral had lofty ceilings, wooden pews, red and purple accoutrements, stained glass, candles, and incense and I loved it. Of Jeremy Cameron and Louis Lindsey, there was no sign. The pews were packed and no one paid me attention, which was odd, I thought; I deserved some. Nicholas McBride delivered a homily and celebrated the sacraments. I felt smug for knowing what those words meant.

Afterwards I found Hugh Pratt and followed him into a back room. Robert Wallace was there, and so were five others. It was a conference room; on the wall was an oil painting of pallid Jesus holding a lamb.

Hugh Pratt straightened his bowtie. "Mr. August, this is a quorum of vestry from the church. Everyone this is the private detective I mentioned, Mackenzie August."

I sat down. The temperature of the room felt sour and grim.

"Mr. August, after the initial accusations surfaced I chose not to inform the rest of the vestry. Not immediately. Only Robert and I knew. I hoped you would find something immediately to prove or disprove the claim of sexual harassment, and I could go to the vestry with more information. However, since I received your video I felt compelled to share everything. I personally informed each member and showed them the video. So now here we are."

"The video proves nothing," said a feisty woman. Her pale eyes were ablaze behind reading glasses. Her hair was gray and blue and held in a tight perm. Her dark dress had flowers and a white lacy collar and she wore a golden cross brooch. She stood up and waved a fist at no one. "We should have been told immediately about the absurd accusations. *Absurd*. Honestly, who's ever heard of such a thing."

"The video is horrible," said a second woman. Younger, a sad face looking down at her note pad.

"Of course it's horrible. It's a horrible job Father Louis has," said Gray Perm. "It takes horrible tolls and produces horrible gossip."

"I didn't know Father Louis could be like that and say those things. In the video, he looks...corrupt."

Gray Perm made a snort and rolled her eyes and sat again.

Hugh Pratt said, "Detective August, would you update us with everything you know, please."

I told them. All of it. Took less than ten minutes. At the end there was some silence that felt accusatory.

Eventually the woman muttered, "Like I said, the video is damaging but it only shows an angry man. Nothing *gay*."

"He's drunk too. And threatening people," said the sad woman.

"Who among us hasn't had too much to drink, Sarah? Land sakes, grow up," said Gray Perm.

"Mr. August, you believe Father Louis has something to do with the missing boy? Alex Ward?" Hugh asked.

"No," said Robert Wallace. "No way."

"*Alec* Ward. I can prove nothing. But Louis hinted at violence."

Gray Perm uncrossed and re-crossed her arms. "You can't prove anything, not really. Of course he didn't take the boy, that's madness straight from the devil."

"Father Louis's not gay," said Robert Wallace.

"Three reputable sources say he is. His alleged homosexuality seems well known outside these walls," I said. "I was hired to find out if Jeremy Cameron is lying. None of the evidence indicates he is. All of it indicates he's more trustworthy than Louis."

"The video is bad. Gotta be dealt with. But the gay stuff, that seems flimsy to me," said Robert Wallace, the old bull.

I remained calm. It was no use arguing with people who didn't want to listen or learn. It only served to ossify their defenses. Cognitive dissonance was, in my opinion, the worst.

"Hugh, I like August," Wallace continued, drumming hard fingers on the table. "August is an honest man. Says things straight. And if he hasn't found anything conclusive... in light of recent ongoings, maybe it's time his investigation concludes."

“Alec is still missing,” I said.

His mouth turned down. “Father Louis doesn’t have him. No way.”

Hugh took off his wireframe glasses and scrubbed at his hair. “And, Mr. August, that isn’t why you were hired. Let the police deal with Alec. This is all just…It’s getting to be too much.”

I read their faces. A collective awkward misery.

“There’s something else. What happened?” I said.

Hugh slipped the glasses back on. Glanced at Robert Wallace, who remained stoic. Gray Perm made another snort.

Hugh said, “Jeremy Cameron was jumped last night.”

“Jumped.”

Wallace nodded. “Beat up. Bad. He’s in the hospital.”

“Dammit,” I said and Gray Perm flinched. “What happened? Who did it?”

“We don’t know.”

“Which hospital?”

“Carilion.”

“Louis told me this would happen, I said. “Friday night on the phone.”

“He called you?” Hugh asked.

“In the video he says he’ll crush Jeremy. Then, Friday night he calls to tell me the suffering will get worse. Now Jeremy is in the hospital. And still you protect Louis.”

“You have no *proof* of anything,” said Gray Perm. “And if we are protecting *Father* Louis, so what. He’s our rector. He brings in the sheep and raises our funds. So we extend grace.”

“If Father Louis is guilty of any of this then we will extend grace but fire him immediately,” said Hugh and then he carried on over Gray Perm's stammering. "Mr. August, the phone call Friday night. Did you record it?"

"I didn't."

"Do you have the call log on your phone?"

"I do but it only shows a blocked number."

Someone down the table chuckled.

"Poor kid," said Robert Wallace. "I wanted Jeremy fired, not assaulted. I don't like violence against clergy."

"He'll be fine. Father Louis will visit and pray for him when he returns from his prestigious speaking engagements. Then Jeremy Cameron should be sent elsewhere. It's high time he move on," said Gray Perm.

I stood.

"Anyone familiar with the phrase white-washed tombs?"

Robert Wallace chuckled. He knew. Everyone else looked blank.

I said, "I am angry with you, All Saints. The church deserves better. So does Jeremy. So does Roanoke. So does Alec Ward."

27

The nurse outside Jeremy Cameron's door didn't want me to go in. But she was young and new and fragile, and I was tall and scary, and I showed my detective credentials and she didn't bother scrutinizing them.

I said, "Won't take long. Just a few minutes."

And I smiled. The kind of smile that set off heart rate monitors and caused young and fragile nurses to swoon and float.

"I'm coming back in a few minutes, sir, and you need to leave then," she said. Poor thing, must be near-sighted.

I entered. Closed the door. His room was quiet, like a sepulcher. Out his window I saw an air vent and a brick wall. The television was on but muted.

Victims never look good the first day after. The contusions are purple and green, and swelling is at full tide. Jeremy Cameron looked like an extra on The Walking Dead.

I told him so. He smiled but it caused his upper lip to ooze. A wound in his lower lip had been stitched. His left eye was nearly closed.

"They'd let me go home today," he said in a croak. "Except they're monitoring for internal bleeding."

"They stick a spear in your side, see if blood and water come out."

"Hah."

I held the insulated cup of water to his face and he sipped from a straw.

"No idea who did it?" I said.

"Two bigger guys. Never saw a face. They didn't say anything. Or if they did, I forgot. Believe it or not, I think it only took twenty seconds to make me look this way."

"I believe it. Looks like four to the face and a few to the abdomen."

"How do you know that?" he said.

"Beneath my beautiful exterior, I am a sum'bitch with a nasty history. I made guys look like you once upon a time. But with boxing gloves."

"Doesn't really hurt."

"It will. I think you should stay at my place after discharge. My roommate never uses his bed," I said.

"My mother is on her way. She's a nurse, so I'm in good hands. But thank you."

"I'm sorry about this, Jeremy."

He tried to sit up. Winced and quit the effort.

"You think Father Louis did it?"

I nodded. Stared at the air vent through the window, feeling rotten. "Someone else, on his behalf."

"Don't be sorry. I'd do it again. Doesn't this confirm he needs to be fired? He'll do anything to protect his job. I can't believe I worked with him for two years without seeing what a maniac he is."

"He's a very skilled predator, which means he can act and he's patient. He's narcissistic and delusional and desperate and hedonistic. We all are, but his power and influence have given his vices a blank check."

"He's an asshole," Jeremy muttered.

"Can you say that?"

"I can say that. Eventually I'll forgive him and accept that he's broken and wandered from the faith. But not today."

"I'll get him. I'll pin this stuff on him sooner or later. He's going down, Jeremy. Okay?"

"I trust you," he said. "Hey. That video you sent me, of him and George Saunders. I forwarded it to our bishop. Like, *believe me now?* He called yesterday afternoon. Finally. We prayed on the phone and he's going to speak with Father Louis soon. So that should help."

I watched him lying there, in pain, purple, staring at the ceiling, relieved someone finally believed him, that help might arrive *soon*.

And Alec Ward. Where was he? His nightmare wouldn't end *soon*.

Jon Young had only been given a month.

We sat without speaking a few minutes. He faded but his eyelids snapped open every time he drifted to sleep, maybe reliving the ordeal.

The door opened. The young nurse had brought reinforcements—a not-young nurse at her back.

I stood and patted Jeremy's foot under the blanket.

"I have to go. Horrible women are here."

"Thanks for coming," he said and then his face changed. He pointed over my head. "Look."

On the silent television, WDBJ7 news was reporting Alec Ward's disappearance. A big picture of his face over the anchor's shoulder. Kids vanished all the time, but they inevitably surfaced at a friend's house within forty-eight hours. Alec had been missing a week—finally newsworthy.

"It's weird," said Jeremy.

"What's that."

"Why did Father Louis kidnap Alec but only rough me up? Assuming it was actually him. Between me and Alec, seems like I'd be the better person to remove."

"You know what, Jeremy..."

"What?"

"That is a great question."

"Sir," said the young nurse. She stuck her chin at me. "This man needs rest."

"Want to feel my muscles?"

The mean nurse behind her said, "Maybe later. Right now? Out."

In the parking garage, on the way to my Honda, I noticed Jeremy Cameron's car. The bumper bore a Vanderbilt sticker, and the window had a cross.

The kid must've driven himself to the hospital after the hell was kicked out of him. He hadn't called an ambulance.

I admired the guy.

Something on the door got my attention. I slid between cars for a closer look.

Big ragged letters had been keyed into the paint. Sending a message to the young clergyman...

LIAR!

28

Manny, Kix, and I ate breakfast together early Monday morning. Manny heaped our plates with a sausage, bacon, egg, and cheese mixture that he claimed was, "Full of good fats, *migo*. Healthy for you."

"Fat is healthy now?"

"Good fat. Always been healthy. Read the research."

I pointed at the Amazon Alexa speaker and said, "Are we listening to Frank Sinatra?"

"Simon." He pronounced it *see-moan*, which meant Yup in Spanish. I knew all the good words.

"Isn't it a little early for Frank?"

Kix nodded sleepily.

It's definitely early for Frank. I did it my way? I'd go back to my crib.

"It's never too early for Sinatra. Sinatra's a great American and don't forget it," said Manny, my strangest roommate. "You seeing señorita Ronnie today?"

"I am not."

"Por que?"

"She's engaged, that's por que."

"Cutest mamita in Roanoke," he said.

"You told me. I did not dissent."

Girl's fly as heck. Don't know if I want her as a girlfriend or as a mother.

Manny watched Kix. "What's he saying?"

"Not sure. Something about a banana, maybe."

Kix threw his juice and shouted.

I've got yoooouuuu. Under my skinnnnn.

I picked up the bottle. "Bad decision, son."

Give it back immediately.

"You decided to throw it. No more juice."

You think this is funny? I'll wake the neighbors.

"Kix—"

Juice! This instant!

"Ay caramba, that's loud," he said.

"This is no time for compliments, Manny."

Kix turned a little purple with exertion and volume.

"Maybe you should give him a banana," Manny observed.

"I do not negotiate with terrorists."

"So no Ronnie today. You gonna bust a priest?"

"Wheels are in motion. Gears are turning," I said.

"But..."

"But it won't happen fast enough. He's still loose and publicly innocent, free to harass and harm. If he took Alec Ward, and if Alec Ward is still alive, then the boy's time is short. I need more evidence against Louis. I need his feet over the fire. You free today?"

"Por supuesto."

"Good," I said.

"Means, of course."

"I'm aware. Follow Louis today. I think he'll be expecting me, but won't notice you. Perhaps wear a hat. And a mustache."

"You think he'll lead me to the tower where he's got Alec Ward chained?"

"That'd be my first choice."

Manny pointed at Kix. "You think your *mijo* will ever stop shouting at us?"

"I expect him to tire out. But his persistence is commendable."

"Give him the juice. See what happens."

Give me the juice. See what happens, Father.

"If I give him the juice, he wins."

"Are you winning now?"

"I am not," I said. "Nor is the entire neighborhood."

"Watch how it's done." Manny took the juice off the table and placed it on Kix's tray. "Kix. Mi amigo bueno. I'm giving you the juice as a peace offering. So don't—"

Kix backhanded the juice with the power of Serena Williams and the grace of Roger Federer. The bottle arced across the room, spilling a rotating contrail of apple juice.

"Look at that," I said. "He's got natural topspin. Gets it from me."

I WENT to All Saints with the noble intention of intercepting Nicholas McBride, the clergy being harassed by Louis but refusing to admit it. I needed his testimony. And he needed the freedom truth would bring.

The polite receptionist explained that it was Nicholas's day off. She didn't know who I was, else she'd be less polite and dreamy-eyed.

Drat—Nicholas was slippery.

Instead I swung by the station and picked up xeroxed

police reports. Attached to the top of the pile was a note from the sheriff, asking me to drop in. So I did. She was on the phone in her office but she curtailed the conversation and waved me in.

"I need to respond to emails first," she said. "Sit. Look over the reports and we'll talk."

She started typing. I opened the files. Police officers' handwritten notes are inherently illegible, so I focused on the typed copies.

Jeremy Cameron had been beset by malfeasants outside Fork In The Market late Saturday evening. According to him it happened at 11:30 p.m. He'd been there with friends from church and he departed before the others to prepare for Sunday services. No one witnessed the assault, and no traffic or security cameras captured it. Police were made aware of the incident when the hospital alerted them. No suspects. Nothing was taken; it hadn't been a robbery. It had been a message.

Next report.

Alec Ward's abduction. The police knew even less about this. He walked home from school most of the time, and on this particular day he never arrived. That's all there was.

Stackhouse finished her emails.

I indicated the reports. "You are terrible at catching bad guys."

"Don't I know it. You were right—Alec Ward was in counseling with Father Louis for depression. I personally checked his alibi and it's flimsy. Louis says he was with his wife the afternoon of Alec's disappearance. She corroborates his account. Vaguely."

"Vaguely," I repeated. But with resonance.

"Patrick Henry parking lot security footage shows Alec leaving in a group after school last week, walking west along

Grandin toward All Sports. School administrators identified the group and we grilled the kids; they all agree Alec was nearby but not really part of their group. They moved into the neighborhood and he kept going on Grandin. That's the last anyone saw him. Detectives are knocking on doors along his normal route home. We're pulling footage from nearby traffic cameras. Thousands of cars, but maybe we'll get lucky. We called all his friends and teachers. We're asking for leads on the local news. Amber Alert activated this morning. Hopefully something will pop."

"Louis needs to pop."

She sighed at my single-mindedness. "Louis's a person of interest. But he's got an alibi and the connection to Jon Young is loose. The man might be sexually aggressive but that doesn't mean he abducts teenagers, babe."

"He's your primary lead."

"No, just the first one. And probably means nothing. What are your thoughts?"

"Alec Ward's parents wealthy? Seems so, if Louis carved time out of his schedule to counsel their kid," I said.

"Not especially."

"Then Alec Ward must be a good looking young man, to get Louis's attention. Better than the photo I saw on television," I guessed.

"Yep, handsome kid."

"Ah *hah*."

"Again, probably means nothing."

"Not to a sexual predator."

"According to Louis's assistant, he's counseled several teens over the years. Maybe, babe, that's just part of his job."

"It's interesting," I said, "that Louis's wife only offered a vague recollection of her husband's innocence."

"I agree."

"Is there marital disquiet at the Lindsey home?"

"Marital disquiet." She grinned. "Only you, Mackenzie, say this crap."

"I'll rephrase. Is there a kerfuffle at the Lindsey home?"

"Hell if I know. Marital disquiet and kerfluff-whatever is your job, not mine. But if the rumors are true, how could there not be?"

It was nice, I thought, to be known for one's specialities.

She said, "What about the assault on Jeremy Cameron? Anything stand out?"

"Louis called the night before it happened. He said people were going to get hurt and it was my fault. And the next day, Jeremy is hospitalized."

"You and Louis are mired in your own fluke-car-full," said Stackhouse.

"Bless you. It's *kerfuffle* and maybe let the unflinching and gallant private investigator handle the large words. How did Louis's goons know where Jeremy was going to be Saturday night?"

"Assuming it wasn't a random mugging."

"It wasn't. Nothing was taken," I said. "And I'll tell you how. The church *friends* Jeremy was with. Louis has informants. Someone is leaking information to him, and he or she or they have been for two weeks."

She pulled a pad close and scribbled a note. "I'll get a detective to discuss that with Jeremy."

"The attack was quick and brutal. Professionally done. I know a lot of professional goons local to Roanoke. I get time, I'll do some probing and deduction. I find out who did it, I'll get them to admit they were hired by Louis."

"Look at you being helpful," she said.

"I am nothing if not boosterish."

"That's not a real word. And I'm swimming in work, so our meeting is concluded."

"You're jealous, Sheriff, of my diction."

"Better watch your mouth with the sexy talk, Detective. I'm dating your father."

"You wish. Dating implies an ongoing activity," I said. And I stood. I read the signs—time for a hasty retreat.

"I called him my boyfriend yesterday." She smiled and it was a sight to behold. "Felt girlish and good."

"Shhh. I'm leaving. Hastily."

"Want to know what we'd just finished doing?"

"Playing chess fully clothed, I assume, and I hope Louis gets you next."

29

At my office I read over the reports again and made a few notes. The best notes.

My phone rang.

"Your boy, Padre Louis?" said Manny Martinez. "He's getting coffee at Sweet Donkey. Sitting outside on the patio with some kid."

"Kid?"

"Young hombre. Or younger than us. Maybe thirty years old? It's hard to tell with you white people."

"Handsome guy in a boyish way?" I said.

"Ay caramba, I don't know."

"Hang on." I surfed to the church's website, took a screen shot of Nicholas McBride, and texted it to Manny. "I sent you a photo. Is that the young handsome guy?"

"Sí, that's him."

"That's the clergyman to whom Louis is applying sexual pressure. What are they talking about?" I said.

"I can't get close, so I'm reading lips. Or trying. They were talking about the Bible, then about Jeremy Cameron, and now I think it's retirement."

"Retirement."

"Or maybe he's saying free firemen? Re-tire-ment. Free-fire-men. Hard to tell."

"Keep at it," I said and we hung up.

As I debated driving to the coffee shop and tailing Nicholas McBride with the intention of ambushing him when he was alone, my inbox pinged. New email.

The letter was from Jeremy Cameron. There were no words, only a link. I clicked and was taken to Louis Lindsey's website. It'd been updated this morning with an announcement. Dr. Louis Lindsey had a new book coming out, *Staying Spiritual in an Unspiritual World*, and he was going on a nationwide speaking tour in the fall. How to stay healthy and holy, with or without the church, when the world turns against you.

Written specifically for milquetoast, I thought.

Was Louis making exit plans? An escape hatch?

I grabbed my keys and stood, prepared to follow Nicholas McBride, but Hugh Pratt called me first. I'm soooo popular.

"I call with big news, Mr. August," he said over my speaker phone.

"What's that." I sat down and eyed my computer monitor, Louis's website still on screen.

"Father Louis is going to retire."

"That so."

"That's so. He spoke with the bishop last night about that damn video and he met with me early this morning. The agreement is unanimous; it's time he moved on. His lawyer helped him draft a letter with his reasons for making the decision, and we'll release the letter—"

"What are his reasons?"

"Ah...well...I suppose I can read it to you. I have the first draft on my screen," he said and I heard a keyboard clicking. "Okay, let's see…here we go…" More clicking and he cleared his throat. "…*My dearest friends helped me realize the clerical responsibilities are weighing heavier than they should. Years of tending to diocesan duties and ignoring my own soul's need for renewal have taken their toll. I suffer in unexpected ways, such as anger issues, anxiety, trouble sleeping. Wine may make the heart glad, but I've grown too comfortable with an occasional second glass. After prayerful introspection, I've decided it's in the best interest of All Saints and the best interest of my family to step down after my replacement has been found…* Blah, blah, you get the idea, Mr. August."

My grip on the armrest tightened.

"The purpose of this letter is to drum up public sympathy and get ahead of the damaging video. If it's ever released, it'll be old news," I said.

"Of course. Nothing wrong with good business decisions. Father Louis was reluctant. Not ready to retire, but the church is giving him a fat severance package, enough to keep him and his wife comfortable a couple years. They should be fine; he's got a book coming out, and he's not far from retirement age, so he—"

"It is not Louis we should worry about, Hugh."

"What do you mean?"

"What about the men he victimized?"

"Allegedly victimized. This is great news for them."

"How so."

"Because he's *retiring*." Hugh said it with a half snort, like I was an idiot.

"Is he moving?"

"Not that I'm aware."

"What about the men he'll victimize in the future?" I said.

"Oh Christ, August. What do you want me—"

"Your plan is to pay him off. To handsomely reward him and take away his responsibilities so he has free time to pursue his hobbies. Or his obsessions, I should say. This is not good news for the men he harasses. This will accelerate and intensify his efforts."

"No, I don't—"

"When does he retire?"

A pause. "This time next year. These things take time. He'll need to train his replacement and the church—"

I was grinding my teeth. "What about Alec Ward?"

"The missing kid? He'll show up. The police will—"

"You're a coward, Hugh."

"*Enough!* Listen, August, I know what you think of me. That I don't care about the victims. That I just want this thing over and done with. That my focus is too narrow, that I'm a hypocrite. You might be right about some of that. But here's the thing, Mr. August. Who said I'm any good at this? Who said I have a clue what to do when a junior clergy is making accusations against the senior? Because I don't. Not a clue. I don't know how to solve this thing, and I don't know how to help the victims. Alleged victims. I was put on vestry and charged with preserving and growing the church, and so that's what I'm doing. Is my focus too narrow? Am I potentially ignoring the pain of others? Yes, maybe so. But I don't know how to save everyone. I'm doing what I can. And in this case, preserving the church means getting Father Louis to retire peacefully so that All Saints doesn't split and dissolve. These things have a way of wrecking a community, wrecking lives. And it appears as though we are skirting that disaster. So, no, I'm not perfect. I wish I had the answers, I wish I could solve every problem. But this is the best I can do."

I took a deep breath. Let it out in a blast at the ceiling.

"I can respect that."

"Thank you," he said.

"You keep doing what you do. Preserve the church. And I'll do what I do—find enough evidence to haul Louis before a judge."

"That won't be necessary," said Hugh.

"Oh it's necessary."

"I'm writing you another check, Mr. August. Right now as we speak. This is from the church, not from me. It's a thank you. You were a big help."

"Predators don't stop. Louis will stalk other men," I said.

"You are released from your obligations to All Saints with our sincerest gratitude. You'll find that you've been more than fairly recompensed for your time and tipped well on top. With the financial obligations fulfilled, we immediately terminate our professional relationship with you."

"He needs to pay. And he needs to be stopped, Hugh."

I could hear him breathing. He started and stalled a defense twice before getting his footing.

"This church is important to me. Saved my life in a lot of ways," he said at last. "It's even more important to Rob Wallace. We'll do anything to keep it intact. We love Father Louis. And now we're sending him away—prematurely, in my opinion—and it's hard and it's awful and I hate it. But at least the church will survive. And that's enough."

"Comes with a high cost," I said. "Too high."

"I think I'll retire too. From vestry." His voice sounded soft and elegiac. "This is too hard."

Unceremoniously he hung up.

30

Jeremy Cameron lived in a condo/townhouse downtown within walking distance of everything. I parked across the street, paid five dollars for the privilege, and entered the building's lobby, which serviced four units. I knocked on Jeremy's.

The door opened two inches until the chain caught. A woman regarded me through the gap. From what I could tell, she wore flowery nurse scrubs. Her hair was dyed brown and cut into a short bob.

"Can I help you?"

"You must be the mother of Jeremy Cameron," I said.

"Gloria. Who're you?"

"A fan."

"I've had it up to *here* with fans of Jeremy," she said.

I opened my wallet and handed her my license.

"I'm a private detective working on behalf of your son," I said. Not entirely a lie. It held a grain of sterling truth.

"Mackenzie August. He mentioned you."

"Did he mention my resemblance to Tom Hardy?"

"The actor from Mad Max?" said Gloria.

"Indeed. May I come in?"

"That's the exact question Father Louis asked me last night, standing where you are."

"Did he," I said and my fingers twitched. That guy.

She produced a gun. Looked like a silver Smith & Wesson .38 special. Pointed at my gut. "He did. He tried to force his way in until I showed him this."

"Please do not, and I can't stress this enough, pull the trigger by accident."

"I almost didn't show him the gun. I *wanted* him to break the door open so I could kill him."

"If it makes you feel better, there's a chance I'll do it for you."

She watched me coolly a long moment while I wished more revolvers came with safeties.

"Jeremy said I could trust you," she said.

"If I give you my gun, maybe you'll believe him."

"You're carrying?"

I was wearing a leather jacket. I pulled it back to reveal the 1911 in my shoulder holster.

"Have you ever used it?" she said.

"I have."

"Shot anyone?"

"Tons of people."

She smiled. Closed the door. The chain released and she opened up. To my surprise, after closing the door, she hugged me. Pressed her face into my shoulder. Her right hand, behind my back, still held the pistol.

"Thank you. For caring about my son. I brought him home yesterday evening."

"How is he?"

"This time next week he'll be pain free. Until then he'll rest and drink fluids and not go near an opioid."

She led me to a set of couches near a television. Jeremy's place was eclectic and cheap, as a young bachelor's dwelling ought.

I said, "What did Louis want?"

She said, "To pray for Jeremy. His words. But I've been around evil men before. Their eyes turn wild when they don't get what they want. Father Louis, he's a selfish son of a bitch, and I hate him."

"You have good taste."

She shook her head. "Members of his church came to visit too. This morning. They brought bread and cookies. I didn't let them in and I threw the baked goods away. I don't trust a single Christian."

"We're not all bad. My guess is, you can trust the cookies."

She arched an eyebrow. "We?"

I nodded.

"Is Father Louis outside, watching Jeremy's place?" she said.

"My friend is tailing him. Louis left a coffee shop an hour ago and now he's at All Saints. But all the same, maybe call me when you need to go out and I'll accompany you."

"No need." She set the pistol onto the table between the couches. "I can handle it."

"Got a license?"

She nodded. "Scored a 205."

"A cutie with good aim? There's so few of us."

She did not think I was funny. Poor thing, maybe she was deaf. She said, "I'm requesting an emergency protective order to keep Louis away from here."

"Good idea. I have connections inside various law enforcement offices to help it get through. Plus I know a great attorney. She'll do all our work pro bono."

"Is that why you're here? To help my son?"

"I came to update him and discuss his options."

Gloria leaned forward until her forehead was resting in her hands and she gripped her hair. "His *options*. I want him to get the hell out of here."

I nodded. And I didn't blame her.

She said, "I never realized how *helpless* victims of harassment feel. It seems like nobody cares. No one is helping him." Her voice got louder with anger. "The police don't care. His friends don't care. His co-workers don't... I mean, his *boss* is trying to break in, to *molest* him. Jeremy told people, which will cost him his job, and...nothing! *Nobody* cares."

"Louis is clever and he has allies. I've been working for two weeks on this, maybe a little less, and I can't pin anything on him beyond reasonable doubt. Not yet. And without proof, who will people believe? The kid? Or the local hero, an established priest? It's tough."

She raised up and jabbed a finger at me. "Tell me this, Mackenzie. Is All Saints a cult or what? Everyone from that church strikes me as full of shit. How does this get to happen? I didn't want Jeremy to go into the ministry. I was raised Catholic, so I'm acutely aware every other week a priest is exposed as a pedophile. That's one reason I left. Is All Saints no better?"

"I don't attend All Saints, but it has the same disease all the other churches have.'

"What disease?"

"Humanity," I said. "Churches would be a lot safer place without us people."

"Well, All Saints seems more evil than most. The priest, the people, the vestry or whatever you call it, they don't care about my son. They care about themselves and that's it," she said.

"I'm not excusing All Saints. In fact I'm working hard to topple its leader. But all humans are broken. Even the best ones. We build institutions like All Saints to protect ourselves and our comfort zones, and then we serve the institution, not each other. We are protected but others are sacrificed, though we don't realize it. The vestry isn't evil; they are human. Sacrificing Jeremy to save the church is an unfortunate necessity in their eyes. It will preserve the church, and that's not wholly ignoble. It's cowardly and sanctimonious and ultimately a pyrrhic victory, but it keeps hands clean."

She was trying not to cry. Glaring at the chair and jutting her chin. But the mother's tears came anyway. "What do we do?"

"That's up to Jeremy. It is him who bears the burden."

"I don't want him to," Gloria said. "Those bastards."

"The only thing necessary for evil to triumph..."

"Jeremy *is* a good man. But he shouldn't have to do this."

"I agree. And he doesn't have to. He can leave."

"Shit. I'm tired of crying." She wiped at her tears like they'd betrayed her. "He did this as a kid, too. Jeremy's father is...he's not a man I wanted around my son. Every so often he'd show up, and once Jeremy realized the damage it caused...he stood up to him. Can you imagine, a thirteen-year-old standing up to his father? A man he worshiped and adored and missed? One night, Jeremy's father was drunk and he came around and he hit Jeremy. *Hit* his own son. That's when I got this." She nodded at the .38. "I'll kill him. I don't care if he's Jeremy's father. I told him I would and he believed me and he hasn't come back."

"There's another evil man in Jeremy's life now."

She choked down a sob. Placed her hand over her mouth and nodded.

"And his mother can't solve this one," I said.

"I know."

"But he was raised well."

"Thank you."

"He's 'man' enough to handle this guy. With our support."

"But why," she said, crying freely now. "Why Jeremy?"

"Because he was the one hurt. Because he's innocent. And he's the only one strong enough to."

The bedroom door opened. Jeremy shuffled out. His mother tried to stand but Jeremy placed his hand on her shoulder and he lowered next to her.

If anything, he looked worse today.

"You two," he mumbled between swollen lips. "Talk too loud."

"You listened?" I said.

"Yes. But say it again."

"Louis is retiring. He'll spend the next twelve months training his replacement and going on a national speaking tour to promote his new book. The church is giving him a severance package."

He made a hmph noise through his nose. "He's retiring to make the investigation go away. Satisfy the bishop and vestry that justice has been done."

"It's bullshit," said his mother.

"Yes," I said. "To both."

"It's not enough. If nothing else, he needs to be publicly exposed," said Jeremy.

"At the minimum."

"Can you do it?"

"I have been fired."

He smiled and winced. "What took them so long."

"So you're no help anymore?" Gloria asked.

"Didn't say that. I'm obdurate."

Jeremy blinked. "What's that mean?"

"It means he's stubborn," replied his mother. "What? I read books, I learn words."

"If Jeremy is still in this, I'm still in this," I said.

"Let's bust his ass."

"And maybe save Alec Ward."

Gloria got up and came back with water. As Jeremy drank from the straw, or tried his best, she said, "You think that kid is tied up in a van somewhere? Waiting to die?"

"I don't know exactly. The police don't either. But coincidences usually turn into something else. I think this is related. If it's like last time, Alec is still alive."

"How do you find him?"

"Follow the only lead I have—Louis Lindsey. Pull and poke enough, I usually find answers. Other words, if I apply enough heat to Louis, I might find Alec."

"His poor mother," said Gloria. "I bet she hasn't slept in a week."

31

Kix and I went for ice cream at Blue Cow. We sat outside on the patio after dark and watched the Roanoke River gurgle and swirl. The same water had previously rushed by Ronnie's apartment, a mile north. I got lost in my thoughts and in the strawberry bovine largess, and was surprised to find Kix had fallen asleep in his chair, still gripping the kiddie spoon.

I cleaned him, got him in his car seat, and we drove home.

Except we didn't. I blinked and we were in the parking lot outside the River House where Ronnie lived. I hadn't intended to, but some kind of autopilot assumed control and driven where I subconsciously wanted to be. Five stories aglow and glazed with cheer. The attached Tap House was active, patrons arriving for dinner or a nightcap. Many of the large industrial windows were uncovered, giving partial insight into the residents' living rooms. Televisions flickered on walls and music drifted down.

I checked the map on my phone—Ronnie was home.

The day's accumulated aggravation weighed on my

shoulders. I'd been fired. It felt like a dishonorable discharge, even though my client was satisfied. I didn't need the approval of Hugh or Robert, but I did need the approval of myself. And I withheld it. Louis was free and Jeremy Cameron was bruised and battered and Alec Ward was still missing and both their mothers were scared.

It wasn't a game, yet Louis was winning.

That made my skin crawl. Would keep me awake with despondency. Would drive me to Ronnie's.

My phone buzzed. A text.

>> **What man art thou that, thus bescreened in night, so stumbles upon my apartment's balcony?**

I smiled despite the ache and replied, **That's not how Shakespeare wrote it, Ronnie. And you don't have a balcony.**

>> **I know, but you love that play.**

>> **I'll try again.**

>> **Imagine my delight at checking your location and finding you at my doorstep!**

>> **I'm cleaning my apartment at the speed of light but it'll take weeks.**

>> **Instead you should come up and ignore how many clothes I own.**

I closed my eyes. Forced myself to keep the car's engine running.

Behind me, Kix sighed in his sleep.

I texted, **I cannot. Though it's not because I don't want to.**

>> **Meet me at the door.**

>> **We will...what do the kids say...we will Netflix and chill.**

>> **On my couch. And then again in my bed.**

I replied, **I have Kix with me.**

>> **Even better! I'll fix breakfast in the morning and hug and kiss you both for hours. I'll earn my way into your heart through hospitality.**

>> **I'm at the door now. Where are you?**

I saw her then. She stood in the spilling light at the River House's lobby. Waiting to let me in. Her hair was held up with a clip. A couple guys left the restaurant and went into the lobby, moving around her. They took second looks. And a third. Her nightgown didn't amount to much. She was worth third glances even fully clothed.

She called my phone.

I answered and said, "Your father would be ashamed of the outfits you prance around in."

Her voice, the rosiest of notes, was warm in my ear. "My father thinks my appearance is a tool I should use more often. Like I'm doing right now."

"It's working."

"I was thinking about you earlier, Mackenzie. And about Christmas parties."

"Objection. Counselor Summers is befuddled."

She said, "I think it's sad you don't get to go to any. You work alone. No co-workers. No bosses, no employees. No parties. No peers."

"Especially no peers."

"Which can be ideal. Except for the times when it's not. Your profession is difficult, and you do the work because you're good at it, but also because very few can, and it's necessary. That's honorable and virtuous. But I was thinking, I'm sure Mackenzie gets lonely."

"Maybe. I don't have to do gift exchanges, so that's good."

"Are you lonely now?" She said it in a half-whisper and the hairs on my neck stood.

"I am."

"I know the cure for that."

"No you don't. You offer a temporary respite."

"But if we hurry, the respite can be administered twice, Mackenzie. Please come inside."

"Are you lonely?"

"I think I am more lonely than you'll ever realize."

"Does your fiancée know you're lonely?" I said.

"Who cares."

"I do. Because I care about all things pertaining to you."

A frustrated sigh in my ear. "He knows to some extent. But he's not the kind of man I would admit it to."

A car parked and a girl got out. Ronnie knew her and opened the glass door for her and they chatted a moment in the lobby.

I watched her smile at her friend. Watched her lips move. Watched her perfect posture and proud shoulders and her long legs.

I dropped the car into drive and motored out of the parking lot.

Ronnie's voice returned to the phone. "That's you leaving. Isn't it."

"That's me. Running for my life."

"You break my heart, Mackenzie."

"You're far too lovely a person to enter a marriage wrecked from the start, Ronnie."

"Say my name again. I like it."

"No."

"Did you know a big storm is coming? It's called a nor'easter. My girlfriend just told me. A cold front is building in the tundra and heads south through Canada soon. Meteorologists say it'll collide with warm air up from the warm Atlantic and cause a big storm. Isn't that appropriate?"

"You and me."

"We're a beautiful disaster waiting to destroy everything," she said.

"In your scenario, you're the hot front coming north, aren't you."

"Of course. Did you see my outfit? Those two boys almost tripped over each other."

"I don't blame them. I'm having a hard time staying on the road," I said.

"I'm wearing you down. Soon, Detective, you will be in my arms."

I didn't reply. But we listened to each other breathe until I got home and parked, and I willed myself to break the connection. The sounds of her breath remained in my ear a long time as Kix and I sat in the car without moving, and I wondered what the hell was wrong with me.

32

My father had claimed I was in a slump and the All Saints case would break me out of it. And yet...

I sat in my office, ankles crossed, fingers laced. Staring at the inbox on my computer screen. I had a few emails from clients and a couple phone calls to return. Nothing important, though. Nothing of consequence or stimulating. Nothing that constituted even a week of work.

Sure felt like I was still in a slump.

Even if something urgent beckoned, I knew I wouldn't focus on it. I couldn't shake Jeremy and Louis, even though I was no longer in the employ of All Saints.

At least not officially.

As I read the mundane emails again, I peered through them and saw the bruised face of Jeremy Cameron and the missing face of Alec Ward. Part of me knew that I'd taken this too personally. That very little evidence existed to suggest Louis had anything to do with Alec, that being a sexual predator didn't necessarily mean Louis had the capacity to abduct and murder a teenager. That I was using the disappearance of Alec as fuel and as an excuse to destroy the priest because I was angry at him.

But what was an intrepid and handsome inspector to do? Give up? Surrender Jeremy and Alec to the winds of fortune on the fear I was overstepping my professional boundaries? No chance. I had a reputation of being obtuse to uphold.

Unconsciously I consigned myself to the slump a few more days. Because busting Louis would solve a lot of problems.

I'd left messages for Dr. Wesley Stevenson, none of them returned. He was the dean of Ashdown Forest, the boarding school attended by Louis Lindsey in his youth. Bonus points for Dr. Stevenson—he had attended Ashdown as a child at the same time as Louis. They knew each other.

I grabbed my jacket and headed north on Interstate 81.

The trip took two hours from Roanoke. Ashdown Forest was north of Charlottesville, tucked away in the gentle green hills of central Virginia. Only forty-five minutes from civilization, yet the campus felt a world unto itself. Like driving into the clean air of aristocracy. The trees were noble and ancient, the columns white and stately, the buildings brick, and the breeze smelled of old money. A few boys played catch on a central lawn.

I parked at the administration offices and went inside.

Dr. Wesley Stevenson himself received me in the deserted main office. He was mostly bald with tufts of gray above his ears. Reading glasses perched on the Roman nose. He wore a tweed vest with notched lapels, and the sleeves of the shirt beneath were rolled up. He had the eyes of someone who'd read more books than me, which I resented.

"Mackenzie August," I said, shaking his hand. "I was in the area and you haven't returned my calls."

His smile didn't falter. "Haven't I? Doesn't sound like me. One doesn't get to sit in my dusty chair by not returning phone calls. My apologies. Please come to my office."

I did. And I swooned. So many built-in wooden shelves, so many leather-bound books. The top pane of the window adjacent to his reading chair was lowered, and next to the chair was a small table with an ashtray and pipe.

"How can I be of assistance, Mr. August?" He sat at his desk and I sat across from it. The chair was ancient but comfortable and I wondered if Edgar Allen Poe had once planted his butt here.

"I have questions about Louis Lindsey, a mutual acquaintance."

His face, I thought, darkened a shade. "Do you? Old Louis. That's a name I've been hearing more and more."

"You two attended school together," I said.

"I arrived as a sixth year, and he was in seventh. We stayed friends through college and a while after. When you called, did you mention Louis?"

"I did."

"That could explain it. My receptionist is a Dr. Lindsey devotee. She listens to his sermons online and gives me the rundown. She's twenty years older than me, if you can imagine, and has arrogated herself the privilege of passing on only those calls she deems worthy. We're lucky she's not here today; most students and staff are home on holiday. We can speak freely and not trigger her wrath. I'm afraid I've forgotten Louis's whereabouts. Where is he these days?"

"Louis lives in Roanoke now. And he's causing mischief."

He pursed his lips and nodded. "I'm grieved to hear it."

"Some of it serious. Some of it very serious. As the dean of Ashdown, there are things you cannot divulge. But I'm hoping that, as a childhood friend of Louis's, there are things you can."

"Such as?"

"I won't know until I hear it. Potentially nothing."

"You're a detective," he said.

"I am."

"And you're on the hunt for a clue."

"At this point, more like trying to understand motivation."

He stared through me at the great yawning beyond, the locked cosmos of his childhood and all the years since. After a moment he stood and went to his office door. Softly closed it and stood at the adjacent window looking out.

"What kind of mischief?" he said.

"Would you care to guess?"

"I've already guessed. But I won't utter it."

"Sexual harassment," I said.

He grunted. Took a deep breath and let it out against the glass. Clasped his hands behind his back, and looked ten years older.

I had struck a nerve.

"Do you see the box, Mr. August, behind my chair marked 'Birthday'?"

"I do."

"Inside the box are birthday cards from parents. Sent to students who specifically requested they not be delivered. So I keep them. Do you know why the students don't want to receive their own birthday cards?"

"I have a guess but won't utter it."

"Because if it's discovered that today is your birthday, the older boys give you an ice bath. It's a longstanding tradition. I banished it, just like the dean before me, but the ritual endures. An innocuous birthday celebration. But painful none the less. Most boys wish to avoid it, especially the younger ones, the more easily traumatized."

"Not entirely innocuous, it appears."

"I misspoke. *Seemingly* innocuous. As the recipient of an ice bath hazing myself, I vouch they are unpleasant."

"You still remember it, forty years later," I said.

"That memory is the primary catalyst for my acceptance to the position of dean. That and other memories like it. Many of them far more sinister, I'm afraid."

"You took the position to prevent little kids like you from being hurt."

"Not exactly." He swiveled at the waist far enough to look at me. "I want to prevent little kids like me from growing into bigger kids like I became. Not long after mine, I was the one preparing the ice bath. And relishing the pain I caused."

"Ah."

"The child held under the icy water is innocent. The bigger child above is not. But in some ways, both are equally helpless. Too many adults today attend counseling as boarding school survivors. And I believe it's often the pain they *inflicted* which leaves the more indelible scar."

"Classic PTSD. A disgust of self."

"Very good, Mr. August. Boarding schools such as Ashdown Forest have strong track records of producing excellent adults and citizens. But what you won't hear is that we also manufacture terrible husbands and fathers, if you'll allow the distinction. There's too much relational rage. Too much PTSD, as you say."

"You want to remedy this."

"I do."

"How goes it?"

"It's an uphill battle. Impossible to achieve total victory. Recently I became aware of a form of punishment the students administer. If a boy gets out of line, a 'firing squad' walks by his dorm room and hurls cans of soda inside. The sodas erupt against the wall and soak everything in Sprite. And if the boy gets hit by a fastball? Even better for him to learn his lesson. I know of no way to entirely eradicate this type of mechanism," he said.

"And Louis? How does he fit into this?"

He returned from the window and sat in the chair. Crossed his legs and played with the hem of his pants.

"Louis was brilliant. More intelligent than the rest of us. It caused him all sorts of problems. He eventually realized he had to quit showboating but by then it was too late. He was a marked boy."

"He was disciplined," I said. "By the students."

"For varieties of reasons. He was spoiled, a brat. Most boys who attend Ashdown are, but...he was beyond the pale. He didn't have the good sense to adapt."

"Was he violent? Did he hurt others?"

"No. And that might've contributed to Louis's torment. He didn't have the backbone to fight or defend himself."

"Was he gay?"

"So you know about that. Yes he was gay. Though not openly. When we went into town for girls, he came too. But I could tell he was bored. Unsatisfied."

"He still is," I said. "Part of the problem."

"I attended his wedding. With mixed emotions. That poor bride; though I got the impression she knew. It was a marriage of power and influence, not love. He was a rocket ship gaining speed, clearly destined for the stars. It's easier now to be gay than it was back then. I wonder how things would've been different if we'd been more...tolerant isn't the word I would pick. Kind. If we'd been more kind."

"That wouldn't have made him straight."

"No no. That's not what I mean. He didn't want to be straight, he once told me, but he had to hide his sexuality. A man who can be himself is healthier than a man in disguise."

"As soon as I mentioned his name, Dr. Stevenson, you reacted as though you knew what was coming. You were already sad, though I hadn't explained myself."

He steepled his fingers and bumped them against his lips. Nodded. "This isn't the first mischief he's caused. The previous occurrence that I'm aware of...I was consulted, yet I was reticent with information. I regret it, because I didn't help. And clearly help is needed."

"Does the previous occurrence have to do with his career change? From hospitals to churches?"

"The sudden lurch into the ministry? Yes. Although I believe that entire incident, including the mischief, brought genuine change. I think Louis, in his late thirties, truly wanted to better himself, to cease the infidelities, to grow, to obey the prompting of a higher power. And he did change, to my knowledge. He did live up to the lofty standards set by his profession for many years. But then..."

"But then came fame and fortune and influence, and the commiserate blank check?"

"Too much power is bad for anyone. It corrupts, as the saying goes. And it's especially bad for men like Louis. Not because he's gay, but because he was obsessed with himself. Much better for him to remain humble and obscure, I think."

"The power was a wine in his blood."

"Are you quoting something?" asked Stevenson.

"Yes. But botching it."

"Now he's a man of importance in the church, abusing his position, isn't he. Like so many others before him. These influential megalomaniacs, the shooting stars, they don't turn evil overnight. It's a slow accumulation of minor deviations. And soon enough... Men like Louis truly believe the targets of his infatuation want to be pursued. He believes he deserves them and they enjoy it. By that point, disaster is unavoidable."

"You're around this a lot," I said.

"I shepherd many children of disaster. I think, despite my best efforts, boarding schools will continue to foster intimacy issues."

"One reason I left the police force is my disillusionment with institutions. Not much has changed my mind since," I said.

"Poor Louis." His voice caught and he looked down at his hands, clasped in his lap. "Kids are scared at move-in day. Understandably so—they're staring at months without parents. I still remember Louis's face as a child. Neither his mother nor father accompanied him to drop off; it was his nanny. Worst day of his life, perhaps, and he was sent off with a caretaker. He didn't graduate from here, did you know that? Finished his final semester at home. Couldn't endure the abuse, because during his senior year his secret got out, and the boys were brutal. They soaked his pillow with urine for weeks."

"Seems unhygienic."

"His final day here, four boys held him down. Each gripped one of Louis's appendages. Luckily a professor arrived just as the fifth boy prepared to sodomize him with the handle of a toilet plunger," he said.

Mackenzie August, caught off guard.

A tear rolled down Dr. Stevenson's cheek.

"We weren't even disciplined. Boys being boys, you know. I apologized to Louis several times for that. Each time he told me to forget it, all was forgiven. But I've always wondered about the permanent damage I caused. From which we can never fully heal."

33

A gusty April wind rose from the hills and buffeted my journey home under dark scudding clouds. Nothing is ever easy, Mother Nature explained. Or simple. The big rigs swerved and fought the wind coming over Afton Mountain, and the rest of us stayed clear of their fishtailing trailers. And Alec Ward remained missing.

Dr. Stevenson hadn't provided any significant help. I wasn't sure what I hoped to find, but it hadn't been empathy. Yet that's what I returned with—a deeper understanding of Louis's pain.

I'd already done my homework on Louis's wife, Celia. She was born into the illustrious Simon family, a name mentioned in reverential tones in Virginia. Celia's father and grandfather before him owned factories and fields in Virginia, Kentucky, Tennessee, and North Carolina, and they sold millions worth of feed to cattle ranchers in the south and midwest. I'd found archived photos of Celia Simon riding horses in her youth, going to church with her sisters, and attending formals at Chatham Hall. Her wedding ceremony had taken up half a page in a Richmond newspaper. It was easy to discern that the Simons were Virginia royalty, and it was only slightly less easy to note Celia had dropped out of favor with her family. The black sheep, fallen from grace.

I parked near her house after lunch, after learning from Manny that Louis was at a luncheon. Before I could exit my car, Celia left her home in a little white Mercedes. I dropped into drive and followed. She didn't go far; she parked on Crystal Spring and walked into Tinnell's Fine Foods, the breeze momentarily wrapping her knee-length skirt tight against her thighs.

Celia was younger than Louis but not by much. I knew from prior research that she attended yoga and aerobic classes at the Y, gaining the trim shape of women who ate little but exercised and drank red wine, both to excess. Her posture was good, her chin tilted up.

She came out of Tinnell's with a bag and stepped next door into The Second Yard.

I ground my teeth and gripped the steering wheel. This was not helping Alec Ward or Jeremy Cameron, and my anxiety collected at the base of my neck. However, I waited.

Celia Lindsey came out of The Second Yard with a larger bag. She stopped and her head swiveled my direction. She wore oversized Prada sunglasses but I knew we were staring at each other.

Did I squirm and fidget?

Not I, man of steel with aureate intentions.

But I did sweat a little. I hated coming off as a stalker.

She turned my way. I got out of the car. Without speaking we met at the rear and she raised her bags to me. I popped the trunk and set the bags inside. Closed the lid and held open my passenger door. She slid gracefully in and smoothed her skirt. I closed the door, went around, and got behind the wheel.

"Where to?"

"Here is adequate," she said. She didn't remove the sunglasses and she stared straight ahead. Her perfume smelled expensive. "I am not staying with you long."

"You know who I am and what I'm doing," I said.

"I do. Louis told me not to speak with you."

"I'm not trying to ruin your life."

"My husband is a homosexual and I married him anyway. I ruined my life a long time ago, Mr. August. But you are, from my point of view, causing more damage than necessary."

"It might get worse, too."

"Because of you he's retiring early. He's losing his prominent position in the community. How much worse can it get? I was told the vestry cut ties with you," she said.

"They did."

"Then why are you following me?"

"I am stubborn. And I have an affection for the truth."

She opened the clasp of her purse and withdrew a small crystal vial. The silver top unscrewed off, and she used the attached micro spoon to scoop a tiny amount of white powder from the vial. She raised the micro spoon to her nose and inhaled, the powder disappearing into her nostril. She continued the inhalation with her eyes closed. All of it done as a dainty and classy woman should.

"You know it's strange. I'm not even angry with you." She finally turned to face me. Sniffed once. "You're a big man. Strong. Attractive, in a blue collar sort of way. Not usually my husband's type. Nor mine." She replaced the lid and offered me the vial of cocaine. "Indulge."

"No thanks. I get my kicks and the ensuing crash from watching baseball now."

"And sex?"

"Thank you but I'm trying to quit."

"I wasn't offering," she said. Then a pause. Her features had softened, even her posture, the cocaine wiping away some harsh realities. "You are trying to quit sex?"

"If I tell myself that, it's easier to cope with the lack thereof."

"You're too young to start down that road, Mr. August. Find someone you love and who loves you. Trust me."

"Why'd you marry Louis?" I said.

She laughed without humor. Awful sound. "That's a story I've never told anyone. Not once."

"Letting it out will be cathartic. And my lips are sealed."

Another sniff. And a cruel smile. "Louis was in the right place at the right time during my...rebellion. I let a sweaty fraternity brother at UVA impregnate me in '82. His name was Carl. *Carl.* I panicked. I'd met Louis the year prior, through friends. I knew he was queer and that he was destined for money and a mildly prestigious career as a physician. I also knew he needed a wife. My mother and father, on the cusp of disowning me, approved of the union. Especially after I told them Louis knocked me up. He did his best. He still does. Treats me with respect. Raised our son like he's his own. Or he tried."

"Would you do it over again?"

Her mouth pressed into a grim line. Her face was without blemish, the beneficiary of botox injections and dermaplaning and fillers. She had fewer wrinkles than I did.

"My lifestyle is comfortable."

"Are you—"

"But my son moved away. He refuses to talk to his father.

Louis, I mean. I have few friends. My husband is not in love with me. I think his career is ludicrous. My family disowned me anyway. But…it's all I have, Mr. August. And you're trying to take it away. What would we…would *I* do? You don't understand. I'm invisible. You're male and young and beautiful, so you can't… Who am I? I'm nothing other than the wife of Dr. Louis Lindsey. People don't even see me. When I was younger I was beautiful. I was noticed. I had lovers. And now? Do you know what I am? Nothing other than the wife of a homosexual. Not even worth speaking to at the grocer."

I watched and listened and felt a little like Hugh Pratt. Hugh Pratt, the senior warden of his church's vestry, telling me on the phone that he wished he could solve everyone's problems but he didn't know how. To do his job, his focus had to remain narrow.

I had no succor to provide for Celia Lindsey.

She said, "Why are you doing this? He's gay, so what. Louis is causing no harm."

"The men accusing him of assault and battery have been harmed."

"Louis has lovers. He's human—I can't blame him, even if I hate him for it. That doesn't mean he assaults them," she said.

"You've been with him a long time, Celia. You've seen this before. Haven't you. This is not new behavior. You know the accusations are true."

"You're trying to take away everything from me."

"Did you know Jeremy Cameron spent a day in the hospital? At Louis's orders, Jeremy was jumped and beaten senseless. Because Jeremy stood up to him."

"You have no proof." She said it rote, as though she'd heard her husband use the line before. She knew to play defense.

"He's going to become invisible, Celia."

"Who?"

"Jeremy. Louis has the power to crush his career. No one will hire him ever again. He'll have to move and switch professions. You know how that feels, to become invisible. Jeremy will be destroyed. Disowned. But he did nothing wrong," I said.

"Then he..." She stopped to collect herself. To avoid showing any emotion. "Then he should stop telling lies. How can I not take it personally?"

"There's someone else who'll become invisible. Alec Ward. Do you know him?" I said.

"No."

"He's missing."

"I heard. I don't *know* him. But I know the story."

"Did Louis take him?"

"Of course not. The missing boy isn't at our house, don't be stupid," she said.

"I didn't say he was. Do you remember Jon Young? He was murdered a few years ago."

"Yes. I remember." Her voice had grown soft. The world reflected in her sunglasses.

"Do you think your husband, to maintain his secrets, to maintain his lifestyle, to keep his grip on everything, could kill someone?"

She opened her mouth but the words didn't come out. She paused a long time, staring straight ahead, watching through the sunglasses.

"No." A whisper. "Maybe. I don't know."

"You don't know."

"Loneliness, collected over the years, maybe even decades, is a powerful thing. An awful thing," she said. "Sometimes I feel insane. And later I feel numb. Loneliness and hurt make us do things and feel things we never imagined when we were young and beautiful. So I don't know the answer to your question, Mr. August. Maybe he could. And that should worry you."

"Why's that?"

"Because Louis is an obsessive man. And right now, one of his obsessions is you."

34

That evening I sat on my front porch and sipped a margarita made with fresh limes, Manny's Casamigos tequila, Grand Marnier, and blended ice. Why? Because vive la vida, that's why.

And I needed a strong drink to wash away the day's hurt.

Temperatures were in the fifties, possibly too chilly for a frozen drink. For lesser men. Beside me on the windowsill, Kix's monitor hissed quietly. Manny left earlier but he texted, said he'd return tomorrow morning. Timothy August was on a date with someone who should know better.

I rocked alone, watching the video of Louis Lindsey storm around the backyard of George Saunders, cursing and threatening everyone. The scenario on my phone screen was a testament to the power wielded by men like Louis. George or Dianne could have called the police but it never occurred to them. George's wife, despite her anger, was essentially hiding. Filming from the protection of her house. George, taller and stronger, huddled with his arms crossed like a scared little boy.

Louis's words hit like hammers, even slurred. His accusations were whips and I found myself wincing as I watched. Years in the pulpit had given him a stentorian voice and iron armor and fiery eyes.

Whoa.

Mackenzie August, a little dramatic. Slow down on the margarita.

Two cars motored by on Windsor.

I kept watching. The ending of the video intrigued me. Louis finished his rant and he was leaving, stumbling to the gate, but at the last moment he turned, as if to say, "And another thing!" but the video stopped. I might be imagining it—I dragged my thumb across to scrub one frame at a time. Slow motion replay. I convinced myself Louis had said more that Dianne didn't capture. A shame. It might've helped.

A man approached, walking the sidewalk across the street and whistling. Car keys bounced on his palm. Despite the late hour, and despite his good humor, he didn't strike me as drunk. I couldn't see his face; he wore an Atlanta Braves baseball cap.

I snorted. Braves. Those dummies.

He opened the door to a car parked on the street, one house down. Closed the door. The engine tried to turn over but failed. The telltale *ruh-ruh-ruh-ruh* of a dying battery, too exhausted to fully engage the starter.

The battery in my Accord was not exhausted. And I had jumper cables. And also, I was a good Samaritan.

No. A great Samaritan. The best Samaritan.

I set my phone down and met him on the street as he popped his hood.

"Dead battery," I said.

He looked up. "Sounds like it, huh."

"I got jumper cables."

"That'd be helpful," he said.

"I'm a great Samaritan."

"Great what? American?"

"Both, come to think of it."

He paused. Paused some more. And then.

Someone hit me in the back of the head. I'd been running my mouth, like a great American, and hadn't heard the approach. The someone caught me at the base of the skull. A shot crunching both bone and muscle.

Getting hit in the head activates all the senses. For reasons unknown, my head filled with the scent of a childhood kickball. Strong nostalgia, strong rubber odor, and I tasted it too. My ears rang. I saw red and white flashes.

The man behind wore brass knuckles. The searing imprint felt stronger than from a mere fist.

Guy in the Braves hat hit me too, put a right hook into my stomach. Not a great punch but I was out of sorts already. Grabbed my collar. Pivoted. Threw me into the side of his car.

"Don't know when to quit, do you," said Braves Hat. "You were warned, asshole."

He tried to hit me in the mouth, a left jab, but I rolled. He jabbed my shoulder instead.

Pressure built at the base of my brain. The world swayed. Streetlights burned and hissed in my eyes. I couldn't see well, but well enough to find the guy with brass knuckles. Much taller and broader than Braves Hat. Brass Knuckles was a black man; Braves Hat was white, maybe Italian.

Diversity in the workplace, I thought, was good.

Braves Hat tried again. He threw an ineffectual right, which I caught on my bicep. A result of luck and muscle memory, and I shoved him. It was a good shove; I was bigger than him, and he fell.

"You guys from the cable company?" I said.

It was funny and I'd be proud of it later. At the moment, the words hurt. Like shoving bricks into my ears. The big guy's sucker punch had been world class. Brass had torn skin and blood trickled down my spine.

Braves Hat got up. Glared at his partner. "The hell you doing? Hit the guy! What, you're too pretty?"

"I *did* hit him," said Brass Knuckles. "Give him the message and let's go."

I knew the voice. My access to memory, however, was disrupted. I squinted into the night.

"A sissy boy, you know that," said Braves Hat. Glared at both of us. He made fists and rolled his shoulders, like preparing for a title fight. "All muscle and a pretty face. No heart. A got'damn sissy."

"I almost took his head off, look," said Brass Knuckles. Big guy, but not a big voice. I knew him. Somehow. "Tell him and let's go."

"Message ain't properly delivered yet."

Braves Hat came on. He kinda knew what he was doing. He didn't loop or exaggerate his punches. He knew to keep his hands up, keep them in front, he knew to snap the fists. He knew to work quick. But knowing doesn't make one adept. The punches landed around my shoulders and neck without stopping power. No real damage done. Had my head been clear, I'd have broken his teeth already.

I tried to back up but his car was behind. Tried focusing. Saw double. I ducked a right and he hit my ear.

Brass Knuckles watched.

Braves Hat made a mistake; he stopped.

Put a finger in my face. "Know what's good for you, jackass, stop your got'damn investigation, understand me? Next time we—"

He was too close. I brought my foot up in a straight-leg kick. My shoe went between his legs; my knee connected solidly with his crotch. Not my best work. I'd bruised balls more effectively in the past. But it worked.

"Oh shit," he said. Or tried, but it came out a wheeze with smeared syllables. Getting hit between the legs is like being electrocuted—there's nothing to be done; no way to fight back, no way to alleviate the pain. You let it pass and hope you don't die in the wait.

He laid down and moaned more syllables at Brass Knuckles.

"This about Louis Lindsey?" I said.

Brass Knuckles nodded. "It's about Louis."

"Not very priestly of him, hiring guys like you."

"You gotta back down."

"Do I?" I said.

"Yup." He took a step closer. "Or I gotta hit you more. Get it?"

The ache in my head made my teeth and tongue throb but I had some fight. I moved away from the car, got my hands up.

"I shove the brass up your nose," I said, "it'll make your apology to Louis more embarrassing."

"Hell you will."

He looked better than Braves Hat. He had a longer reach, more muscle behind the fist. If I caught one of those in the chin or nose, fight was over. But I got the impression he was uncomfortable. Didn't want to do this.

The neighbor's dog started barking. Kept at it.

I moved sideways and back. Giving way. Hands up, ready to parry. My head still swam. Should probably run, but...

Death before dishonor, and all that.

Stupid Marine Corp, getting us gallant idiots killed.

With a clear head, my odds went up a lot. But I didn't have a clear head. Still I might be the favorite. Not my first rodeo.

We moved under a streetlight.

He paused. Leaned forward, seeing my face in the light.

"August?"

"That's me."

"Mack August? Ah shit." Said it like shee-yit.

"We know each other."

"Naw." He lowered his fists and backed up. "No you don't. Shit, he didn't tell me your name. Told me you were just some guy."

"Braves Hat said I was just some guy? Hurtful."

The neighbor's dog wouldn't shut up. The noise bounced around my head, red hot.

"Listen, August, I'm gone." Kept backing. "He didn't gimme a name. Sorry about...you know. We good."

"Who the hell are you?"

"We good? We're done. Aight?" He turned and moved quick. Ran.

I wanted to chase him down. But my head throbbed and the world swayed. His first punch had nearly removed my head.

Also, as he'd turned I got a decent view of his profile and I placed the face. Name was Russel. I'd find him tomorrow.

I stopped beside Braves Hat, still unrecovered. I lowered next to him and the redistribution of blood made my neck hurt worse.

His hands were between his thighs. I patted him for a gun. Found a revolver on his belt and I took it. He complained until I hit him in the nose. A sharp chop, connected sideways, like trying to take it off instead of shove it in.

A gout of blood spurted onto the street and he made a gurgling groan.

"The Braves? You deserve it. Come back," I said, "and I'll rip your ears off. Stick to bullying guys smaller than you."

I walked stiffly back to my porch. Finished the margarita in one drink.

The normally docile dog behind my house still howled. Last time the dog'd done that we had an intruder.

I checked the revolver. It was loaded. I stepped into my living room, let the door close softly behind. Cleared the main level.

Dog still baying. Head still throbbing.

Went upstairs, revolver held low and ready.

Rooms were empty; no one here. Kix slept, unaware his old man's head was splitting. I turned to go.

I spotted it then. My heart froze.

A pink toy was in Kix's crib. New. Not there earlier when I put him to bed. Someone had been in here. I picked the thing up. A stuffed goat.

Outside, the dog was losing energy. He'd seen an intruder. Warned the world but I'd been busy. The interloper was gone now, and so the dog ceased the siren.

I squeezed the toy and fumed.

A goat? What on earth.

35

I immediately burned the toy goat on my grill. Nothing sinister inside, no cameras, no needles. I gave Kix a thorough examination; he was fine.

Louis was the intruder. Had to be. He'd waited until I left the porch to offer jumper cables and he snuck in. Sonofabitch went into my kid's room. Watched us fight through the blinds.

Sonofabitch went into my *kid's room*.

Louis was an old pro at stalking. He would've worn gloves, or else touched nothing. He hadn't been in the house long. A few minutes at most. I scanned everywhere, looking for other *gifts*, but didn't find anything.

Timothy August came home, pink and pleased from his date. I didn't tell him about our intruder. I swallowed Tylenol and took an ice pack to my room.

I slept. But not with any grace or bravura.

The next morning, Kix quietly ate bananas and dry cereal and he watched Paw Patrol. I drank coffee and plotted murder.

Manny returned without fanfare. His shirt was torn, his

jacket missing. A bruise swelled under his eye and his lip was cut. Scratches and burns everywhere, like he'd been dragged. He got coffee and said, "Ay, migo. Back of your head is bloody. What happened to you?"

"Me? Happened to you?"

"There was a bad man. Needed apprehension."

"Just one? By your appearance, he must've been a ninja. Or Darth Vader," I said.

"He was resilient."

"Ah."

"Hear that? Resilient. Good, right?" said Manny.

"Sure. For a kid in seventh grade, that's a good word."

"Somebody hit you in the head?"

"Russel Devine."

"You're joking," said Manny.

"I am not."

"Muscle Russel picked a fight with you?"

"Eighty percent sure. It was dark. He didn't know it was me."

Manny sat at the table. He tried to laugh at me but it made his face hurt so he quit. Even battered, Manny's good looks bordered on cartoonish. "You hit him back?"

"He realized his error and took off before I could."

"Russel mugs people now?"

"He was sent by Louis to scare me," I said.

"Bet it didn't work."

"It did not. I am more angry today than I was yesterday."

Manny sipped coffee. "Muscle Russel maybe moved to Mexico by now. Always been scared of you."

"While he pushed me around, Louis came inside. Left a toy in Kix's crib. Least I assume it was Louis."

Manny lowered the mug. "Louis came into my house?"

"Our house."

"Ese cagaleche entró en mi casa?"

"*Our* house. And that's not a sensitive name to call someone," I said.

"Mierda, Mack. We gotta kill him now."

"Might. I need to visit Muscle Russel Devine. Make sure I got my facts straight."

"Sí. Then we kill Padre Louis."

"First I need him to tell me and the police what he knows about Alec Ward," I said.

"He broke the rules. Came into my house."

Our house. Jeez, said Kix.

Muscle Russel Devine got occasional work as a fitness model. He had bulk in the right places, made for a good photograph. But most days he worked at a junkyard in the morning, ripping cars into pieces for parts and scrap. A legitimate business that sometimes serviced unsavory clients. In the afternoons he worked out at a local mixed martial arts dojo and gym. He helped manage the place in the evenings, every other day.

We drove by the junkyard but he was gone. Found him at the gym.

The place wasn't fancy, just free weights and a ring. No locker rooms, no saunas, no machines. Meant for fighters. A couple guys were at a bench press near the front.

Russel Devine was in the back, at the fighting ring. His feet were up, ankles crossed. Bright pink sneakers and a matching Nike tank. He was eating a salad with chicken. Talking with two other guys.

He saw me and Manny approaching and he lowered the fork.

"Ah shit," he said. Like shee-yit.

"Russel. Easier to see you in the daylight," I said.

Manny wondered, "That a racial thing?"

"It is not. It is a vision thing."

Russel had two friends with him. There for support; I'd been expected. I knew them, they knew me. Some mutual respect existed. They kept their eyes on Manny, not pleased with his presence.

My head still hurt but the pain was a tight angry ball at the base of my skull, instead of a big dull ache. I pointed beyond the ropes. "Into the ring, Russel."

Russel Devine was taller than me by an inch. Good breadth of shoulders. His arms were covered with tattoos and burned designs that were airbrushed out of marketing photos. He wore colored contacts that made his eyes bright green. "August, don't be an jerk. I tole you. They never gave me your name."

"Into the ring, Russel. Get on your gloves."

"I apologized. Last night. We good."

"We good?" I said.

"Fine, aight, you can hit me back. One time."

"Get your gloves."

"Hey, stupid and more stupid," said Manny and he nodded at Russel's two friends. "Go sweat somewhere else."

"Maybe we stick around, Manny," said the first guy. Around town he was called Johnny Roofer. Because, get this, he helped put on roofs in the winter.

Manny pulled his marshal badge. Walked in real close. Pressed the silver badge into Johnny Roofer's cheek. Hard. Manny's other hand was on the butt of his Glock. He pressed until Johnny's head was against the wall, his lips smushed together. The other guy watched; most guys steered clear of Manny the Marshal.

"Johnny Roofer, you didn't hear?"

He had a hard time answering. "Marshal—"

"Johnny Roofer, you didn't hear me? I said go sweat somewhere else. You breaking probation? You behind on child support? You want me to beat you with my pistol? Want to spend a couple days in jail? Cause it looks like you do."

"Marshal, we cool. We're leaving," he said. Through his mushed lips, it came out, *arshaw, ee coo. Ee eevin.*

"Shit," said Russel again, watching the betrayal.

I got into the ring. Took off my jacket and gun. Placed them in the corner, and I pulled on gloves. Russel's two friends moved to the far side of the gym.

"You acting a jerk, August," said Russel. "Why you doing this?"

"So you don't get to tell anyone you hit me and got away with it, Muscle Russel."

"I'm not telling nobody."

"This goes deeper. And you know it," I said.

"Deeper?"

"You need to know. I need to know. The guys watching need to know. And then they need to tell everyone. You don't hit Mackenzie August in the back of his head."

Manny, watching at the wall, said, "You use third person now?"

"I'm angry and I have a headache. Not thinking clearly," I replied.

"Ah."

"Get your gloves on, Russel."

"August! Knock it off. I got a shoot coming up, I can't be boxing."

"I'll wear gloves. You don't have to. Makes it fair," I said.

"You don't get in this ring right now, I'll come out and beat you worse."

He ducked into the ring and made an unhappy grunt. "I ain't a fighter, August."

"What about last night?"

"I tole your ass, I didn't know it was you. Times are tough, I needed some extra scratch. I model. I don't box. This isn't fair, August," he said. With great and overflowing misery.

"Neither is hitting someone in the back of his head, Russel. Get your hands up." I'd been angry for hours, adrenaline already hot and flowing. I closed the distance. He didn't move, hoping a preemptive surrender would save him.

"August—"

Quick left, popped him on the nose.

"Gonna be a long few minutes, you don't get your hands up," I said.

He grabbed his nose. "*Gee*-zus."

Hit him a left-right. The right was a tight hook, flush against his jaw.

Wearing brass knuckles, with the element of surprise, Muscle Russel could square up against me. Now, in the light of day, no chance. He wasn't stupid; he was banking on me not beating the hell out of someone who refused to fight back.

He spat some blood. "August, you sumbitch, now my nose's gonna swell. I don't do this stuff."

"You just sucker punch at midnight?"

"I said sorry! We good now! Okay? The hell else you want—"

Hard left into his stomach. Another right hook. His head snapped back and he fell onto his butt. Rolled to his side and held his face. Doing his best impersonation of a woebegone loser.

"This isn't much fun, Russel."

"You knocked my teeth loose, dammit."

"Get up. Try to hit me back."

"No. We good, so you can go to hell, August."

"You talk," I said, "and give me answers I want to hear about Louis, I'll stop."

"Cause I'm a damn snitch?"

"Cause you don't wanna get hit anymore. And we'll talk quiet so no one hears," I said. "Louis sent you."

"This stays between us, August."

"Sure."

"I mean it. I ain't repeating a word to the police or anyone else. I'll spend the weekend in jail first."

"Yeah yeah." I made a *hurry up* gesture.

"Louis talked to Hazel. Said a guy needed to learn a lesson. Hazel asked me to tag along." He sat up, still holding his mouth together.

"Hazel? Guy in the Braves hat is named Hazel?"

"His real name's...I don't know, August. We call him Hazel."

"You're gay, Russel. That right?"

"You already knew that. Not exactly a secret, is it," he said. "So?"

"Louis's gay too."

He chuckled and stood up. Held the rope for support. "Thought *that* was a secret. At least from ugly straight people, like your ass."

"Hazel, too? That how you three know each other?"

"Yeah. Pink Mafia."

"Pink Mafia?" I said.

Manny, close enough to listen, made a snorting noise.

"What? You jealous?" said Muscle Russel. "We'd let you in, Marshal. Trust me."

"Louis is a member of the Pink Mafia." I said it out loud. So weird I needed to hear it. "Secret group for gay men?"

"Obviously. And you can't join. Just Manny."

"Manny's straight," I said.

"Still."

"Louis hired you to beat up the kid?"

"What kid?" said Russel. His nose made a honking nose when he talked.

"He's a friend of mine. Jeremy Cameron, Saturday night. Ended up in the hospital."

"Ah hell, August, I didn't know," he said.

"So you did."

"Me and Hazel. But Hazel did the work, mostly."

"Louis talk to you about abducting someone?" I said.

"Like kidnapping? No. I don't do that shit."

I glared at him. Gave him the good stuff. "You think Louis kidnapped Alec Ward?"

"Who?"

"Alec Ward. Good looking boy, still in high school."

He frowned some. Touched his swelling lip with his tongue. "No he didn't. That's offensive, August. Being gay doesn't mean you a pedophile."

"I didn't say it did. I'm not asking about an entire group of people. I'm asking about one man."

"No. No kidnapping. Father Louis doesn't hurt anyone," he said.

"Yeah? My friend Jeremy Cameron spent the night in a hospital."

"I said Louis doesn't. Didn't say nothing about Hazel."

"Louis paid you."

"Paid Hazel and Hazel paid me. But that ain't why we did

it. Father Louis's part of the Pink Mafia. We help each other. 'Sides, who cares about Jeremy Cameron. The sumbitch is a snitch."

I pulled off the boxing gloves. "I care."

"Why."

"Because he's willing to tell the truth. Even when it hurts."

"The jerk's a snitch, August. He's trying to out someone. Trying to ruin Louis's life."

"He's not *outing*. He's fighting a predator."

"Predator." Russel said it with a mocking smile. "Grow up, August. Two consenting adults."

I thought about hitting him again. I'd enjoy the crunch his nose made more without gloves.

I said, "A married supervisor hitting on an underling who wishes he'd stop? That's a predator, Russel."

"Wishes he'd stop?"

"Louis's sexual advances are not welcome."

He shook his head. "Not what I hear."

"You heard it from a tainted source."

"Maybe. Maybe not." He took a step away and slid out of the ring.

"It's not just Jeremy Cameron. Multiple persons are accusing him of sexual harassment. Is that acceptable in the Pink Mafia?" I said.

"Course not. We aren't perverts. We a support group."

I slipped between the ropes to leave. "I'm taking him down, Russel. He's a predator and he's gonna pay. Stay clear. You get it?"

"You got proof Father Louis molested some people?"

"Yep."

"Damn. Aight, sure, I get it." Russel moved in front of a mirror and looked at his nose. "Listen, August, for real, sorry about last night. We good. And about the kid we jumped, you know? Won't happen again. We thought we were protecting someone."

"And the abducted boy?"

"I swear on my mother's grave. That ain't the Pink Mafia."

"Ask around. I need answers."

"I hear something, I'll call you. Or maybe I'll call Manny," said Russel.

I headed for the exit. Manny joined me and said, "Not a very exciting fight."

"You go hit him then," I said.

"Meh. Not my type."

36

The local WDBJ7 news update on Fox Sports Radio mentioned Alec Ward's Amber Alert and gave a number to call with leads. He was still missing; nothing had 'popped' yet.

The subsequent weather update stated the oncoming nor'easter would develop near the coast and then move inland. Roanoke would be hit hard, starting Friday. Today was Wednesday.

If Alec Ward's abductor was the same guy that abducted Jon Young, and that was still a big *if*, then he might dispose of the bodies in a similar fashion—dumping them into the river and letting them be found downstream days later. And if the guy was smart, he would take advantage of the swollen waters inherent with a big storm.

Which meant maybe—maybe—Alec Ward had forty-eight hours to live. If he was still alive.

In my office, I left a message for Sheriff Stackhouse. She returned it an hour later.

I told her Muscle Russel had confessed; Louis hired goons to jump me and Jeremy Cameron.

"Can you prove it?" she said.

"No. Told Russel I wouldn't rat him out."

"This is law enforcement, babe. Not the damn virtue police. We lie all day long."

"I can't use him. I get a bad reputation and no one talks to me anymore," I said.

"You're worried about your reputation?"

"Only reason Russel told me in the first place is he trusts me. Called integrity, Sheriff."

"I gave that up years ago when I got the boob job," she said. "Why're you calling me then, if I can't use it?"

"I'm being collegial. Sharing information is wise. Maybe you should write that down, I'm giving you pearls here."

"Proof. I need proof. His attorney would chew my ass and spit me out if I brought him all this stuff I can't prove." She took a deep breath in my ear. "I hope you're right about this, kiddo. You turn into a nutcase conspiracy theorist, I can't recommend you out anymore."

"Working on it."

"I didn't know Russel Devine did hits like this."

"He doesn't usually. Times are tough. Ever heard of the Pink Mafia?"

"Sure. They throw great parties," she said.

"Louis's a member."

"Not surprised. It's a good underground support group for guys like him. Guys still in the closet, I mean."

"Russel said the Pink Mafia wouldn't be involved in a kidnapping. Said they aren't violent."

"He's right, babe. Bunch of sweet guys, mostly. Never give me trouble. And I mean it about the parties. Best in Roanoke. Even you'd like them."

"*Even* me? I like parties."

"No you don't."

"No I don't."

I hung up and dialed Manny.

"You find Louis?"

"Sí. Left the church twenty minutes ago. Guess where he's been."

"Jail. Surrendered himself out of respect for me."

"He left church and drove slowly by your office. Then drove even slower by my house. I thought about shooting him then," said Manny.

"*Our* house."

"This guy's obsessed with one of us."

"He spot you?"

"Maybe. Hard to be coy in a neighborhood, *migo*."

"I bet he didn't. People are obtuse and they make mistakes when they're fixated."

"Like you with señorita Veronica?"

"No. Not like that," I said.

"Coy. You heard I said it? Coy's a good word."

"Where's Louis now?"

"Coy. I use it right?"

"Yes Manny. You are clearly the world's foremost authority in neurolinguistics and morphophonology."

"In Spanish I know a lot of big words. I just don't use them out of respect. Something for you to think about."

"Where's Louis?"

"At Sweet Donkey. With that guy again—Nicholas. I'll tail him a while longer then I gotta go arrest someone."

"Actually do what you're paid to do?"

"I don't get paid near enough for what I actually do, *migo*."

We hung up and I rubbed my forehead. Thinking about Nicholas McBride. The target of Louis's ongoing advances. I should've talked to him days ago but he's evasive. Clearly unwilling to give testimony. I needed to crack him somehow. While also being sensitive to the fact that this ordeal was already awful for him.

The stairs leading up to my office creaked and groaned. Multiple sets of footsteps.

Robert Wallace came in, followed by two other guys, one of which I knew. Robert didn't give a cautious or polite knock, just walked in. I liked that about him. He was dressed in steel-toe work boots, Dickies, and a flannel shirt. I was reminded again of an old brahma bull, shaggy and powerful.

"Mr. August," he said. "Need a moment of your time."

I stood. "You got it."

Robert inclined his head to the younger man, maybe forty, to his right. The younger man looked a little like Robert. "This is my nephew. Darrell. Son of my brother."

I shook hands with Darrell.

I shook hands with the other man, too. Friendly guy, shaved head. Shirt a little too tight across his protruding middle. A black man with great teeth.

He said, "You recognize me?"

"You're Omar Bell. Elected Roanoke's mayor last year."

His smile widened. "Mayor, and also proud parishioner of All Saints."

"August, I want you to listen," said Robert Wallace. "Listen to this story, and then we'll talk. Darrell works for me. Helps process lumber. Or he did, now he's in the office. Couple years ago, his foot gets crushed by two big oaks. Wasn't being careful. Those trunk sections weigh two tons each. Maybe more. Pulverized Darrell's foot."

Darrell verified the story by pulling up his left pant leg. His sneaker was attached to his leg by prothesis. Darrell said, "The pain was awful, Mr. August. I got depressed and addicted to Oxycodone. Tried to kill myself twice. Worst year of my life. The only reason I'm alive, Mr. August, is Father Louis. Uncle Rob told him about me, and he started visiting every week. Prayed for me. Convinced me to go to Mount Regis for rehab, and got the church to help pay for it. I'd be dead without him. He's a great man, Mr. August."

Robert Wallace kept his gaze on me during the story. He said, "I could bring a couple dozen just like him, August. Testify to the character of Father Louis."

"I too sing his praises, Mr. August," said Mayor Omar Bell. "Through his intervention and counseling, my marriage was saved. I haven't touched a drink or a woman other than my wife in five years. Father Louis is a saint, if you ask me."

"You get the point, August?" said Wallace.

"That a sexual predator can be good at his job? I never doubted it," I said.

Wallace's face darkened. "Father Louis isn't gay, August. You were hired to find him innocent."

"No. I was hired to discover the truthfulness of Jeremy Cameron's accusation. And he's telling the truth."

"That doesn't make *sense*. Father Louis is clergy."

"But more importantly, he's human," I said.

"You understand the Apostolic succession, August? We trace the lineage of our bishops back to the original apostles. Not just anyone can be clergy. It's a sacred and holy thing."

"Agreed. But it involves people; it's inherently flawed."

"Clergymen aren't like the rest of us," said Robert.

"Jeremy Cameron is clergy. Why is he exempt from your pedestal?"

"I didn't say they don't make mistakes. Cameron's still a boy."

"Jeremy—"

He spoke over me. "You were fired, August."

"Fired, but obstinate."

"You're tearing down All Saints."

"I'm protecting the people within," I said.

"You don't understand how hard it is to keep a church together. I've been tending the church for fifty years, and my family before that. It's the center of our community. We need it."

"The leader of your church is corrupt. And the blind accommodation and idol worship will corrode outward until the walls cave."

"You can't *prove* he's corrupt," said Wallace.

"Did you forget your church has a missing kid?"

Robert made an eye roll. "Father Louis didn't take Alec Ward."

Mayor Omar Bell said, "Mr. August, what do you want? What would it take for you to leave this alone?"

"A signed confession from Louis and big fat severance packages for Jeremy and Nicholas, so they can start over somewhere else."

"That's preposterous. You're a private detective. Probably licensed, I assume?"

"Proper as heck."

"Considering that you are no longer in the employ of All Saints, I find it disturbing you are still investigating Father Louis. Having him followed. Making unfounded accusations. Haranguing his wife on the street. This sounds suspiciously like harassment to me."

"Harass his ass all the way to a grand jury."

"Mr. August, you are to cease your investigation immediately. This very minute. Do you understand?" said the mayor.

"Yes and no."

"Yes and no?"

"Yes I understand, and no I won't."

"I'll pull your license and have the chief of police arrest you for harassment. Don't think I'll hesitate," he said.

I made a gasping noise.

He glowered. Terrifying.

He said, "I heard you were a smart-mouth jackass."

"Phrase you're searching for is, pithy with a formidable intellect. Trouble is, Mayor, those threats are not things you can do. They are cute threats only."

"Watch me."

"The chief might bring me in to placate you, sure. Maybe even shout a little. But that's all he's got. Besides, he owes me a few favors. This might not go your way."

I didn't tell him it would be impossible to do my job if the police hated me or if my reputation was ruined. He could conceivably wreck my career in the long run. If I hadn't done that myself already.

"You're a piece of shit, August," he said.

"I heard a rumor that your assistant makes more than you, Mayor. Is that true?"

"If we—" he said.

"It's true. I looked it up. Just wondered if you could admit it."

Robert Wallace's deep voice interrupted our pissing contest. "There's still time, August."

"Oh?"

"Father Louis retired to get you off his back. Because you were embarrassing him. He sacrificed himself for the good of our church. If you back down, maybe he'll return," he said.

"I like a lot of things about you, Robert. Including your

FJ40 and your determination to preserve what's noble and holy. But Louis Lindsey isn't a noble person. He's not who you think he is, despite the good he's done. The truth will come out soon. It's going to be rough. But necessary."

Robert's nephew Darrell leaned forward, his face a little red with anger. "Father Louis *is* a good man. I am alive because of it."

"Good deeds do not a good man make. You fellas ever cracked a Bible? Worship God, not men."

"Stop your investigation, August," said Wallace.

"No."

"Yes," said the mayor. "Yes you will."

"This is a fun circle we're going in."

For a dangerous moment I thought Wallace might come around the desk. He owned his own company, kinda ran the church, was used to getting his way. Looked like he wanted to cut me down like a tree. But the anger and fight passed like a rain cloud.

With unexpected hurt, he said, "You're ruining the church. And for some of us, the church is family."

He turned to go.

The mayor sniffed. "Life's gonna get hard on you, Mr. August, you keep this up. Maybe I can't arrest you, but I can ruin your reputation, got'damn it. Make sure everyone knows not to hire you again." And he followed Wallace to the door.

Last to go was Darrell, Robert's nephew. He moved with a limp to accommodate the prosthetic. His descent down the staircase was exaggerated and slow.

I remained standing. My head hurt and I felt rotten.

Mackenzie August. Ruiner of families.

37

The next morning I didn't leave the house early like I usually do. Instead I sat on my couch and stared blankly at the television while Kix stacked blocks in his playpen.

Before my father left, he stood fixing his tie at the mirror near the front door. "One of the teachers at Crystal Spring Elementary attends All Saints. She asked me if I was the father of the detective trying to ruin her church."

"Ouch."

"That's what I thought."

"What'd you tell her?"

"I said my son doesn't ruin things, especially not churches." He picked up his leather satchel and paused at the door. "Was I correct?"

"Verdict's still out."

"Son, apparently a lot of people aren't happy with you. You're toppling a celebrated treasure. Are you taking this case too personally? Are you causing needless and irreparable damage to your career?"

"Ask me again in a week."

He inspected me like he would a troublesome third grade student. Declined to speak further. And left. There was education to administer.

Manny was at the marshal's office. He was a deputy marshal and there were criminals to apprehend.

And me? I was an investigator. And there was coffee to drink and families to ruin. Churches to crush. Careers to damage. Lives to destroy. Potentially my own, if I was wrong about this.

At the moment, my job made my stomach churn.

Kix's block tower collapsed. He glared at the mess and then at me.

Your self-pity is off-putting.

"I am being melodramatic, Kix. Do you mind?"

In fact I do. It is beneath you.

"I have earned a few minutes of despair."

Clock's running. Hurry it up.

I pulled out my iPhone. No pertinent messages waited. No clues. No confessions.

I punched up the video of Louis rampaging through George and Dianne Saunders's backyard. He stormed about, swilling wine, until the video ended.

I needed to speak with Nicholas McBride. Should've done it days ago. But his was another life that could be ruined. Nicholas had admitted the abuse to Jeremy. But refused to talk with the vestry. Why?

Fear. He had a family to feed, a wife and baby.

But it was more than fear. His account along with Jeremy Cameron's would be enough to force action. Two testimonies were powerful. Nicholas wouldn't be acting alone; because of Jeremy, he would be believed. He wouldn't lose his job. So why did he let Jeremy face the terror alone?

I watched the video again. Louis shouting. George Saunders hunched, arms crossed. Embarrassed at the madman in his backyard.

That was it, wasn't it. Nicholas was embarrassed. I knew Jeremy was. Nicholas would be too, obviously. Embarrassed by the attention. And potentially by his own behavior? One reason Nicholas might be more embarrassed than Jeremy Cameron was if he'd done things that warranted greater scrutiny and scorn. The victims of abuse often did, at least in their own eyes.

I thought about this. Stewed over what I knew concerning predators and prey. Watched the video again. George Saunders, hunched, was embarrassed because of his sexual history with this man. Because he'd been complicit in the past. A past he wanted to forget but Louis wouldn't let him.

George Saunders wanted Louis caught but didn't want to expose himself to the scrutiny. To the potential humiliation and shame.

Was this true of Nicholas? Did he want Louis caught but didn't want to expose himself or his family to scrutiny and shame? How far had his relationship with Louis gone?

The video ended as it always did. Louis was about to leave but then he didn't; he turned back, and the video stopped. So frustrating. I needed to know what Louis said next. A terrible time to cease recording.

Or was it?

Maybe it wasn't terrible, maybe it was intentional. In fact, maybe she hadn't stopped filming but she'd gone back and edited the video to make it appear so. She edited out the things that she didn't want me to hear. Or that her husband didn't want me to hear.

That made a lot of sense.

She'd privately admitted her husband's past to me.

The way Nicholas privately confessed to Jeremy.

Both done out of the public eye. To remain hidden.

She'd given me the video but nothing on it was damaging, because she worried it might get passed around. Which is exactly what I'd done, like a nitwit.

There was more of the video. I was suddenly certain.

I needed to see the rest.

I stood.

"Kix," I said. "I have a plan."

George's truck and Dianne's minivan were parked in the driveway. Luck was on my side.

Wind swirled down the street and clouds scudded overhead. The radio informed me the Canadian cold front would pass through soon, headed toward a fateful crash with warm air on the coast this evening. The resultant storm would expand and reach us not long after. The nor'easter, they said, would be a doozie.

I knocked on the front door and Dianne answered it, her mouth a grim line.

"You," she said.

"Sorry."

"I'd rather you not be here."

"I get that a lot. May I come in anyway?"

"Why?"

"I need help," I said.

"I already helped you. We saw Louis's retiring. Isn't that enough?"

"You tell me."

She didn't respond other than to narrow her eyes. It was not a look meant to make me feel good.

I said, "You helped me. But I need you to help someone else."

"Oh good Lord."

"Let me ask the question," I said, "before you give the answer. And if the answer is No, I'll leave."

"We say No to Louis, but he doesn't leave," said Dianne.

"I'm not like Louis."

She pushed the door wide. "Oh fine. Come on."

I stopped inside the front room, their television room. Dianne was wearing socks and sweat pants and a long t-shirt. No makeup. Laundry waited to be folded in the corner. George stood in the kitchen, watching us, carrying the baby. George was in jeans and a Home Depot shirt, barefoot.

"Make it quick and then leave," said Dianne. "We're trying to forget this shit."

"There's more to the video than what you showed me," I said. It was a guess. But a good one.

Her back straightened. Chin up. Defensive.

"No there's not. And if there was, it wouldn't be your business."

"There's someone who needs your help. Another man in the same situation as George. He has a wife. And a young baby."

George said, "Who? Maybe I know him."

I held up my phone. On the screen was a picture of Nicholas McBride. Sharing this with them wasn't ethical. Or fair. But I'd potentially already ruined my career and reputation, and I was out of time.

Alec Ward was out of time.

I said, "You know him?"

"I do," said Dianne, getting a closer look. "That's what's-his-name. From church. The worship leader guy."

"Nicholas McBride. He's being sexually abused by Louis."

The air seemed to go out of George. He set the baby into a high chair at the table. Gave the kid some dry cereal and came into the television room and sat down on his couch.

"Nicholas is afraid to admit it because he might get fired," I said. "Home Depot won't fire you. But the church might fire him. And he has a family."

George's head was down but he nodded.

"Well that's sad. I feel bad for Nicholas. But so what? I don't see how we help," said Dianne. "We got our own problems."

"If Nicholas confesses the abuse, potentially at great personal cost, Louis is finished. Louis will be defrocked, humiliated, cast out. The justice system will get involved."

"Oh," she said. "Well. That's something."

"But he won't confess."

"What's this got to do with our video?" she said.

George made a grunt. He stood up but didn't look at either of us. He scratched his left forearm. "Does Nicholas McBride know about me?"

"Not that I'm aware," I said. "Far as I know, Nicholas thinks Louis is abusing only him and Jeremy Cameron."

"Nicholas thinks he's alone. Or mostly alone," said George. "That's a bad feeling."

"You know about that, the loneliness."

"I do."

"He's embarrassed too."

"Yeah. He is." George bent to pick up a stuffed toy. A pink tiger. "Father Louis gave us this. Gave it to Bryan, our son. Said it reminded him of Dianne. I wanted to throw it away but Bryan cried without it. I hide it sometimes but Bryan looks for it. So now we're stuck."

Bryan was, in fact, watching the toy from his high chair. He munched on cereal with one hand and silently reached for the pink toy with the other.

George said, "Give him the whole video, Dianne."

"What! Why?"

"Cause it'll help Nicholas. Don't you get it?"

"No. What the hell should I get?" she said.

"He thinks he's alone. He hates himself, thinks it's all his fault. But he sees the video, he'll realize. It ain't all his fault. It's Father Louis's fault."

"The part of the video you cut out," I said. "Louis says things that'll humiliate your family. Right?"

Dianne wiped at sudden tears. "If people see that video, we might have to move."

"I know being gay ain't a reason to be humiliated," said George. "Nor is being abused. Nor is having a...dirty history. God forgives me. Dianne forgives me. I forgive myself. That's all behind me. Like I said, I know I shouldn't be embarrassed. *We* shouldn't be. But somehow, we will be anyway. If that video gets shown around."

"If you share it with me, I'll only show one person."

"Nicholas McBride," he said.

"Right."

"And he'll realize the truth. It ain't his fault. And maybe he'll be willing to take down Father Louis."

"And then you will delete the video," said Dianne and she poked me in the chest with her finger.

"Yes ma'am. Trust me," I said.

"Damn it." Dianne took the phone out of her pocket and shook her head. "Damn this whole thing. I'm sick of it."

"Hey, tell him," said George and he paused. He ran a hand through his hair and looked at the ceiling. Deep sigh. "Tell Nicholas. If he's willing to talk to the vestry, or whatever, or the police, then I will too. Tell them Father Louis won't leave me alone. Maybe it'll help."

"The message will be conveyed, George."

He handed the pink toy to baby Bryan. Bryan ate more cereal.

Behind me, the door shuddered and the wind whistled against the window. Air currents shifting direction.

The cold front was passing overhead.

38

My luck held. Louis's Audi wasn't in the parking lot at All Saints, but Nicholas McBride's car was.

No more running, Nicholas. The bell tolls for thee.

Temperatures had dropped fifteen degrees and a lesser man would've hurried from his car to the church's office. But not I. Real men freeze.

The reception area was small and warm. A small and warm woman smiled from her desk.

"Welcome to All Saints Episcopal Church, how can I help?"

"I didn't see Jeremy Cameron's car. He still at home with a ruined face?" I said.

"Um," she said, less warm. "He's not here today, that's true. Can I help with something?"

"Please alert Nicholas McBride. Mackenzie August is here to see him."

"Oh," she said. "Do you have an appointment?"

"I don't need no stinking appointment," I said.

"Sir—"

"Call his office. Tell him Mackenzie is waiting and it's going to get loud if he's not out here in sixty seconds."

Her hand paused above the phone. She looked a little frozen.

"Don't call 911," I said. "I know all those guys and they'll be irritated with us both. Tell Nicholas please."

She raised the phone, pressed a single button, and murmured into the receiver.

Nicholas arrived quick. He wore stylish duck boots, tight jeans, and a button-up cardigan. He had all his hair, kept shortish, going slightly gray but it added to his boyish charm. Sharp features. He didn't venture in. Stayed near the door leading to the staff offices.

"Mr. August, I'm swamped at the moment," he said. "If you make an appointment I can try—"

"You know who I am, Nicholas. We're having this conversation. And it'd be better to have it privately. Agree?"

He didn't respond. Glanced between me and the receptionist. I thought he was holding his breath.

Quietly the woman said, "Should I call the police?"

"I think," I said, "he'd rather speak with me, and not with them. Nothing needs to be public, Nicholas, until you're ready."

He took a deep breath. "Come to my office then."

I did. His desk was too large for the smallish room. In the corner a Martin guitar stood like a musical totem. His carpet was deep red and he'd chosen religious paintings on the wall to match. He sat. I sat. On the side of his neck, his pulse visibly raced.

"I know," I said.

He swallowed. "You know what?"

"I know about Louis. About Jeremy Cameron. About you. And about other persons Louis is hurting."

He leaned back in his swivel chair. His breathing sounded ragged and he stared at a spot on his ceiling.

"I don't know what you mean, Mr. August."

"Yeah. You do. Let me tell you what I know. I know coming forward with this stuff is almost impossible. It feels like weakness and betrayal. It's humiliating and I don't blame you for your reluctance. I understand why you've ducked me for almost two weeks. But I know the time for running and the acceptance of abuse is at an end."

He tried not to cry. Closed his eyes. Pressed lips together. A squeak emerged anyway.

"Jeremy Cameron got the hell beat out of him. His career verges on collapse. Louis will fire him soon. But he's still fighting. I got jumped too. Louis burgled my home. Guess what, Nicholas. You're next, if we don't do something."

"I can't..."

"The truth is, you don't *want* to. Because it'll hurt. But that's different than *can't*."

"Fine then. I won't." The words came out high and tight. "He warned me. Told me you would find me. Told me you were trying to break our careers. Said I'm not allowed to discuss this with you."

"Of course he said that."

I set my phone on his desk. The video was cued.

"This video was taken a few days ago," I said.

"I've seen it."

"Not all of it." I pressed play.

He didn't move. But he watched through half-closed eyes and he listened.

On screen, Louis rampaged and threatened and stormed off. But then he came back.

"*You and me, George. We had something. Something...something special.*" Sounded like sum'in smeshel. "*You left me. Left me! We were animals, George. Doing what our bodies told us. But inside it we found something special. How can you leave...how can you pretend it didn't happen?"*

Nicholas closed his eyes and made another squeaking noise. I wondered if he'd heard Louis use similar words before.

On the video, Louis described a couple of their nights together in graphic detail. His wine was gone and he pointed at George with the empty goblet. He used it as a lewd prop to demonstrate sexual congress and laughed at George's discomfort.

Nicholas heard enough. He slapped at the phone until it turned off.

"I don't want to listen to that," he said.

"I don't blame you."

"Show it to the vestry. Father Louis will be fired and that's that. You win. That's what you're after, correct?"

"I can't show it."

"Why not?" he said.

"I promised I wouldn't."

"But you have everything you need! Leave me out of it."

"The man in the video, George, he's embarrassed just like you. But he said he'll come forward if you will."

"Oh God." He placed both hands over his face. "Oh God."

"I understand the shame. But you've got to realize it's a lie, Nicholas. You were preyed upon."

"You don't...you don't understand," he said. I worried he might hyperventilate.

"Maybe not. Let me guess. You want him to stop. Except some days, when you doubt yourself and you doubt everything else, maybe there are times when you don't want him to. You don't know why. Everything started normal. You admired him. He was wise and kind, and you became better friends. Somewhere along the way, you savored the approval and friendship so much that you pretended the growing intimacy wasn't inappropriate. The feelings were weird but everything got jumbled and mixed together. The lines blurred between friendship and desire. It was all one big overpowering emotion and you didn't know how to resist. And when you tried to, it was too late and you found you didn't know how. He said he needed you. More and more, and on deeper levels. You found yourself doing things or saying things that humiliate you. But you didn't stop. The most shocking part, you enjoyed some of it. You're angry at how malleable you were. And now you're stuck and broken and there's no way out."

His face was in his hands. His entire body seemed to be flexing and shaking.

I said, "Even now, your emotions are conflicted. You dare to hope for relief. But you're scared. For yourself and for him. You're angry at me, angry at Jeremy, but you know you shouldn't be. Probably on some level you can't grasp, angry at your wife. But it can all start to go away. Beginning today."

"I can't...I can't make him stop," he said.

"I can."

"He'll be ruined."

"That's the plan."

"I'll be ruined. My family..."

"Don't count your chickens yet. We can work on that."

"He...he has evidence that we..."

"Tell me about the evidence," I said.

He looked up with red eyes. Raised his hands. "Nothing's happened. Between Father Louis and me. It's all... emotional. But there's a trip soon and..."

"Tell me about the evidence."

"He bought me a burner phone. Makes me text him every night before bed. He asked me to text him encouragement. Then he changed it to...texting things I liked about him. I told him I didn't want to, but he demanded it. So I did, for weeks. Then he asked me to compliment his appearance. That's where we are now. He writes me emails that...they aren't...they appear to be innocent at first glance. Just innuendos. You know? But then they started getting worse and worse. I delete them. When we're alone, he's affectionate. But so far, nothing...he hasn't raped me or anything, I mean."

"Maybe not you. Chances are, you and Jeremy aren't the first. I know of at least one more. Probably others in his wake."

"We don't know for sure."

"Trust me."

"But—"

"If we go forward with your testimony and the record of your texts and his emails, he's toast," I said.

"I don't want to."

"I understand that."

"I have a wife. She'll be destroyed if she reads the things I've said. If she sees the things he's written to me," said Nicholas.

"I'm no expert on marriage. But seems to me, she has a right to know. And if you want a healthy union for the rest of your life, you can't hide it from her."

"Is there no way to do this without me having to come forward and spill everything?"

I heaved a sigh. A long and profound and thoughtful sigh.

"I was hired to prove Jeremy Cameron is telling the truth. I have collected enough evidence to do that. Handily.

Between you, Jeremy Cameron, George, George's video, the Pink Mafia—"

"The what?"

"—I have oodles of evidence. And I could find more. Trouble is, I keep promising you guys I won't use it."

His smile was commiserate. "Very noble of you."

"I'm a softy who likes a challenge."

My phone buzzed. An incoming message. I read the note—it was encouraging. I remained calm. Would deal with it soon. Slipped the phone back into my pocket.

Nicholas said, "Father Louis is going to retire, you know. This will all go away...?"

"Good men don't sit around and wait for evil to go away, Nicholas."

He flinched.

I said, "You don't have a year. You have a sinister trip with Father Louis coming up soon."

"Maybe I could—"

"Alec Ward doesn't have a year. He has days. Maybe less."

"You think Father Louis took Alec Ward?" he said.

"I do."

"No way. Trust me, Mr. August. He's not like that."

"He had Jeremy Cameron half killed. He hired men to attack me. Don't defend him, Nicholas. It is unbecoming."

"I didn't—"

"The police have no leads. I have one, so I'm chasing it hard. And I have an idea of a way to procure evidence against Louis I can actually use," I said.

"You do? How?"

"If you rattle someone, they make mistakes. I want to scare Louis. Spook him. See if he errs. If he does, we'll apply enough pressure to get a confession out of him. Enough to save Alec Ward."

Nicholas nodded. Looked unsure.

I said, "For it to work, you can't alert Louis."

"I wouldn't!"

"Yes you would. You're compromised. He has tentacles in you. But you can't."

"I won't," he said.

"Where is he?"

"It's his personal day off. We never know where he goes. What's your plan?"

"I'm told you two meet in the mornings for coffee."

"Yes. Tomorrow morning, in fact."

"Perfect. You're going to skip the meeting. And instead go to the gym."

His countenance fell like a chastised dog.

"Father Louis won't like that. He gets possessive."

"Nicholas, my boy," I said. "I'm counting on it."

39

Louis's wife Celia sat in a swinging bench on her front porch and watched the maelstrom approach. Her face was blank and she wore a small white dress, like a bride in mourning. I parked in the driveway.

"I knew you'd come," she said, very soft, as I came up the wooden steps. She didn't look at me. "Even if I didn't want you to, not really."

"Where's Louis?"

"You think he tells me where he's going? Probably a truck stop."

"He frequents those?" I said.

"No. It is the slow ruination of innocence he enjoys, I think. For him, sex is more than carnal."

"True for all of us, Celia. Your text message said you could help me but didn't explain how."

"You are still investigating, I hear."

"I am."

"And?"

"Tomorrow's an important day. If it doesn't go right, your husband will ruin lives because of jealous rage," I said.

"Mine's been ruined for decades."

"He might kill a teenager."

"He wouldn't. Louis doesn't have the balls for it."

"You know what it means to be invisible," I said. "It's a crushing and helpless feeling. If Louis gets his way, no one will hire these kids again. Their livelihoods will be ruined. One of the guy's married with a kid."

"Nicholas, you mean. They're doomed for failure."

"Not yet. You gave up a long time ago. His wife hasn't. Tell me why you texted."

"Why are you still trying? I don't understand. Your services were terminated. You should be invisible too."

"Not everyone cares about the victims. Hardly anyone cares about the snitch. But I do."

"Trying to save yourself, Mr. August?" A bitter mocking smile. Could have learned it from her husband. "So you don't become invisible. Save yourself, along with everyone else?"

"Maybe on some level."

"Who am I kidding. You're a man. A handsome one, and you'll age well. You will never be invisible."

I spread out my hands, like—why am I here?

She still wasn't looking at me. "Perhaps, Mr. August, as you said, on some level I'm trying to save myself." She stood. Smoothed her dress and placed a hand on the door knob. "Let me show you something. Let me show you how deeply mad my husband is."

She led me inside.

The carpets were two decades out of style. The walls were papered. She'd decorated the corners and surface tops with pottery and porcelain knickknacks. No plants, no photographs. The home of the wealthy and the lonely.

I followed her downstairs, through an unfinished

hallway with low ceilings, and into a hidden office. Cramped but richly furnished.

"I'm not allowed in here, you understand," she said. "But sometimes I profane his holy temple for spite."

The room smelled faintly like the musty basement of a hundred-year-old house, but more like incense and furniture polish and good leather. A Bible was open to the New Testament on a side table. Next to the book was a vial of cocaine. On the wall, a wooden crucifix. Below it, a framed photograph of Louis with his arms around the neck of his son.

I had the creeps. A room of warfare, and the soul of Lindsey was the prize. Also, if this was an ambush it was a good one—no one outside would hear gunshots.

"This book," she said and she placed her hand on a leather binder next to Louis's laptop. "This will make your toes curl, Mr. August."

I flipped it open. The book was filled with printouts of emails. The first page was dated fifteen years ago. I didn't recognize the email addresses. Within a few sentences it become a love note. I flipped the page. The next email was less a love note and more a short story of debauchery. The third page contained a lewd photograph of a man tied in bondage straps and smiling.

"Louis prints them and deletes the digital copy. So even if you subpoena for the records, the evidence is long gone," she said.

And yet, I thought, it was also under my fingers. My shaking fingers.

"Take what you like, Mr. August." She paused to pick up the vial of cocaine adjacent to the Bible. She smiled, shook it a little, and slipped it into her dress. "Maybe the things in this office will help you. I always liked Jeremy and Nicholas. Even if Nicholas's wife is a bitch."

"When does Louis return?"

"Your guess is as good as mine, Mr. August. You should hurry. Also, on his laptop, you'll find a folder marked *Scripture*. It's not scripture. It's full of photographs he takes with a high-powered camera. Photographs of his obsessions. Never...never of me. Who knows, maybe you'll find yourself."

She left. The stairs made no noise as she ascended, she was so thin.

I stared at the plethora of evidence before me. Few men were less fit for a Christian clergy collar, I thought. He had dozens, maybe hundreds, of lovers beyond the boundary of his marriage vows. How much of Louis's cybersexual *historia* involved harassment? I didn't have time to peruse. Nor the inclination. I hadn't been hired to humiliate someone. Would any of this be admissible in court? Maybe if I had an attorney with a sterling reputation with the judge...

The binder of Louis's escapades was arranged chronologically, so I flipped to the back. Found a couple pages from Nicholas that I ignored momentarily. Kept looking, kept scanning...but saw nothing that struck me as originating from Alec Ward.

I didn't want to take any evidence that would arouse Louis's suspicion. Ideally he'd walk into the office and notice nothing amiss. But also I wanted to remove any notes written by Jeremy or Nicholas that Louis could use to ruin them. Would he notice the theft? Maybe, but only on close inspection and I had to take the risk. I removed three emails from Nicholas. I searched backwards until 2015 but saw nothing related to Jeremy Cameron. Thank God.

I'd been here too long. Time to go.

Mackenzie August getting a little antsy. And Celia had been right—my toes were curling.

On the computer, I located the file marked *Scripture.* I opened it and found hundreds of photos. Far too many to search through. Did I need to? Would any of this help?

Maybe not. But it'd be nice for the police to see, if it came to that.

I found an old flash drive in his bottom drawer. Dusty, hadn't been used in years. I plugged it in and copied the photos to the flash drive and pocketed it.

On the way out, Celia said, "Goodbye, Mr. August. I hope we never meet again."

Which, I thought, was hurtful.

40

Alec Ward was experiencing the initial effects of white torture. He knew this because of a recent unit in his modern history class, where he learned about interrogation techniques around the world. The isolation and sensory deprivation had settled deep into his bones. He experienced loneliness and confusion so pervasive that sometimes he forgot what he looked like. Frantic minutes passed while he fought to remember his mother's name. If he opened his eyes, the dizziness was overpowering and he would dry heave.

A more appropriate term would be black torture. He was in a dark room underground; not a white room, like he'd learned about at school. He wasn't being interrogated. He felt forgotten.

He was thirsty again. He'd been hungry for two days.

His only companions were the flies and insects that penetrated his bunker to inspect the bucket of urine.

Today, however, as he surfaced from unconsciousness, he realized he wasn't alone. The muffled echoes of the room were different. His scuffles caromed into the corner and died there.

A man was with him. Silent and unmoving.

Alec recoiled but was too disoriented to speak for a full minute. When he did, his voice sounded like a frog's and the words were unintelligible.

The man in the corner twitched. And stood.

"You're awake," he said. "Good. I brought water and food."

If Alec had been in a more sane frame of mind, he'd note the man's voice was thick with emotion. He'd been crying.

Alec croaked again.

"This was supposed to be simple," said the man. "I wish you weren't still here. But he won't stop, so what am I supposed to do? I won't do nothing."

Alec cowered from the enormous voice. His shoulder bumped against the water bottles.

"I have to kill him," said the man, still sad and angry. "I don't want to. But he's blaspheming. He brought it on himself."

Alec didn't understand. After the prolonged silence, the words sounded like ear-splitting thunder in his ears.

A door opened. Cold air rushed in. Some of the flies escaped.

Outside, rain didn't actively fall but it had. The steps were slick and a rivulet of water overflowed the doorframe to trickle into Alec's dungeon.

The man watched the puddle and then looked at the sky devoid of stars. Heavier rain would fall. A lot of it.

"The rivers will swell. To wash away...our sins. And anything else." A pause and he repeated, "I have to kill him. Soon. Then it's over."

He closed the door and left Alec alone again.

41

Nicholas McBride sent Louis Lindsey a text stating he would not meet him for coffee and their personal relationship was over. He was taking the morning off to exercise at the gym and clear his head.

I crafted the text myself. It was an elite message. Obviously.

Nicholas arrived at Crunch Gym at nine in the morning and he hustled inside.

Louis Lindsey showed thirty minutes later. He circled the lot twice and found Nicholas's car near the back. He eased his Audi to a stop next to Nicholas's Civic.

The wind ripped off the last spring petals from the dogwood and cherry trees. Roanoke was being canvased by far-reaching bands of the big nor'easter, bringing intermittent bursts of downpour. The satellite picture looked like a hurricane. The center of the storm churned violently over the Chesapeake Bay, but strong wind and rain would extend into West Virginia and Ohio. Like all of Virginia, Roanoke would be walloped. It had poured last night, but at the moment the cold air howled with only scattered droplets.

Louis braved the wind. He stepped out of his Audi to glare into Nicholas's Civic. He tried the doors but they were locked. He marched for the Crunch Gym entrance, changed his mind, and returned. Checked his phone. Nicholas wasn't answering his calls. Wasn't responding to his messages. His face purpled in anger. He made another attempt on the gym, but discretion warned him off once more. Logic barely winning against a jilted lover's madness. He came back and slid into his Audi to wait.

An hour later, Nicholas emerged from the gym. He walked quickly, head down, hands shoved into his wind breaker.

He nearly reached the Civic, but Louis sprang his trap. Emerged from the Audi in all his sordid glory. Nicholas froze, ashen faced.

"Nicholas, stop."

"Father Louis, I—"

"I know Inspector August came to the church. I know you spoke with him alone, Nicholas. After I ordered you not to. He told you lies."

"Stay away from me, Father Louis."

"How long were you alone with him? You had your office door closed."

"That...that doesn't matter. I'm leaving."

"We must talk. About us," said the elder priest.

"*No*. We are colleagues and that's it."

Louis laughed. Cruel and mocking. "Don't be absurd, Nicholas. You feel much more than that. Don't give in to fear now."

Nicholas made a move for his car door. Louis lunged forward, his motions sudden and desperate.

"Nicholas, stop!"

"I'm leaving."

"He lied to you, Nicholas. Everything was fine, *we* were fine, until August began to pry. What did he say?"

"I won't have this conversation with you, Father Louis. Not here, not now. You need to back away."

"He's convincing, isn't he. He has the silver tongue of a serpent. You like the way he looks? You like him more than me?" said Louis.

"This is ridiculous."

"That's it, isn't it. You prefer him to me. Admit it."

"No. I don't prefer him to you."

"Love me." He said it in a whisper.

"What?"

"You love me, Nicholas. You told me so. It was a breakthrough and released you from the bondage that society drops on us."

"I..."

"And I love you. I need you," said Louis.

"I don't love you, Father Louis."

"That's dishonest. A deceit August has filled your head with."

"I only said things because you made me."

"Lies!" He shouted it, but they were alone in the parking lot. No one heard. "Lies from hell. You are deceived and you need my council. You need to be righted."

"No I don't think I do. I love my wife."

"No you... So *what*. She doesn't deserve you."

"I won't listen to this. I'm leaving."

"No! I need you, Nicholas. Please. I'm...I'm out of sorts. It's all crashing on me at once. It's spiritual warfare and I can't do it alone. The boy at our church is missing. My retirement. Celia and I aren't getting along. Inspector August is ruining my life. But you, Nicholas, are all I need."

"Do you know where Alec is?"

"Please, Nicholas. Get into my car and we'll talk."

"I'm going home. Back up or I'll hit you."

"You'll *hit* me." Louis said it with a sneer. His persona swung between anxious paramour and stern mentor. "You'll hit me. Are you sure you want the police involved? Are you sure you want them to see what you wrote to me? Get in the car, Nicholas."

The clouds rushed overhead. A strong gust pushed both men off balance and the sprinkling increased.

"I'm not getting in your car," said Nicholas.

"Your career depends on it."

"What do you mean?"

"You know what I mean," said Louis. "We hold each other's future in our hands."

Nicholas didn't reply. Louis pressed his attack. He spoke louder over the storm.

"I'll leave her, Nicholas. I'll leave Celia. I swear I will."

"Why?"

"Because I love you. That's why."

He stepped closer to Nicholas. Close enough to touch.

The Chevy Malibu I sat in had tinted windows. During his wait, Louis hadn't seen me from his Audi two spots away. Partially because I'd been reclined.

I sat up, opened the car door, and stood. My camera still pointed at them, recording. It had been for six minutes.

The shock nearly knocked out Louis's knees. He placed a hand on the Civic for support. Nicholas looked as though he released a breath he'd been holding for an hour.

"Thanks for shouting," I said. "You're a director's dream. Easier to hear."

Louis and I locked eyes, and he knew. He'd been caught and I had it on video. He saw it all collapse, the severance package, the prestige, the celebrity, the book tours, the secrets and lies.

Like a chameleon dropping camouflage, Louis seemed to change skin. He'd vacillated between pleading to domineering, but now looked almost reptilian. It was my imagination, but he became hideous and deformed. His eyes paled. His mouth seemed to widen, his nose flatten, like a snake.

"You," he said.

"Me."

"The brave inspector, pretending he knows right from wrong, good from evil. Thinks he's caught the *bad* guy."

"Not bad. Just broken," I said.

"Going to hit me, Inspector? Maybe that'll erase all your fear. Will that fix things? Hold me down and hurt me?"

"Nicholas, get in your car and go."

"No, Nicholas, I think not," said Louis.

Nicholas looked miserable.

I came around the Civic, closer to them. Still recording with my iPhone.

"I can't hit you, Louis. That would help you, after all, with the police. But if you prevent Nicholas from getting in his car, I'll shove you all the way to McDonalds."

Louis thought it over. He had options. He could cause a scene. He could flee. He could snatch at my phone or fight me. None seemed geared toward a positive outcome, so he remained where he was, between Nicholas and the car door. He'd only give an inch if forced.

I came around Nicholas. Intended to grab Louis's shirt in a bunch, press him backward. I got close, however, and he retreated.

"You did your job well," he said. "Filled my employees

with your deceit, like the serpent in the garden. And look, you're filming the moment. Like a true desperate American."

Nicholas ducked into his car. Fired the engine, reversed, and left in a hurry.

I ceased the recording. Dropped the phone into my pocket.

Louis said, "So my career is over. Congratulations, Inspector. You win this round."

"Where is Alec Ward?"

"It's a shame you had to interfere with my church. Lives are imploding because of your false journey to redemption. Poor Nicholas will have to find a new line of work."

"Alec Ward. Where is he?"

"Your obsession with the young man is disturbing, Inspector."

"You want this video deleted? I can bargain."

The malformed man had climbed back into the smooth exterior of the Episcopalian priest. It was Father Louis who regarded me, not the monster of pain beneath.

"Ah. You have the video. I have lives and careers in my hand. We can reach a symbiotic agreement perhaps. Though, to be honest, the idea of watching you drown with guilt and grief fills me with perverse delight, Inspector."

"I want Alec Ward," I said.

"Delete the video and I'll take you to him."

"No chance. One of us here has integrity and he's not the one forcefully coercing his church staff into sex. You take me to Alec Ward and I won't share the video. You enroll at a rehabilitation clinic and I'll delete it. You have my word."

He blinked. Twice. "A rehab clinic."

"Yes."

"You believe homosexuality is like alcoholism, Inspector.

Like drug abuse. I can cure it with some well grounded-therapy. That's what you think?"

"No, I think the trauma you suffered in your youth has never been dealt with."

"The trauma of my youth," he said.

"At Ashdown."

His hands balled into fists. His nostrils flared. For the second time, he thought about fighting me. Again, decided against it.

"Aren't we a busy little bee."

"Just stubborn."

"No, I don't think you'll find Alec, Inspector." He turned for his car. "Looks like this round goes to me. We both leave unsatisfied. Perhaps I'll clean out my desk."

I was out of options. So I decided to hit him in the teeth until he confessed.

Before I could, he turned and said, "Run along to that hot young blonde. You know the one. Life's short, after all. Eat, drink, and be merry while you're young. While you can."

It's not often I was stunned. But this was one of those times. The world tilted under my feet.

Hot young blonde. He'd said that before. Previous conversations came flooding back, flashing between my ears...

Louis had asked about my sexual obsessions.

He asked about a hot young blonde running through my mind.

He noted my Princess Leia had blonde hair and blue green eyes.

He mentioned a griffin. A *griffin.* The mascot of William & Mary, the alma matter of Veronica Summers, was a griffin.

And...

In Kix's bed, he'd left a toy. I assumed it was a goat but I was wrong. It was a pink ram. He called me a ram, too. Ronnie had also attended VCU for undergrad. The mascot? A ram.

Good hell.

Louis had been threatening Ronnie for weeks and I was too dense. And now he was telling me to enjoy her while I could.

I returned to my senses as Louis's Audi reversed with a squeal of tires. His car jumped into my rented Chevy Malibu, collapsing the Audi's rear bumper and destroying my car's driver side front tire. A stupendous noise. The rubber ruptured and metal groaned. The tire went instantly flat, maybe torn from the axle and struts.

He dropped the Audi into drive and fled the parking lot. His rear tire smoked as it rubbed against the crumpled fiberglass.

Wish I'd gotten *that* on video. I hadn't sprung for extra insurance.

I retrieved my phone and dialed. Manny answered.

I said, "I need you to pick up Ronnie."

"It's important?"

"She's in danger."

"I'm on the way," he said. "You're, ah, in a disposal?"

"*Indisposed*. And yeah," I said, inspecting the wrecked rental. "I am. Calling for a tow."

"Humiliating for you."

I nodded.

It was.

42

That evening the heavens opened. Rain fell like the world was ending, the nor'easter's full anger reaching us.

Ronnie and I cooked chili in the kitchen, watching the weather channel and listening to sheets of rain hammer our windows. She browned the grass fed beef and I cut fresh tomatoes and peppers. We combined the full list of ingredients into a pot and set it simmering with the top on. Then I mixed cornbread while she played with Kix and listened to my account of Father Louis.

In a hurtful coincidence, she wore a blue hoodie embroidered with VCU's logo, Rodney the Ram.

I told her everything she didn't know, which included my foray into Louis's basement, and she said, "He had photographs of both of us on his laptop?"

"Took your photo as you arrived at your office one morning, looks like."

"That's horrifying."

"You look okay in the photo."

"That's not what I mean. What will you do now?"

"Louis's career is over. He knows it. Trouble is, however, he can only be charged with minor crimes at this point. Trespassing and battery. Not enough to terrify him, because he's already lost his job. If Jeremy and Nicholas are willing, we can get him for workplace harassment. But..."

"Those are misdemeanors. A slap on the wrist. Especially if he moves to Florida or some far off land of retired exploiters," she said. "And you're still not positive he actually took Alec."

"Correct. He could be bluffing with the hope that I'll back down."

"But you doubt it."

"But I doubt it."

"And the vestry?" she said.

"Hugh Pratt is in Charlotte and his flight was canceled, so he's driving in tonight. I'm meeting him at his house in a couple hours. Show him the video. He'll call Louis and reason with him. If that's unsuccessful, we see what help Sheriff Stackhouse can provide. I told her to anticipate a late phone call from me tonight."

She had Kix on her lap and he watched the storm churn on screen.

"You're worried that Alec might be killed soon, because of the flooding rivers. And you're worried Louis will hire men to hurt me. Thus your urgency."

"Yes."

"I suppose I should spend the night in your bed. For safety."

"I suppose you should."

She made a happy gasp. "Be still my heart."

"I didn't say I'd be in it, Ronnie."

"Don't you dare get a girl's hopes up and then hide, Detective," she said. "I'll come find you."

"Maybe," said Manny, reading a book in the corner chair, "you two crazy white people can wait until after chili to talk dirty? I'm losing my appetite."

THAT NIGHT RONNIE put Kix to bed but he was restless and fussy, so I took the second shift. The rain pounded hard enough to form white noise and that took some getting used to, but after reading *Goodnight Moon* and some Shel Silverstein poems he consented to being tucked in. He gazed up peacefully from his crib.

There's a girl in your room, father.

I paused, a hand on the rail. My heart, the coward, thundered.

What will you do with her?

"I don't know," I told him. "I don't know what to do."

I'm sure whatever you decide will be for her good. You've always been a good father.

"You're cute when you're exhausted," I said.

And when I'm not.

"Goodnight, Kix."

I pulled his door shut and stood in the hallway. Ambient noise from the television drifted from below—Manny watching baseball. The Nationals were in Los Angeles.

Ronnie was on my bed. Her legs were tan and long and shapely with muscle. She still wore the blue VCU hoodie as a night shirt. She held up a book of essays from my nightstand.

"Reading Mishka Shubaly? What do you think?"

"Fascinating guy," I said. "He has more sex than me."

"Well that's your fault, not his." She patted the bed next to her.

"I have to meet Hugh Pratt soon."

"Mackenzie, I can tell you're stressed. I know that my pursuit of you is one of the causes. So if you sit down and let me rub your shoulders, I promise to release you unmolested."

I didn't acquiesce immediately. I watched her. I watched her watching me, and I wondered if all girls would transubstantiate my bedroom the way she did.

And I doubted it.

I sat on the edge of the bed and she slid close. I faced away from her, toward the mirror over my dresser. We made eye contact through the reflection. Her legs went around my waist and she pressed her thumbs into the tender flesh near my neck, along the spine.

"You're upset because it's true," she said. "Everything you didn't want to be true about Louis, it turns out, is."

"Something like that."

"Good grief, Mackenzie, you are thick with muscles. And they're knotty and hard. You need regular massages if you carry stress like this for long. I'm willing to play masseuse if you'll be my patient."

"Maybe stick to bartending," I said.

"Why?"

"Your fingernails hurt."

"Wimp," she said. "Are you mad at God? Because of Louis?"

"I don't know what I am. Maybe."

"Talk it through. I'll listen."

"What is your hourly rate?"

"The Law Office of Veronica Summers charges three hundred and fifty dollars an hour," she said.

"Oh my."

"But because my pants are off, the rate goes up."

"I'm not mad at God. I don't think. Because the problem isn't him. And the problem isn't church, not even the Episcopal church. The problem isn't sex, or sexuality, or even homosexuality. The problem is us. The people."

In the mirror, I saw her nod.

"We're evil. That's why I can charge so much," she said.

"We're sick. We're broken. And we break things that are good."

"Things that are good?"

"Baseball, for example. Sports are good, but there was a fight last night and now guys are suspended and the pitcher from the Dodgers has a concussion. Sex is good but we pervert it. Church is good, but...there's guys like Louis growing on it like a cancer, feeding off the goodness, and he infects and desecrates it. The church lets him remain, lets him take what he wants, as long as he's making it grow."

Her hands had paused.

"Does this apply to us?" she said.

"I think so."

"You think that..." She sucked lightly at her lip, frowning thoughtfully and teasing the small hairs along my neck. I watched her do it. She was reasoning this through, trying to see the world as I did. "You think, if you give into me then you're breaking something good."

"Yes."

"Me. By taking what you want, you'll be breaking me."

"Yes. And me. And us."

"And my potential marriage," she said. "And our potential future."

I nodded. My hands were on her feet, massaging. I didn't remember putting them there. They were strong, the feet of an active person, not a couch potato. Good arches, active toes.

She said, "If you give in to me, if you take what doesn't belong to you, then you're almost as bad as Louis. At least in your eyes."

"Which are, in some ways, the most important eyes."

"You have a tough head to live in, Mackenzie. I'm always impressed by your perspective on things, but holy shit, maybe you think *too* much. That's why you're so angry at Louis. Apart from all the perfectly good reasons, you're mad because you see yourself in him, and he doesn't have the courage to resist temptation. It makes you worry about yourself."

Maybe that was true, but I didn't want to think about it too long. I didn't want to admit Louis had crawled that far under my skin.

"All I want is you, Ronnie," I said.

Her breath caught. An absence of warm air near my ear.

"But if I give in, you and I are two ticks without a dog."

She replied in a whisper, "I don't understand."

"A better analogy is, we'd be two lawyers without a client."

"Oh my word. Why would we...what an awful thing to consider."

"We'd be going through the motions. Both needy. But without any basis, nothing to sustain us. It couldn't last."

"That's remarkably profound." She pushed her hands under my arms to give me a tight hug from behind. I enjoyed the impression she made on my body. She kissed my neck and said, "I think I get it. I don't like it, but I get it. You see too much brokenness in the world and you can't let yourself be part of it. All those men at the church should have done the right thing but they didn't, and now you have to. Which means you have to stay above reproach, especially in light of Father Louis."

"I haven't earned the right to take him down, otherwise."

"That's not accurate."

"I know. But I feel it."

"You're like a paladin," she said.

"And you're a succubus."

She laughed but it was half forced. "You're joking but I have enough self-awareness to detect the truth beneath it."

"Only a little."

"I don't throw myself at men like this. No girl does, at least not the girls I know." She leaned her head on my shoulder. "But the chase was part of the fun. The temptation and forbidden romance makes me wild. You are worth the work."

"*Was* part of the fun?"

"If I know you like I think I do, you're considering staying at a hotel. The temptation will be too great when you return. Right?"

"I already checked. The Hampton Inn downtown has rooms."

A soft sigh from her.

"I have to stop," she said. "I know I do. A girl can dream, but eventually she has to wake up."

"Ronnie—"

"Come home after talking with the vestry guy. I promise I'll behave."

"That's no fun," I said.

"If you're lucky, I'll flash you."

I disentangled myself and stood. Turned, took her face, and kissed her. Neither of us expected it, one of those sudden eruptions that's better for it. For half a minute we lost ourselves and admitted without words the hurt and the affection and the longing. Might be ill-advised; the pain was bad enough already.

I released her and stepped away. Steadied myself.

"You're engaged. So that was platonic."

"Didn't feel platonic." She laid backwards, flat on the bed. Her voice wavered with emotion. "I can't breathe."

We both knew. We had to stop. Had to grow up.

I picked up the three printed emails in case Hugh Pratt needed more convincing.

"Good bye, Ronnie."

As I left the room, she took my pillow and covered her face.

43

Hugh Pratt lived in South Roanoke, only half a mile from Louis. I got to his house before he did and I waited in the drive, car running, windshield wipers throwing rain but not making a difference. The cheery lights from his house smeared back and forth.

He arrived ten minutes later. I got out and hustled into the passenger seat of his Porsche Boxster. He held the weariness that came with a prolonged drive.

"Cats and dogs," he said and he yawned.

"This car is tiny."

"It is you, my friend, who are too big. Don't blame the Porsche."

"You want to go inside, first? Kiss your wife and kids?"

He said, "No, I want this settled. I won't go into my home with guilty hands. Why couldn't you text me the video?"

"I made that mistake once. I won't distribute the evidence again."

I passed him my phone. He pressed play and watched the parking lot encounter between Louis and Nicholas. His shoulders slumped and he seemed to shrink as Louis's tirade bounced around the Porsche's cab. Hugh's face shimmered with bleary light coming through the deluge, and his wire-framed glasses reflected the scene.

"A lie. A lie August has filled your head with."

"I only said things because you made me, Father Louis."

"Lies! Lies from hell. You are deceived and you need my council. You need to be righted."

"No I don't think I do. I love my wife."

"No you don't. And if you do, so what. She doesn't deserve you."

"I won't listen to this. I'm leaving."

"No! I need you, Nicholas. Please. I'm...I'm out of sorts. It's all crashing on me at once. It's spiritual warfare and I can't do it alone. The boy at our church is missing. My retirement. Celia and I aren't getting along. Inspector August is ruining my life. But you, Nicholas, are all I need."

At the end, Hugh bent forward until his head rested on the steering wheel.

"The poor young man," he whispered. "He's scarred for life. Him and Jeremy. Thank God Jeremy had the courage to come forward."

"Yup."

"This is my fault. I wasn't the man...I'm *not* the man the church deserves. I let this happen."

"Don't place blame. Let's end this ordeal. And maybe save Alec Ward."

"You still believe Father Louis has him? You're the only one who does," said Hugh.

"I'm stubborn. And nothing has convinced me otherwise."

"We need to show Rob. Then...then confront Father Louis, I suppose," he said in a small voice. I almost didn't hear him over a thunder peal.

"Tonight."

"Poor Rob, he'll be crushed. His grandfather founded All Saints. He's the final remaining grandson and he took it upon himself to protect the sanctity of the church. Think about it from his point of view. After the arrival of Father Louis, church attendance tripled. Tithing skyrocketed. All Rob's hard work, all his sacrifices, paid off when Father Louis arrived."

"He wants to preserve the church, he'll see reason."

Hugh returned the phone, dropped the car into reverse, and twisted to look over his shoulder.

"Let's do it. I've delayed doing the right thing for too long."

44

Robert Wallace lived near Franklin County, off Naff Road. This was a different world from Hugh's wealthy neighborhood; this was the country—farms and stately manors with a hundred acres of cattle and horses. The drive lasted twenty-five minutes, during which Hugh tried not to hydroplane and I yelled above the downpour thundering on his canvas top. I told him about the Pink Mafia and George Saunders and the printed emails.

He pulled off Naff onto a paved drive marked by twin brick columns. The columns were topped with electric lanterns, and the drive wound up a steep hill and into the trees.

"Robert's rich," I said.

"Rob's very rich. He owns the logging company."

Robert's house was a luxury two-story log home, the kind families rented in Aspen for ten grand a week, sprawled across the crest of a broad hill. Wrap around porch, attached four-car garage, majestic view of lightning in all directions. I saw his blue FJ40 in the garage's first bay—two of the garage doors were up.

"He's richer than you."

He almost smiled. "We haven't compared. But I work hourly."

"Not many lights on. Robert's asleep?"

"If he is, we'll wake him; this is important. But he's a night owl."

Hugh parked at the wide flagstone steps and we ran to the double doors and the shelter of the wide front porch. During the intervening three seconds, I gained two pounds of water weight.

At the top of the steps a German Shepherd waited and nearly ripped out our throats. Or would have if he hadn't been on the other side of the glass double doors. He deemed us unwelcome. The dog barked and fumed, fogging the glass and spraying spittle. Beyond him, through the dark entrance hall, I could see part of the dimly lit kitchen. Hugh tried to soothe Samson (the dog) but progress was not made.

Hugh rang the bell, further enraging the sentry.

Robert did not appear.

He called Robert with his cellphone and shouted over the rain, "Rob! I'm at your front door and Samson won't let us in." A pause, a hand over his other ear. "I have Mackenzie August with me." Another pause. He stepped back and glanced around the porch. "Okay, I see them. Be there in a sec." He hung up.

"He's home," I said. Intelligently.

"Around back, working on furniture in his shop." He pulled two umbrellas out of a decorative canister. Gave one to me. "This will ruin my Allen Edmonds."

"Want a piggyback ride?"

"I'll let you know."

We walked under the safety of the porch around the south side of the house. The back yard was wide and deep, the grass cut short. An impressive workshop glowed near the tree line, reached by a stone walkway and gravel service road.

Samson followed our progress on the inside, howling as we passed windows.

We hoisted umbrellas and walked the stone path, often through standing puddles.

"Let me do the talking," said Hugh over the drumming rain on our umbrellas. "He's not thrilled with you. Then we'll show him the video."

I spotted Robert through the shop door's viewing window. He set down a big chunk of wood and went out the back again.

The forest lit up with flare and shadow as lightning raced overhead.

Hugh yanked open the door and we stepped into the dry, orderly woodworking shop. Robert had a lathe, miter saw, reciprocating saw, big belt sander, planer, shop vac, and other stuff I couldn't name. In the corner were newly turned legs for furniture, already stained. He came back in and set down another large chunk of tree, still with the bark attached. His arms were bunched with knotty muscle.

"Rain's gonna ruin my walnut," he said. "Making a new table for the church's prayer chapel. Can't let it get too wet."

"Rob, I got some bad news for you," said Hugh.

"This is about Father Louis, isn't it." He indicated me with his chin. "That's why you're here."

I nodded.

"It is."

"Well. I'll listen. Tell me while you carry walnut." He went through the back door again. We followed into a partially covered lumber yard. Chunks of wood stacked above our heads against the shop and more in a raised shelter across the sodden grass. He pointed to the dark shelter and picked up a felling ax with wooden handle. "Those big chunks. Don't lift more than you can handle. I'll cut them smaller."

"It's bad, Rob. And we've Father Louis on video. Confessing it, essentially."

"You got him on video. How about that," said Robert.

We walked across the grass near a descending staircase with metal rails leading to an underground storage bunker, maybe for more lumber.

I was an ass. Looking back on it, that's the only conclusion—I was an ass. I let my mind wander. I allowed Hugh to lead and I started thinking about Louis. I trusted Robert, like an ass, and got lulled into the trap. Professional mistake. Enormous fallout.

We passed the staircase and Robert put his big left hand on Hugh and shoved. Shoved hard. Hugh weighed eighty pounds less than Robert, shorter and slim. Hugh flew like a rag doll, not touching down until near the bottom of the concrete staircase. He landed awkwardly on his shoulder. His clavicle snapped in half; Robert and I heard it. His body somersaulted once and collapsed in a heap on the lower landing.

I was entirely caught off guard.

Someone inside the underground storage bunker shouted.

Robert was swinging the ax. It moved with sick ease in his powerful right fist. He aimed at my skull with the flat butt, because the blade would carom off. I got my hands up, mitigating the damage. He connected anyway. Dented the parietal bone above my ear.

Maybe fractured it.

I staggered to my left, near the stairs.

Felt like the universe split in half. A burst of stars.

The lights dimmed.

And I…

…I WAS BEING DRAGGED down the concrete steps. I couldn't hear, but I felt the scraping against my back, and my head dropping over and over.

Thunk.

Thunk.

Thunk…

VISION WOULDN'T FOCUS.

But my ears switched back on.

Head hurting…I couldn't remember why. My eyes ached despite the dark.

I was in…I didn't know where I was.

Two men sat on a dirty floor across from me. One of the guys, I knew his name but… The guy had thrown up on himself. His shoulder hung at a grotesque angle and he tried to hold it in place.

The other man, I knew his name too…his name was… Louis. Louis was shouting.

Louis was here? Did I know that?

Where was I? What happened to Hugh?

Hugh. That was his name. The hell happened to Hugh? His face was white.

Another guy arrived. Filled the entire doorway, holding an ax and a chunk of wood. He set the wood firmly onto the ground vertically and sat on it like a stool.

Robert. I always liked him.

"Robert!" Louis shouted the word and my head rang. "For God's sake, get ahold of yourself!"

"I told you, Father Louis," said Robert in a deep and patient voice. He set the head of the ax on the ground and let the handle rest against his thigh. "Some things in this world are important. And no sacrifice is too great."

I tried to sit up but my head swam and my stomach lurched.

The move caught Louis's attention.

"August! I swear I didn't know. I'm as confused as you are. This isn't—I didn't do this. He told me to come over, told me it was an emergency."

"What..." I said.

"He's got the kid, he's got Alec Ward. Right there," said Louis and he pointed into a dark corner. I looked and saw... something. A lugubrious sack of rags. "You have to believe me now."

This room smelled awful.

Outside, thunder crashed. Water cascaded in from the stairwell and overflowed a drain.

"You can relax, Father. August is no longer a threat to you. Now that we're all here," said Robert and he paused to consider his ax. No longer the venerable guardian on vestry, now the madman with a weapon. A creature of action, finished with debate. "We will have a vestry meeting. With the only people who matter. And you will listen."

I touched my ear. Then my neck. My fingers returned red with blood. My brain was pressing to escape its skull enclosure.

Robert had hit me with the ax. That's what happened.

"First things first," said Robert. "Address the elephant. Father Louis, are you gay?"

"Am I—Robert, these men need help."

"Are you gay?"

"...No, Robert, I'm not," he said.

"The issue is settled. Clergy don't lie. Okay, Hugh? Okay, August? Now let's move on."

"*Robert*," said Hugh feebly. He wiped his mouth with his uninjured hand. "What are you doing? I don't...I don't understand. You hurt me."

"Robert, Mr. Wallace, my friend, I want you to listen to me." Louis had a wild frantic face, and I didn't blame him. He couldn't take his eyes off the ax, and I couldn't blame him for that either. Terror took the authority out of his voice. "I need an explanation."

"Father Louis, quiet now. For the moment."

"Where—" I said and a wave of nausea washed over me.

"You too, August. Quiet. You talked enough. Father Louis told me you trapped him to get a fake video. He told me you'd come here with the lies."

"Yes," said Louis. "I did say that." He glanced between Robert and me, caught somewhere in the tension of self-preservation and the truth. He still knelt beside Hugh.

"I won't watch your video, August. I believe you have one. I believe you tricked Father Louis into saying things he wishes he didn't. What I don't believe is that those things are the truth."

"Robert, is Alec Ward alive?" I said.

He flinched. "Yes."

"Is that—"

Robert made a groaning noise. He closed his eyes and shook his head, like fighting off vertigo. "I didn't plan...the boy wasn't— It wasn't supposed to happen this way. I don't like hurting people."

"You," I said. "*You* took the kid. Not Louis? Why?"

"That's not," he said and he opened his eyes. Focused on the dirt. "That doesn't matter."

"Is that Alec in the corner? Did you take Jon Young, too? Why'd you kill him?"

Robert gripped the ax handle in both hands. His knuckles turned white. Lifted the head six inches and slammed it on the floor. I felt the impact.

"No more! That doesn't matter. That wasn't... We're here now. You will listen. Listen to how I'm saving the church."

Louis said, "The church. Yes. You're right, Mr. Wallace, it is important."

"Robert, look at Hugh. Look at your friend," I said. "His shoulder is broken. He needs a physician."

"I told Hugh not to hire a detective. I told Hugh to leave this alone. Told him a dozen times. He wouldn't. He deserves a broken shoulder. And more."

"Why'd you take Alec?" I had a gun. It was pinned beneath my rib cage, inaccessible. I tried sitting up a little more. I had a concussion, I knew. A big one. My fingers were numb. At the moment, if I went for my gun, I'd fumble it. Numb and dizzy. I needed more time, needed to stall and let my faculties return.

He ignored me.

"Father," said Robert. "I will not allow you to retire. That's why I called you here. Tonight is perfect. You will find the boy in the river and bring him home, still alive. That way your hands are clean."

"*Find* him? In the river?"

"Yes. You're a shepherd bringing home his sheep. Otherwise I gotta get rid of him soon. Somehow."

"I'm still confused, Mr. Wallace. I'm in shock," he said. "Why do you have Alec?"

"He did it for you, Louis," I said. The fog in my head and

the unanswered questions aligned for a brief moment like open windows, providing an unobstructed view of the truth. And I understood. "All for you."

"What do you mean, *Inspector*, all for me?"

"You're his hero. You're worshipped, just like you wanted. You became a god worthy of sacrifice."

Robert Wallace picked up the ax and placed the head against my chest and pushed.

"You are ignorant of the things that matter, August. I did it for All Saints."

"For All Saints," repeated Louis. He licked his lips, sizing up the danger. He recognized the need to kowtow. Play it calm and cool and always agree with the man holding an ax. "That's worthy and holy work, Mr. Wallace."

"You clean up a lot of Louis's messes, don't you, Robert," I said. "This is making more sense."

"My messes?" Louis raised himself up to look down at me. "You're confused again, Inspector, if you think I arranged any of this."

"Yes you did. Just didn't know it."

"How so?"

"You groom worshippers, sometimes they worship in a way you didn't expect," I said.

"The glorified traffic cop fancies himself a pontificating judge," said Louis. He smiled the mocking smile and moved to physically stand with the man holding the ax.

"Rob." Hugh spoke again, his voice a croak. His skin was white and sweat poured down his face. "Robbie. I don't understand what's going on, but we were wrong about Louis. It's not too late."

Robert set the ax on the dirt floor again. He spun it and he nodded at the kid in the corner, who still hadn't spoken.

"You're right, Hugh. It's not too late for the boy. Or for All

Saints. Or for Father Louis. This can all go back to the way it was, when everything was good."

"What about for Jeremy and Nicholas and the others? Too late for them?" I said.

"They are liars."

"Mr. Wallace, about your plan," said Louis. He spoke like a man venturing onto thin ice. "I already announced my retirement. Perhaps a better idea—"

"You'll change your mind."

"He's done so much for you, Louis. Time to return the favor," I said.

"Done so much for me? Mr. Wallace, what does he mean?"

A muscle in Robert's jaw flexed. He cast his gaze at Louis, standing over him, and looked a little wounded.

"I'll explain," I said. I was flexing my fingers, making a fist over and over. The tingling in my fingertips lessened but I still didn't trust my grip. Nor my aim. "Robert has been tending All Saints forever. And you come along and you're a godsend. Attendance and tithing explodes, and all is well. Except he keeps hearing rumors of your infidelity. And even worse that you're gay, which doesn't jive with his worldview or the history of the church. And then, lo and behold, he hears that you're spending time with Jon Young, who is openly gay. Something has to be done."

"Inspector August, how dare you insinuate—"

"I insinuate nothing," I said, ignoring a headache that flashed as a throbbing light in my vision. "I'm explaining the appearance of a thing. And to you and to Robert, appearance is what matters."

Robert made another grunting noise.

I said, "And so to protect you and the church and the explosive growth, Robert removed Jon Young from your life.

I had to guess, I'd say he didn't intend on killing Jon. But sometimes the evil we do has a way of spiraling out of control. Surely you understand that, Louis."

"Even if that's true, Inspector, I had nothing to do with it. I am innocent. I am not a pedophile."

"Then, a few weeks ago, Jeremy Cameron came forward with allegations. Exactly what Robert had been trying to prevent for years. But the trouble was, Jeremy is clergy and Robert has a deep regard and reverence for clergy. Robert didn't dare hurt him, but Jeremy Cameron mentioned that there's someone else. A source he won't name. Robert went into panic mode, found out you were mentoring another young man, Alec Ward, and so abducted him. Robert's a logger; he sees a tree in the way, he cuts it down."

He picked up the ax again and pushed it against me like a spear.

"The boy is still alive," said Robert.

"Doesn't look like it."

"He's medicated. He's no worse for wear and he'll go home. Tonight."

"Jon Young didn't," I said.

He thumped my chest with the ax like a little battering ram, bruising my breastbone, beneath which my heart thundered.

"You screwed up, August. This would have gone away if you'd quit. Everything would go back to normal. But now it can't. This is your fault."

"Mine? Not the guy sexually harassing his employees?"

He closed his eyes and shook his head, like he did a moment ago. Scalded by his own reflection.

"You were supposed to find Father Louis innocent."

"He's not," I said. "At the minimum, he's broken every workplace law in half. Not to mention criminal charges."

"I told you Father Louis didn't take the boy."

"Yeah but the truth is worse," I said.

"Jon Young was...an accident. I didn't mean what happened."

"Doesn't make him less dead."

Robert ground his teeth.

"*Stop* saying that."

"Rob," said Hugh. He raised his uninjured arm. In his fist he held a cell phone. The hairs on my neck raised. "Last chance, Rob. I know you'll do the right thing. Don't make me call the police. It'll break my heart and break the church. Let's figure out a way—"

"*No* Hugh. Drop the phone," I said. "*Now*."

Robert swung his ax in a horizontal slash. It caught Hugh at the wrist. The bit entered at the joint, separating Hugh's hand from the radius and ulna bones in his forearm. The blade dug into the wall and Hugh's arm was pinned by the heavy ax. Stuck fast. His hand was nearly severed. But not quite.

Hugh screamed and dropped the phone.

He would have bled to death in minutes if the ax hadn't pinned his wrist, pinching closed veins and arteries. Only a small trickle of blood escaped down the ax's cheek.

I went for my gun. The concussion made me clumsy. My vision throbbed. My movements were sluggish. The 1911 Kimber felt too big, too heavy, but I got it out.

Hugh's arm...pinned...God help us.

Robert kicked me in the face with a steel-toed boot. Caught me in the nose. My nose had been broken before and I recognized the feeling.

A bunker of nightmares.

I kept my grip on the gun. Given another half second I

would have shot him. But he moved quick, jerked the pistol free.

I rolled backward and pressed my hand to my face.

Everything hurt. Couldn't think. Blood came out of my nose and welled in my cheeks beneath my eyes.

Hugh...

In the corner, Alec was whimpering.

"Brought this on yourself, August," said Robert in a loud voice. He was breathing heavy, eyes wide like his dog Samson's were. He snatched Hugh's phone and slid it into his back pocket.

Louis stood at the door, hand at his throat. Face white as his Sunday clerical robes. He wanted to run but didn't dare anger the armed zealot. Light from the workshop came down the stairs over his shoulder and made my eyes hurt.

"Watch the video, Robert," I said. My syllables were thick.

"Already told you no," he said. "This is a good gun, August. 1911. Father Louis, do you have one?"

"Do I have...no, Mr. Wallace, I don't own guns."

Robert held the pistol out to him. "Here."

"No...no thank you."

"August has blasphemed. He must die."

Louis rubbed his hands together, leaning against the door frame because he was unsteady.

"You think it's necessary?"

"I do. Think of it as a sacrifice. Otherwise he'll spread his deceit and you'll be defrocked. The nor'easter is the perfect vessel. Maybe even miraculous. They won't be found for weeks,"

"They?" said Louis.

They—me and Hugh, borne away by the swollen rivers.

Robert would get caught. Too much evidence existed. But by then Hugh and I would be dead for weeks.

Louis and I held eye contact a moment—we were dealing with a man off his hinges. Passion and religious fervor made holes in his sanity and logic. But still it was better for Louis to stay in his favor. Pander to the man with an ax.

Hugh's head fell forward onto his chest. Each breath was a gasp. He closed his eyes and mumbled, "My fault. This... this is my fault. August was...dear God..." And he started whispering prayers.

"Okay," said Louis and he swallowed. "Okay, I trust you, Mr. Wallace. To do the Lord's will. I'll go. I suppose that's best. You will...handle things here, I believe."

"I'll carry the boy to your car."

"Alec to *my* car? Why?"

"It's better if you find him. Tell his parents you found him by the side of the road, maybe. God sent you to him," said Robert.

"Maybe, Mr. Wallace, you should do that."

"Has to be you. You're the priest. It's better if people trust you, Father."

"Yes but there is already suspicion that I took him. If I return to the city with him in my car—"

Hugh made a sharp cry and tugged at his arm. His body wasn't in shock yet. Blood was turning his shirt cuff dark crimson.

"Why are you refusing to help?" said Robert. A hint of frustration in his voice. "It's better if we're in this together. A cord not easily broken."

"He's not in this with you, Robert," I said. "Louis's never been in this with you."

"Don't listen to Inspector August, Mr. Wallace. You and I will work together. But it'd be better if you had the boy."

"*Watch* the video," I said.

Robert had my own pistol pointed at me. His finger wasn't on the trigger. Yet.

"No," he said. "Stop saying that."

"But obduracy is my best trait."

"If you mean stubborn, it's got you killed, August."

"Don't you want to know what Louis said about *you*, Robert?"

Both of the men standing above me grew still. Only for a second, but maybe the longest second of Louis's life.

"Mr. Wallace, your idea is a good one. Carry Alec Ward to my car." Louis said it in a rush.

"They talk about me?" Robert's eyebrows bunched together. "In the video? It's full of lies, so I don't care."

"Not in the video. In an email."

"In an email?" said Louis. "Inspector, this desperate and pathetic attempt at self-preservation is beneath you. I've never had anything but exemplary things to say about Robert Wallace, the guardian All Saints deserves."

"Then shut up and let him read it."

"You do not have access to my emails," he said.

"Yeah. I do."

Robert held his hand up for silence. "Where are they? The emails?"

"Mr. Wallace, please. This is the devil's lie."

"I want to see them."

I said, "In my back pocket. Three of them, printed out."

Louis's shoulders kinda sagged and his mouth opened, but he couldn't speak.

"Roll over," said Robert. "You move funny and I'll shoot you in the spine."

I twisted onto my stomach. Blood dripped from my nose into a pool on hard ground. He dug under my rain jacket and came up with the papers, folded in half and creased.

"Mr. Wallace— *Robert*, listen a moment." Louis's words came out weak and landed softly at his feet.

"You have nothing to hide, Father," said Robert. "Right? So hold your peace a moment." He moved closer to the door so light fell onto the first page. His eyes scanned and he said, "This is disgusting, August. And there are no names."

Louis reached for the papers. "Allow me to read the lies first and I will—"

Robert brushed the grasping hand aside. "No."

"Second page," I said, still on my stomach.

Hugh whimpered. "My fault. I deserve...my fault."

Robert shuffled papers. Took a moment to read. Said, "This is an email written *to* Father Louis, I think. Not from him. And there's nothing about me."

"It's from Nicholas. the clergyman at your church. He's replying. Read the bottom of that page. It contains Louis's original email."

"Why the hell do you have this, Inspector?" said Louis, a man considering stomping me to death.

"The truth matters, Louis. And so does Nicholas."

Robert read silently—

My dearest Nicholas,

I have to postpone our meeting this morning. Robert Wallace (the obnoxious homophobe on vestry) has requested prayer for his nephew, an asshat addicted to painkillers. I'm afraid I must, because that wrinkled old fool holds surprising sway over the church. He thinks All Saints is special because of him, and sometimes these petty fantasies must be coddled.

But afterwards, my young friend, I will call...

Robert flipped the paper over but Louis hadn't printed anymore of that particular email. His flat gaze shifted to Louis, who backed against the doorframe again.

"Petty fantasy?" His voice rumbled like the thunder outside.

"*Lies*. August typed it."

"This is dated three years ago," said Robert. He tapped the timestamp with a thick finger. "We prayed for my nephew Darrell. I don't remember the exact date...but this is close. How would August know that?"

"Mr. Wallace, he has clouded your mind. You must trust me."

Robert flipped to the third and final page. I thought I heard teeth grinding. He read only a little and said, "You write like this to other men?"

"Of course not."

"But you're married. So is Nicholas. And you said... You said..." Robert lowered his arms. The papers fell into the mud at his feet. "I don't understand, Father."

"No. You don't. But I will explain."

Poor Hugh, pinned against the wall, made a whimpering sound. He whispered, "He's lying to you, Robbie. I see it now."

"Give me the video, August."

"No!" said Louis. "It's lies!"

Robert grabbed a fistful of Louis's shirt and hauled him deeper into the dungeon.

"Stay here, Father. Stay here...*Louis.* This wrinkled old homophobe wants to see the video."

From my place prone on the floor, I held up my iPhone. The video was cued.

Robert snatched it. Returned to his wooden stool, sat, and pressed play.

"Mr. Wallace, please—"

"Quiet!" His shout sounded like a gunshot.

The video played. Four and a half minutes of it, while Louis fidgeted. Robert sat still during and after. Dangerously still, and he gripped my pistol on top of his thigh. He opened his mouth to speak, changed his mind, and played the video again; he held the screen close, like looking for tampering evidence, but not too close or he couldn't make out details. The video ended. Using the hand holding my pistol he scratched at the stubble on his jaw and chin for a while. For a long while. Five minutes maybe. For Hugh and Louis, I bet it felt like a lifetime.

Finally he said, "I can't tell."

Louis cleared his throat. "Mr. Wallace, listen to your clergy. Listen to—"

"I can't see anything. Need my glasses."

He stood and limped out, stiff from sitting.

Slammed the door behind him, leaving us in darkness.

45

"Louis, where's your cellphone?" I said.

Louis was standing. In the dark, his voice came from above. "In the house, on the table."

"Robert took mine," said Hugh.

"Worthless, the pair of you." I stood. Put my hand on the wall to brace against the roaring pain between my ears. Blood trickled down my neck.

"We're dead, Inspector. You condemned us to hell."

"I was already dead, Louis. Only thing that changed is you're in the noose too."

I blindly made my way toward the heap in the corner.

Louis and I crashed together in the black. He pushed at my shoulder and cursed. I got my forearms up in time to catch a punch, thrown by a panicked man not used to throwing them. I shoved him. He stumbled, tripped over something, and sat hard. Based on the sudden effluvia, he spilled a bucket of piss.

"Oh dear lord," he moaned.

"That's for taking photos of Ronnie."

"Celia let you into my office, didn't she, the bitch. Those photos are a hobby, Inspector. Just for fun."

"Having fun now?"

I found Alec in the corner. He was limp but warm. I blindly probed his arms, his chest, his neck. He wasn't emaciated; Robert fed him. His pulse was strong but he only murmured when I shook him.

"He'll survive," I said.

"We won't, Inspector. So focus on the pressing issue."

"Shut up, Louis, or I'll hit you in the ear."

"The ear?"

"Yeah but really hard. It'll hurt."

"How can you make jokes now?" he said.

"When better." I moved forward. Tripped and stumbled over Hugh's foot. Reached the dungeon door and tried it, but Robert had securely fastened it from the outside. Didn't even rattle when I hit it with my shoulder. The impact made my head throb and nose ache.

"Mr. August," said Hugh. Very soft. "This is my fault."

"Let's get out of here first, Hugh. Then I'll accept your apology."

"Why, Father Louis? Why would...those poor boys. So sorry, all *my* fault."

"The sexual predator bears most of blame, Hugh," I said.

"Oh please, don't pretend you're some Paraclete," scoffed Louis. "Jeremy and Cameron are grown men. They adore me. No one forced them to stay. They could've left."

"They're grown men; they shouldn't have to. They have careers and responsibility."

"I'm so cold," said Hugh.

"You're going into shock, Mr. Pratt, and if that isn't holy justice then I don't know what is."

Hugh had to take deep breaths and speak only a handful

of words on each exhale. "The church needs men like you, August. Not men like me. I knew we should've fired Father Louis, but...I didn't want to. I didn't want the conflict. I hoped it would go away. So did the bishop. We wanted it to be lies. But we knew. We knew deep down."

In the corner, Alec mumbled something in his medicinal fog.

"I want to tell Alec I'm sorry," said Hugh. "Tell him it's my fault. Tell him not to blame the church. Not to blame God. Blame us, the cowards."

I knelt beside Hugh. Untucked his shirt and used my fingernails to rip a hole in the fabric.

Louis gasped. "Oh god, what's that sound?"

"I got bad news, Hugh," I said.

A wheeze. "What?"

"I'm making you a tourniquet." I did my best, trying to tear his shirttail evenly in a long strip. It jostled him and he moaned, and in retrospect I probably should have ripped my own shirt instead.

Through clenched teeth he said, "Why's that bad?"

"Because it's going to hurt. And after it's on, I'm yanking out the ax. And that's going to hurt worse."

"Oh. Shit," he said, and I thought I heard a little smile in the word. "Rob hates it when I say shit."

"Then stop it. Let's not make him angrier."

"Why do you need the ax, Inspector?" said Louis.

"To execute you."

"You're joking again."

"I am. I don't need an ax for that, just a thumb. I'll use the ax to break down the door. After that, to impair our captor."

He sniffed. "Clever."

"No. Desperate."

"You're an irredeemable pain in the ass. How'd you find those emails?" said Louis, sitting in a puddle of urine and being unhelpful.

"Not telling."

"Why not?"

"You don't deserve it," I said. "But let me congratulate you. Your vocabulary is better than I expected. So many euphemisms for penis, I had no idea."

"Why the sudden jocularity?"

"That'll happen when the guy with the gun leaves. That and a salience of mortality," I said.

I wrapped the long strip of shirt just above Hugh's elbow, where there was one bone instead of two. I cinched the wrap and twisted the loose ends tighter and tighter until Hugh was crying with the pain.

"It won't save your life if it doesn't hurt," I said.

"I know."

"Louis, get over here."

"Why?" he said.

"Because I told you to."

"Inspector—"

"An ax is buried in his left arm and his right shoulder is broken. You need to hold this knot in place. We don't have time to do it right."

Louis fumbled his way to us. I placed his hand on top of the makeshift tourniquet.

"You smell awful," I said.

"I'm covered in urine. As you intended."

"Hold this knot tight or he'll die within minutes, and I'll bury you with him."

"You are culpable for this, Inspector. You wrecked it all, including Hugh. The blame is yours."

"Do it," said Hugh. "I'm ready."

"Our Father who art in heaven," I said, gripping the throat and knob of the ax handle. "Please help us."

"Amen," said Hugh. "Amen."

"Everyone hold tight."

"I'm ready."

"This is *your* fault, Inspector, dammit," said Louis and his teeth chattered.

One strong tug and the ax tore free.

I couldn't see much. I imagined a thick wet gout from Hugh's wrist, blood in his arm finding release. I hoped the hand stayed attached but Hugh made no sound. Probably he fainted.

"Keep it tight," I told Louis.

"I am! Good Lord, I am."

The door squealed open and light poured in.

Robert Wallace had returned.

I wasn't ready yet.

Robert's hair whipped in the maelstrom's wind. He held my pistol in one hand, my cell phone in the other. Reading spectacles perched on his nose.

He'd been crying. And he still was.

I wasn't in place, not close enough to hit him with the ax.

He raised the pistol. My pistol.

I did what everyone does when a gun's aimed at them. I held my breath and winced. But he didn't pull the trigger.

"Robert, *wait*," I said and I made a subtle move to place myself between him and Louis/Hugh/Alec. I held the ax in both fists crosswise.

"He lied to me, August," said Robert Wallace.

"I know he did."

"It's true. All of it is true. Isn't it."

I nodded.

"It's true, Robert. He's been lying to vestry, cheating on his wife, and harassing the younger guys."

He jerked the gun. "Move aside. Let me see him."

"Louis needs to go before a judge. He'll face criminal charges for trespassing, sexual battery, assault, and indecent exposure. And civil charges for workplace harassment. He'll be exposed, humiliated, and defrocked."

"That's not enough," said Robert.

"Yes. It is."

"He's behind you. I want to see him."

"Give me the gun and you can," I said.

"He betrayed All Saints. He betrayed...me. Treated the church like a rag. Something to be used and thrown away. I want to know why."

"He's human like the rest of us. Maybe even more so," I said.

"Move."

Behind me, Louis whispered. "He'll *kill* me! Like he killed Jon Young. I need you. You need me. We'll survive. *Please*, Inspector.

I said, "Hugh needs a doctor, Robert. Immediately. So does Alec."

"*Move!*" he shouted and we winced. I was jumpy.

"Patricide would feel good, I admit. But it would make things worse."

He fired the gun. In close quarters it was deafening. Some of the noise escaped through the door but most of it went into our ear canals like knives. Robert grabbed at his ears.

Over the ringing I heard Alec Ward cry.

Robert released his head and said something.

"What?" I shouted.

He repeated it. He was telling me he missed on purpose.

"I know you missed on purpose," I told him.

He spoke again. I read his lips—Move. Let me see him.

Without moving my feet, I twisted to look behind. Hugh was unconscious and bleeding far too much on the ground. Louis had released the tourniquet to cower behind me. He was crying and I didn't blame him.

"Lay flat," I told Louis. He ignored me, or he couldn't hear over the ringing. "Get down."

"August!" shouted Robert. "Let me see Father Louis."

"Come in here and find him."

He looked at me and the ax I held. Shook his head. "I'll shoot you first. So move aside."

"Why?" I said.

"He lied."

"That's the least of his sins," I said. "If there is such a thing."

"He lied to *me*."

"Still, though."

"He desecrated the church. It'll crumble now. He needs to answer for it."

"That's not your call, Robert."

"Yeah it is, August," said the man with my gun. "It's entirely mine."

"Louis needs to answer to the police and Jeremy Cameron and Alec Ward's parents and a bunch of other people. Not just you. And not in the darkness."

"I'm gonna kill you, August."

I could barely hear him over the ringing in my ears, over my pounding heart, my throbbing face.

"I believe you," I said.

"If you don't move aside."

"I can't," I said.

"Why's that."

"Haven't you been listening? I'm stubborn. And somebody, at some point in this whole mess, needs to do the right thing."

"I'll count to two, August. Then you're dead with your own gun."

"Don't do this, Robert. I have a son at home."

"Then *move*. One..."

I didn't wait.

I said a two-word prayer and lunged forward. Tucked and rolled to my right, his left, making sure not to roll on the ax blade.

He roared and fired at the spot where I'd been. And fired again, tracking my evasion. Both misses. Both thunderously loud.

Being shot at is the worst.

I came to my feet. Ax held like a baseball bat. Ready to swing at his hands. I wasn't fast enough, wasn't close enough. He had me. He wouldn't miss this time.

Screaming in the room.

Two more gun shots. Large and deep sounds. But somehow less hard on the ears, less penetrative.

Robert Wallace staggered forward, his eyes wide.

He made a cough and tried to reach around to his spine. Went to his knees and twisted in pain. I saw his back. His shirt was punctured in two places, blooming crimson.

Those final gunshots... Robert hadn't fired; he'd been shot from behind.

Manny Martinez, federal marshal and my good friend, stepped into view. His big .357 issued some gun smoke that the wind caught.

"I shoot the right guy, *migo*?" he said. "Figured somebody needed shooting."

I went limp. Let myself sag onto the ground, ax across my lap.

"You're a little late," I said and my voice only wavered a little.

Robert collapsed forward. Twitched twice. And didn't move again. Manny's absurdly large ammo had probably disintegrated his heart.

"Ay caramba, looks like somebody kicked your face, Mack." Manny held a flashlight and he flashed the rest of our little sepulcher. All threats were neutralized. "Smells terrible."

"Why're you here?"

"I'm fond of you," he said.

"I mean, how'd you find us?"

Manny held up a cellphone.

"Señorita Ronnie's in my car. Your phone tells her phone where you are, she says. White people witchcraft. She was watching you and your dot disappeared here and she got worried. So we came over *muy rapido* and I heard the first gunshot."

"How about that." I looked at my phone in the dirt with renewed fondness. "Sexual obsession saves the day."

"This is no time for eye running museums."

"You mean ironic musings. We need a couple ambulances. One for Alec Ward and another for Hugh Pratt. Not a fun trip in this weather."

Manny dialed 911 and nodded with his chin.

"Happened to him?"

Father Louis Lindsey was dead. I hadn't noticed. Consigned to oblivion by Robert Wallace's wayward gunfire. I told Louis to lay down. Twice. But he wouldn't listen, not even to save his own life. Defiant unto the end. He stared upward, his death visage one of distress.

"Louis once told me the worst part of his job was dodging sniper fire from his own congregation. Prescient words, Louis," I said.

I scooted across the dirt floor. To tighten Hugh's tourniquet and stop the bleeding.

46

The big nor'easter moved up the coast, leaving Roanoke with blue skies, standing water, and swollen rivers. Plus nightmares and broken noses.

Two days after the farrago in the bunker, Kix and I knocked on Jeremy Cameron's door and stepped back so his mother could get a good look at us through the peephole.

I wasn't exactly sure what I was doing here. It had something to do with Jeremy being the client I'd truly worked for. Even though Hugh had written the checks and honorably discharged me a week ago, I needed to close this out with the guy who started it.

I told Kix this.

Closure is good, I suppose. But why do I have to tag along?

"Be nice while we're here. Roxanne doesn't work today, otherwise I wouldn't make you."

From what I hear, bringing your kid to work isn't wise in your profession. I'll be useless when the shooting starts.

Jeremy's mother opened the door but the chain stayed fastened. Through the crack, she said, "Who is this beautiful boy?"

"Mackenzie August. We met before."

"I meant the baby."

"Ah. My son, Kix."

"He's an angel."

"Thank you."

"Appears you broke your nose, Mr. August."

"Rude and hurtful, Ms. Cameron."

"It's stupid, I know, but I'm still afraid to open the door even though it's someone I trust," said Gloria.

"Not stupid. Fear doesn't simply evaporate."

"Especially for the mother."

"Or the father," I said.

She smiled. Closed the door, removed the chain, and opened up. "Please come in."

We did.

Jeremy sat on his couch reading a book. Other than residual discoloration, he looked brand new.

He pointed at my face. "Hey you look like I did."

"A badge of honor."

My son, demonstrating a preternatural sense of good manners, held out his arms to Gloria and she accepted him.

"Look at you. Look how gorgeous. I always wanted another baby, but never got around to it." She took him to the kitchen for cereal. Came back with a bowl of it.

I sat with Jeremy. "You look better."

"I feel better. Went into the office yesterday."

"It was a zoo, I bet."

"Everyone knows Father Louis and Robert Wallace are dead, but no one knows why," he said.

"Police should issue statements soon. It's still fresh."

"You were there? Based on your face?"

"I was."

Gloria said, "Can you tell us what happened?"

"That's why I came. You earned it."

"Yes," she said. "Jeremy has."

"I was wrong about Louis; he wasn't kidnapping kids. Robert Wallace was, in an ill-advised plan to preserve the reputation of All Saints. He heard the rumors that Louis was gay, and he heard Jon Young was too, and he panicked. Needlessly. His zealotry got the better of him and he didn't know what to do after he had Jon, and it ended in disaster. Then he started it again with Alec Ward."

"That's madness," said Jeremy.

"It often is."

"Good thing you stuck with it."

"Well." I shrugged modestly.

"But Alec isn't gay."

"Robert put the puzzle pieces together wrong. Fortunately Alec survived the ordeal. Robert and Louis had a showdown in an underground bunker. In his rage, Robert shot Louis. Then a federal marshal shot Robert."

"That's horrible."

"It was," I said.

"Nicholas called me. Told me about the trap you two set and that Father Louis...*Louis*...fell right in. Wish I could have been there."

"I have it on video. Hugh's seen it."

"One of our deacons reported Hugh's in the hospital," said Jeremy.

"Robert cut his hand off."

"Cut his hand *off*?" said Jeremy in a yelp.

Gloria, the hardened emergency department nurse, nodded calmly. These things happen.

"With an ax," I said.

"I thought those two were close friends."

"Religion, handled without care, does not lead to longterm friendship," I said.

"But still. Yikes."

"Very."

"The bishop called me yesterday. He's coming to town tomorrow and hiring G.R.A.C.E to sort out our mess."

"Grace?"

"Yeah, a non-profit legal team who gets to the bottom of disasters like All Saints," he said.

"Like 'Law & Order' for the church?"

"It's what we need. All our secrets revealed and a fresh start. Until then, I'm the acting rector."

"That's a fancy word meaning you are the lead clergyman at the church," I said.

"Yes."

"You want the role?"

"Not really. But someone's got to do it." He paused. The fingers of his left hand were massaging the wrist of his right hand. "Geez. Poor Hugh. An ax?"

"The hand might be reattached, who knows. I rode in the ambulance with him. He considers it a small price to pay. And somehow the pain will free him of a little guilt, which is good."

"What guilt? He's the only one who believed me."

"He feels like a coward. Accurately, in some ways. He's determined to make things right, especially with you and Nicholas."

"It's a little late for that," his mother said. With a dignified sniff. Kix nodded agreement.

"No it's not. He *believes* me. The truth will be restorative for All Saints and I feel better already," said Jeremy. And he did look a little brighter in spirit.

"The workplace harassment you suffered through should trigger the church's insurance and allow a fat severance package, if you'd like to switch careers," I said.

He nodded. "I might, to be honest, eventually. That'll take a lot of dreaming and praying. Even though the facts will emerge, my reputation at All Saints is permanently sullied."

"Everyone hates the snitch. Unfortunate and true."

Gloria had her cheek resting on Kix's crown. "Where is this perfect baby's mother?"

"Not in the picture."

"Are you dating anyone?"

"A girl broke up with me this morning, in fact," I said.

"Today? With your nose broken?"

"To be fair, she insisted on being my nurse for a few days. The split was for my benefit, and I'm grateful."

"For your benefit? Jeez, Mr. August. I don't know that I'll ever understand you," said Jeremy.

"I didn't have the strength to do it. I shouldn't be with her, and she saw the reality. Plus her fiancée is coming to town later this week. So."

"Her fiancée," said Gloria. One eyebrow went up.

It is hard to remain proper and stoic during a public admission of sin. But I did my best.

"The heart wants what it wants."

"Mr. August, you dirtbag," she said.

"I'm working on it." I indicated a Get Well bouquet of flowers on the side table. "From the church?"

"No. You'll never guess." Jeremy grinned. "Read the card."

I did.

. . .

Jeremy,

Your hospital bill has been paid for.

Get well soon.

All our best wishes!

—The Pink Mafia

47

Manny and I sat in opposing rocking chairs and played chess on a Saturday. Each of us held a freshly squeezed margarita—over ice, because Manny said the good blenders cost a thousand dollars and nothing else would do. So we were saving up.

Kix took his afternoon nap in a reclining bouncer beside me, exhausted from a fifteen-minute protest of being the only guy without a cocktail.

While I waited for Manny's move, I checked the map on my phone. Ronnie had turned off her location sharing; she no longer appeared on my screen. Maybe she realized my life would be easier without the temptation. Or maybe she was taking her engagement more seriously. Both good reasons, and I was grateful.

Her goodbye had been sincere and heartfelt and painful. A bittersweet coda allowing me to move on.

One day soon I'd quit checking the map and hoping.

Manny pushed his knight forward.

It was, I thought, not a wise move.

I told him so and he rebutted with Spanish profanity.

Thusly our game proceeded on the plank of mutual respect and collegiality, until a Porsche Boxster arrived and my ol' pal Hugh Pratt climbed out of the passenger seat; he had a driver.

His left hand was cradled in a sling and wrapped in fancy plaster up to the elbow. But on the bright side, it was still there. His right arm wasn't plastered, but it also rested in a sling, because of the broken shoulder.

He looked ridiculous.

"Hola amigo. How's the hand?" said Manny.

Hugh smiled in a way he hadn't since I'd known him—genuine and lighthearted.

"Hurts! Big time. Replantation is a process best avoided. But I deserve every bit of it."

At the word 'replantation,' Manny looked a little queasy. I knew the feeling; my father and Sheriff Stackhouse were on an extended date this weekend, causing my stomach distress.

"It'll still work?" I said.

"My hand will never be the same. But I'll have partial use, yes."

I fetched him a chair and he sat. Despite the cool afternoon, he was sweating and he adjusted the slings into a more comfortable position.

"I won't stay long. I bring greetings and gratitude from Alec Ward and his parents. He's in a recovery clinic in Pennsylvania and doing well. His parents are searching for ways to thank you two," he said.

I arched an inquisitive brow.

"Both of us?"

"That's what they said."

"Manny was only there for fifteen seconds."

Manny grinned. "That's all it took me, mijo."

"But still."

"Seemed like an important fifteen seconds. Maybe the most important."

"I had it under control," I said.

"That why your face is purple?"

"Tell the Wards to make a donation to All Saints," I instructed Hugh. "Fifteen cents of which can be on Manny's behalf."

Hugh, without speaking, conveyed his impression that we were jackasses. Or idiots. Or both.

"Have you spoken with Jeremy Cameron, Mr. August?" he said, eager to change the subject. "Or Nicholas?"

"Not in over a week."

"Nicholas is accepting the severance package and moving on. I tried to keep him but I think he needs a fresh start."

"He does," I said. "He should take his wife and child and get the hell out of Dodge. Clean breaks hurt, but often for the best."

"I wish him all the best. And his severance package is generous indeed, as it should be. On a happier note, Jeremy Cameron might stick around. After my email to the congregation, the general consensus has shifted in Jeremy's favor. Not only was Father Louis guilty but he's *gone*, making it easier for people to not take his side. So to speak. I spoke with Jeremy this morning. He's considering a well-deserved two-month sabbatical, fully paid for by the church, and then returning to us. Isn't that great news?"

"The greatest."

"It'll be good for All Saints, I know that."

"Is the church on the cusp of falling apart?" I said.

Manny got up and went inside. Came out with a pitcher

of margaritas and a highball glass for Hugh. He filled Hugh's glass and topped mine off.

What a guy.

Hugh, with some pain, was able to meet his right hand halfway and sip his margarita. He said, "Attendance is down. Twenty percent, and the flight will continue. But All Saints will survive, even without our two biggest pillars, Louis and Robert. They were celebrities."

"Maybe churches shouldn't have celebrities," said Manny.

"I'm sure you're right. But I don't know how to do that. We're only people, after all."

We sat in silence a couple minutes. It was comfortable, the way most silences weren't. The three of us had been in that dungeon and seen horrors no one else had. A shared bond we tacitly agreed should be left behind soon. In the meantime, we'd earned some comfortable repose.

My phone buzzed and I checked it—another urgent request for my services. I had a dozen waiting. Demand for Mackenzie August was sky high.

The professional slump had concluded. Even though I considered it a nonexistent slump to begin with.

The personal slump...endured.

Hugh finished half his margarita, stood, and said, "Thanks for the drink. My driver is probably bored and I'm needed at home."

"Good to see you, Hugh."

"And you, hey, I should mention, your face is looking healthier, Mr. August."

"Better than your hand, I bet."

"You got that right." He laughed. "You should see the thing, it's awful. Like Frankenstein's monster."

Manny made a groaning noise.

"Heroes come away with the best scars," I said.

"I'm no hero, but thank you. You and Jeremy Cameron are the real heroes in my eyes."

"Well," I said. "Yes. There's that."

He returned to his Porsche. Awkwardly slid in and rode away.

Manny said, "You're a hero, amigo?"

"Obviously."

"Still a little purple under the eyes. Don't look like a hero."

My phone was on the table. The map was still displayed and I remained the only dot. No Ronnie.

I didn't feel like a hero either.

"It's your move," he said.

I finished my margarita and set it down with a thunk.

Kix stirred. Opened his eyes to peer at me. Smiled at his father, twisted a little bit, and returned to sleep.

It was enough for me.

EPILOGUE

It was an idyllic May. Temperatures in the low-seventies, skies were clear, and business was booming.

Except I didn't want to do any of it. I needed a day off from photographing romantic trysts, searching for missing teenage runaways, and foiling insurance fraud. So I did what all trusty and industrious private detectives do in their downtime; I searched for new grill recipes online and practiced drawing my gun from the holster, Wild West style.

Fortunately for me, and also for the client, I was sitting at my desk when the stairs creaked. Someone knocked softly on the door and entered.

A blonde. She wore a white blouse with an exaggerated collar and one of those skirts already too short and then had a professional slit running halfway up the side. Red heels. No hose.

She was perhaps the prettiest person I'd ever seen in real life.

"Hello, Ronnie," I said.

"Hello Mackenzie. I am in need of a professional private

detective," said Veronica Summers. "Are you accepting clients?"

"I'm your man."

The gravid statement hovered and the air became hot and electric. She inspected me. I watched her inspecting me. Both of us flushed a little. I almost flinched each time our eyes connected.

She said, "Mackenzie. I'm serious. This is a professional call."

"Then you should put on an overcoat."

"But how would you look at my legs?"

"I have a degree in criminal investigation. I'll find a way," I said. "Close the door behind you."

She did.

My heart, the sissy, flip-flopped.

Mackenzie August, wading into trouble again.

Dear reader,

I hope you enjoyed *The Desecration of All Saints* (You did). It was an important stand-alone novel for personal reasons, and it may interest you to know that a portion of the proceeds from this book will go to G.R.A.C.E., a non-profit group helping victims of sexual abuse.

Mackenzie August is the main character of a mystery series I write. If you'd like to read more (you do), find book one of the series by clicking here. Mackenzie is hired by the sheriff to take a job teaching English at a city school in order to take down a villainous criminal within.

The series is free, if you have Kindle Unlimited.

Though *Desecration of All Saints* doesn't fit perfectly into that universe, it takes place approximately between books one and two. A portion of book one is included below.

I live in Virginia with my wife and three children. You can find me in coffee shops or libraries or my office (blah) working on the next novel. I plan on being your favorite mystery writer for the next twenty years.

~

A SNEAK PREVIEW of August Origins, book one of the Mackenzie August mysteries.

THE FIRST DAY at my new office, I sat in the swivel chair and glared at the oscillating fan and ignored emails beckoning from my laptop. Correspondence in this heat bordered on absurdity. It was late summer and temperatures kept touching triple digits. Perhaps I had moved into the new office too early; the air conditioning was noisier here than in my basement.

Like all professional and winsome investigators, I ruminated on the more important things in life. Such as, if Rooster Cogburn was real and alive today, what pistol would he carry? Maybe the third generation Peacemaker, Colt .45. But that gun had some glamor now, thanks in part to Rooster, so maybe a less flashy Smith & Wesson 19? Or would he carry a semi-automatic, like a Glock? I snorted. Rooster Cogburn would *not* carry a Glock.

These things were important to consider.

Also, maybe I should get a bottle of scotch for the bookshelves. Would clients be put off without one?

My office was on Campbell Avenue, downtown Roanoke, Virginia. Second floor, above a bookstore and the restaurant Metro. From my window I could see an Orvis and a river of millennials on cellphones streaming to the local farmer's market. To purchase responsibly grown broccoli. Maybe some elite asparagus. To produce truly exquisite steel-cut urine. All paid for with Apple Pay, pure sorcery.

My building was 1920s classic revival and Beaux-Art, built before World War II. The stairs creaked and the central air groaned but I'd moved with certainty that clients would rush the doors with bags of cash. And perhaps be a princess in distress.

Thirty minutes before lunch, the stairs creaked and snapped. A new client. I remained calm.

Sheriff Stackhouse entered. I recognized the sheriff from recent campaign posters. Approximately fifty years old. Brown hair showing the first streaks of silver. Excellent physique. Rumored to be a hard-ass. Pretty green eyes. She read the name on my door, "Mackenzie August."

"Sheriff. I notice you're not carrying bags of cash."

"I'm hoping you take Apple Pay," she said.

"I don't know how. But you may ogle my new office for free."

Sheriff Stackhouse wore tight khakis, which flared at her lace-up Kate Spades. Her white button-up shirt was tucked in, sleeves rolled up, collar flicked wide. Rumors were, she was enhanced surgically. I'd heard her described as good breeding wasted on public service.

The sheriff was followed by a man who resembled what a police detective should look like; thick, buzz cut, hairy forearms, snub nose, maybe forty-five. Vaguely resembled a Rottweiler. Not good breeding.

Two clients.

He threw me a nod.

"You resemble your father," Sheriff Stackhouse told me.

"Except handsomer?"

"I haven't seen him recently. I don't recollect quite the same breadth of shoulders, though. You played football in college, yes?"

"With varying degrees of mediocrity."

Sheriff Stackhouse sat down on the chair placed opposite mine across the desk. She shifted to accommodate a pistol and badge clipped at the small of her back, and crossed her legs. "At Radford University? Their first team, if I recall."

Buzzcut snorted. "Never won a game." He poked through the stuff on my bookshelves. Probably looking for the scotch.

"In my defense," I said, "we were terrible."

"I remember reading about you in the papers," she said. "I'm glad you returned home."

"Good to be back."

"Do you have a few minutes to chat with Sergeant Sanders and me?"

"I do."

She held out her hand and Buzzcut placed an iPad into it. "I'd like to verify some information about you."

"Sounds exciting."

She powered on the tablet and ran her finger across the screen. "You were born and raised in Roanoke, Virginia. Played on Radford University's first football team and earned a dual degree in English and Criminal Justice. After graduation you moved to California and joined the Highway Patrol. Worked your way onto the Los Angeles police force. Was assigned to homicide. Promoted to detective. Got mixed up in the high-profile North murders. Took a leave of absence that became permanent. Briefly worked in a church before moving to South Hill, Virginia and teaching English for one year. Came home last year, couldn't land a teaching job, so you got your private detective license and contracted out to local law firms. How am I doing so far?"

"I was my apartment building's chess champion in California."

She returned to her iPad. "You fought in underground cage matches in Los Angeles. You were reprimanded multiple times while on the force for insubordination. And last year you shot your coworker."

Buzzcut sniffed, possibly with approval. "Shot the bastard twenty times."

"Am I still accurate?" she asked.

"Essentially. My coworker needed shooting. And try not to make me sound like a cliché."

"You come highly recommend by Brad Thompson Law in Salem. He says your work is so good you're now in demand by other firms. The Los Angeles police captain told me I'd be a horse's ass if I don't hire you. And finally, you have a son named Kix."

"Last but paramount in importance."

She clicked off the iPad and returned it to Buzzcut. "I'm here to potentially offer you a job, Mr. August."

"Not interested in police work," I said.

"Good. I'm not interested in having you in my office."

"Rude."

"Roanoke has a gang problem. A significant one. You're aware of this?"

"Roanoke doesn't have gangs. Roanoke has illegal organized groups involved in territorial disputes."

She smiled. Kinda. "You're quoting me. From the article in the Times a few weeks ago. That's only bullshit I feed to the press. We have a gang problem."

"Oh dear."

"It stems primarily from narcotics. On the East Coast, cocaine and opiates such as heroin are smuggled in from South America, Mexico, and the Caribbean. Although there are many points of southern ingress, much of it is temporarily warehoused in Atlanta, awaiting distribution. But the drugs don't stay there. Unfortunately for us, Roanoke is the halfway point between Atlanta and New York City. Seven hours, each way. Billions' worth of drugs travel up and down Interstate 81, and Roanoke is a convenient meeting place."

Buzzcut Sergeant Sanders spoke up. "Roanoke's a staging area. A shit ton gets stashed here by the local gang."

"Bloods," I said.

"Yes. Crystal meth hasn't hit us yet, thank god. We've got our hands full as it is."

I placed my elbows on the table and steepled my fingers. "You've come to the right place. I'll take care of this gang problem."

She smiled again. Kinda. "Ha ha. It's a bit beyond one man."

I kept my fingers steepled, but I pointed one of them at Stackhouse and then at Detective Buzzcut. "Sheriff's office. And police. You represent different departments."

Stackhouse answered. "This is a joint endeavor. I've taken point but I'll collaborate with the chief of police."

"Lucky him."

"I agree," she said.

"I met the chief. Or what's left of him. We shook hands and I nearly killed him."

Buzzcut snorted and said, "I heard you was funny."

"*Were*."

"What?"

"*Were* funny. Or *are*," I corrected him. "Not *was*. I know it's complicated because *are* and *were* are both plural, but *you* does not take singular verbs."

"The hell you talking about?"

"Don't blame me, Sanders. It's the rules."

"You taught English, huh."

"Correct."

He held up a book found on my shelves. "This the fucking Bible?"

"Better be. Else that's a terribly misleading cover."

"Why you got it in your office?" he asked.

"To pass the time between my affluent and attractive clients."

"You a christian?"

"You got a problem with the Bible?"

Buzzcut said, "I'm a christian. Went to an episcopal church when I was a kid."

"I don't know what episcopal means."

"You go to church?"

"I do not. But I plan on it soon."

He snorted. "Then you ain't a christian, dope."

"Sanders, I'm entertaining the possibility you aren't the world's foremost expert on the subject."

"You say weird damn stuff, know that?"

"Boys, we've gotten off track. Sanders, close your mouth," Sheriff Stackhouse said. "We're here because we need help. I have it on good authority a heavy hitter has recently moved to town."

"A heavy hitter."

"Gangs don't have strict hierarchies or leadership, per se, and in fact Roanoke is even less organized than most. The Bloods are subdivided into neighborhoods, like Lincoln Terrace. But the sets do recognize older and more powerful members. And apparently, the Roanoke Bloods has one. An important one. Nicknamed the General."

"Your sources are local and low-ranking gang members?"

"Correct. Incarcerated and willing to snitch for reduced prison sentence."

"How do I help?"

"By returning to the classroom. I'd like fresh eyes and ears inside Patrick Henry High School. I believe the General is active there."

"You want me to teach."

She nodded. "Yes. Tenth-grade English."

"This would interfere with my thriving private detective enterprise."

"Think of me as a ten-month client."

"You can't afford me."

She gave me a half smile, genuine this time, and shifted in her chair. "Sexy talk for a broke PI."

"That's economic profiling. I'm loaded."

"Yet you live with your father."

"The August boys stick together." I made a dignified fist for visual aid. "Solidarity."

"No interest in teaching?"

"The schools have resource officers. You don't need me."

"ROs wear uniforms. Hard to get fresh intel. You know this."

"I know this," I said.

"I need someone to listen in the tenth grade. That age is beginning to drive. Becoming more active in gangs. I want to identify the new OG."

"Original gangster. Roanoke's new big man."

"Yes. We know you can handle this because of your well-publicized heroics last year."

"I'll pass."

She sucked lightly on her pearlescent front teeth and tapped her index finger on the chair's armrest. "What is your hesitation? You were applying for jobs like this last year."

I shrugged, palms up, winsome smile.

"Now you're being an ass," she said.

"I know this."

"I've offended you. I said something uncouth, but I'm unsure what. I didn't realize men could be so prickly."

"Only us sensitive types."

"You do not strike me as a sensitive type."

"I'm not. But I pass."

She stood and moved to the door. "I'm not giving up on you yet. Okay?"

"You'll need to line up behind my many clients with bags of cash."

"Think about it. Please."

"Because you asked nicely."

Sergeant Sanders shot me with his finger and followed her out. He left the door open and the heat poured in.